GW00674260

the Irish Family Secret

BOOKS BY DAISY O'SHEA

EMERALD ISLES SERIES

The Irish Key

The Irish Child

DAISY O'SHEA

the
Irish
Family
Secret

bookouture

Published by Bookouture in 2024

An imprint of Storyfire Ltd.
Carmelite House
50 Victoria Embankment
London EC4Y 0DZ

www.bookouture.com

Storyfire Ltd's authorised representative in the EEA is Hachette Ireland
8 Castlecourt Centre
Castleknock Road
Castleknock
Dublin 15 D15 YF6A
Ireland

Copyright © Daisy O'Shea, 2024

Daisy O'Shea has asserted her right to be identified
as the author of this work.

All rights reserved. No part of this publication may be reproduced, stored in any
retrieval system, or transmitted, in any form or by any means, electronic,
mechanical, photocopying, recording or otherwise, without the prior written
permission of the publishers.

ISBN: 978-1-83525-082-2
eBook ISBN: 978-1-83525-081-5

This book is a work of fiction. Whilst some characters and circumstances
portrayed by the author are based on real people and historical fact, references
to real people, events, establishments, organizations or locales are intended only
to provide a sense of authenticity and are used fictitiously. All other characters
and all incidents and dialogue are drawn from the author's imagination and are
not to be construed as real.

PROLOGUE

EVIE, 1923

The O'Brien family had barely been home from mass an hour when Evie's mama, Maureen – about to serve the ham and potatoes that had been steaming over the fire while they were at their devotions – froze, peering out of the window. 'Will ye look at that, now?'

Evie's father, Patrick, rose from his chair by the fire to stand beside her. Evie and her two young sisters crowded behind to see what had caught their mother's eye. It was their neighbour, William Savage, thundering up the track, whipping his poor mare into a frenzy.

'What's the daft eejit got in a blather about this time?' Patrick muttered.

Evie hoped it wasn't about the boundary – yet again. The river had divided the two farms for as long as she'd known, and if it carved a different path a yard one way or the other after the storms turned the gently rippling water into a thundering cascade, surely that was in God's hands? Her father couldn't be expected to give up access to the water for his cows, could he? Yet year after year, William terrorised her family with his violent outbursts, accusing them of land theft, as if her father had secretly altered the strip of land through which the stream meandered.

It was well known that William had a temper on him, which made even his clutch of brawny sons wary. The only one who paid him no mind was Molly, his only girl-child. Evie's mam had been heard to whisper, crossing herself fervently, that she wished the girl had never been born, because Molly had been the downfall of her only son, Davan.

It wasn't Molly's fault at all, Evie had to admit. She had exchanged no words with Molly in all the days they had grown up on adjacent farms, but every so often their eyes would meet – across the fields, in church – and Molly would give a cheeky smile it was almost impossible not to echo. Evie understood her brother's infatuation but echoed her mother's wish that it was a shame Molly had ever caught Davan's eye, because she loved her brother, for all that he was a besotted fool who had brought William's wrath down upon himself. Molly was, it had to be said, bewitchingly beautiful. Her mother had been beautiful in her day, too, Maureen said, before long years with William, bearing his children and working his farm, had worn her into early old age.

Evie watched William slide from the shaking animal and barge through the open doorway into their house, his face flushed red with anger. 'Where's my daughter? Where's Davan? I'll kill him, so help me God!' he screamed, spittle forming on his lips. 'What has he done with her?'

'Calm down, man,' Patrick said, which further stoked William's fury.

'Don't you tell me to calm down! My daughter is gone! Your son has taken her!'

'I suspect Davan has done no such thing,' Patrick said, his brittle anger held in check. 'He's back just these two days past and hasn't left the farm. The lad is barely able to walk after what those spalpeens did to him. I doubt yous have any idea what ye did when ye had him sent down.'

'They should have hanged him!' William bellowed, pacing two steps and swivelling in the tiny space. 'Then my Molly would have been safe!'

'Sure, she's safe enough,' Patrick said. 'Why would she not be? Our Davan would never hurt the girl.'

It seemed as if William was about to vent with another tirade, but he clamped his jaw shut and continued pacing, his eyes flashing the whites like a distressed horse.

Evie had heard rumours, of course, that after Davan's incarceration Molly had been *sent away*. She – and everyone else – knew what that meant. Molly had disappeared for several months, visiting relatives, the story went, to return pale and wan, having apparently suffered a bout of the flu, too weak even to attend mass when she came home.

Evie knew it was Davan's child Molly had given birth to, though no other knew the fact, because Davan had admitted, before being arrested, that he had lain with Molly Savage in the rath above her father's farm. He had picked Evie up and swung her around in the small kitchen, his eyes bright with excitement, telling her he loved Molly with his heart and soul and was going to marry her, with or without her father's good wishes. He was so in love, Evie had been able to do little but laugh at his enthusiasm, but unease trickled through her as the declaration hinted at the onset of tragedy.

There was bad blood between the two families, and she couldn't imagine Molly's father would be quite so ecstatic about the possibility of such a union. Even she hadn't envisaged the fury of William's wrath, though. Now, with Davan nearly broken having served thirteen months in Cork jail, and Molly hemmed in by the confining care of her family, it would take a miracle for that to come about. The young lovers would no doubt find themselves married to others in a year or so, and maybe, by the love of God, they would learn to forget what had gone before, because William would never let his precious only daughter marry the son of a neighbour he despised.

Evie loved her young brother deeply – how could she not? Davan had a way with him that often made their father roll his eyes and say he must be a changeling, because no one in the farming community had ever known the like. He was without a doubt handsome, but he was also away with the fairies half the time. He had a gentle way with him that somehow set him apart, and never a bad word in his mouth, not even for Molly's father. He would set off out into the fields to do his chores and disappear into himself, forgetting the day at all, if they didn't mind him.

Evie and her sisters had oftentimes been sent out in search to find Davan engrossed in drawing some tiny creature that had taken his fancy. What with his daydreaming and his sketchbook forever at his side, the family despaired of what would become of the farm after Patrick was no longer able to work. Maureen often grumbled that her son's head was so far up in the clouds, one day it would just float away.

Evie had been lucky, she knew. She had married the brewer from Bantry, who had taken a fancy to her just three years gone, and him with his own house and livelihood. *For when was a brewer ever out of work?* he would say, with a laugh that shook his belly; sure, didn't he have a partiality to his own brew? Evie, only back for a visit after marrying the man of her own choice, was contented enough, her only grief being that after two years, she still hadn't fallen with child. As the oldest of the four daughters, she had assumed she would provide her mother with the first grandchild of many, but it had been her next sister who had done that, much to Evie's chagrin.

Patrick turned to his two youngest daughters and ordered, 'Go and find Davan. I expect yous'll find him in the top field, enjoying the sun. God knows he's seen little enough of it this last year. Bring him here to me now.'

Mary and Clodagh warily slid around William to do their father's bidding and scuttled quickly away. While they waited, William was muttering incoherently like a man possessed. Evie thought he must be a little mad, as in one breath he talked of his Molly as if she were already dead, in the next he ranted about murdering Davan with his own bare hands. Indeed, he paced rapidly back and forth in the small space, bending his riding crop between his clenched fists as if he had every intention of using it on Davan.

Patrick would have cleared things up with talking, but Evie feared that because William was into fighting, there would be no holding him back, and then what would the four women do? Patrick would never stand by and let William do harm to Davan, but he was no match in size or aggression to his neighbour, and Davan was in no state to stand up for himself.

'The devil's in him, God help us,' Maureen whispered, crossing herself swiftly.

Catching the words, Evie wasn't sure she was wrong. William's blaspheming would awaken the dead. Their neighbour had always betrayed a tendency towards irrational behaviour, but at this moment he was surpassing himself.

Evie agreed with her father that Davan had been a fool to be fancying William's daughter, especially her being so young, but she knew that there was no rationale in such an outcome. Oftentimes bemoaned after the event had turned into a lifetime commitment, young love was like the wind; it could blow in like a squall and fade to nothing just as swiftly. She was glad that her own sensible choice of husband left her with no regrets, which was surely a rare thing.

Clearly, Molly had inherited her mother's beauty, and Davan, the little fool, had surely been blinded by lust. Maybe William had been within his rights to call the magistrate back when he found his underage daughter with child, but surely Davan had paid the price? William's honour should be satisfied with Davan's year in prison. That had been a great price for any young man to pay, and him only just on the brink of manhood.

Evie's whole family had been shocked at the harshness of the sentence, but she learned, through her husband's connections in Cork, that the judge who had tried Davan's case was distantly related to William Savage, which demystified the matter. Evie, with her husband's agreement, left her parents ignorant of that fact to avoid exacerbating what was already a tense relationship between the neighbouring farmers, but it left her with a sour taste in her mouth regarding the integrity of those who were supposed to be impartial in upholding the law.

Davan had been hauled away as a fresh youth and returned a year later, bent and grey as an old man, bowed under the weight of his experience. He was so thin his mother said she could have scrubbed her linen on his ribs. Nearly broken, he was, so. It was going to take months for the boy to reclaim his health and get back to the life he should have been living, instead of being locked up with thieves and beggars in the Cork jail. And here was William, back to cause him more grief.

Patrick had been furious at William for not allowing the matter to be settled between them. A little time and a wedding and it all would have been made proper. Surely if the young couple had been allowed to marry, which was what both the daft weans wanted, it would maybe have gone a way towards healing the rift between their fathers, and theirs before. Whatever had caused it was so long ago, neither man had the truth of the matter.

But no, William had to be William.

In fairness, Davan had known he shouldn't have touched the girl, her being underage, but, as he told his family, they had made secret vows and had naively thought it would all work out. The law and Molly's father didn't see it that way. But didn't all the young make the same mistakes, time and time again? Davan just didn't have the experience to know when the glow of passion should be cast aside, when promises were not enough. And to be after William's only daughter, of all the girls in Roone Bay! If truth be known, she guessed her parents would rather Davan didn't marry into the Savage family. It was entirely possible that the irrational behaviour William displayed might have been passed down to his children and, ergo, to Patrick's potential grandchildren.

It seemed that Davan had ample time in prison to regret his actions, and though he came home admitting to having been at fault, he was obviously still wearing the willow for the girl. He'd be best forgetting her, though, Evie thought, because that family were not going to let him anywhere near her, whether she wanted him or no. Her father would have liked nothing better than to shake hands with William, let the past be, but William was equally as determined to fan the flames that had burned for generations. She couldn't help thinking, though, that his present ranting was weirdly disconnected, more so than usual, as if his brain couldn't control the actions of his body.

The man was surely demented.

Her two younger sisters slipped back into the farmhouse, one by one, with a frightened negative shake of the head. They had searched from barn to field, they whispered, and couldn't find Davan anywhere. So, Molly was missing and Davan was missing. There was an obvious conclusion to be gathered from this discovery. Maybe William had the right of it, after all.

Maureen clutched at her husband's arm, and voiced what they were all thinking. 'Oh, saints preserve us,' she murmured. 'He's gone and eloped with the girl.'

At that William paused in his pacing and froze for a moment as if the thought hadn't occurred to him. Then his basilisk glare hit the frozen O'Brien family one by one. 'You're right. They must have eloped. But where has he taken her? Answer me that!'

1

GINNY

When I wake up in my childhood bedroom to the gentle calling of doves, I know the sun is rising behind the hills on the other side of the valley. A vague shadow of a dream about Ben fades in the back of my mind, pushed away by fingers of dawn peeping through the curtains. I don't know if I was recalling Ben, the kind and gentle expert on all things wild, or the frighteningly unpredictable Ben who had surfaced for a brief but significant moment in my childhood.

Sleep will evade me now, so I rise quietly and dress. The basic bedroom – wood-panelled and uncarpeted – is still filled with my childhood clutter. Mam won't clear it until I have a place of my own, she says. So far, I've short-term rented tiny flats or bedsits, as my career makes for a transient lifestyle. Maybe that will change one day, but I'm not holding my breath.

It's strangely quiet downstairs, so I slip on my wellingtons and let myself out. The sun is casting a glorious yellow radiance from under the clouds. It will spread into a canvas of pink and orange brushstrokes before fading as quickly as it arrived. The sunrise is bringing a clear morning on its heels, welcome after all the rain, but the weather can change in moments, so I slip on a waterproof, just in case.

I love this time in the morning. The birds are singing the day in with a scattered chorus that will fade with the sunrise. Ben explained to me that we sing to express concepts and emotions, but birds sing to communicate. Their 'songs' convey information such as availability during the mating season, warn of predators in the vicinity, notify territorial rights and probably so much more, given how little we understand them. Even Ben didn't know why the early dawn prompted such a massive outpouring of sound, though. Perhaps they were just warming up for the day's performance, he joked, stretching their vocal cords like an orchestra tuning up.

Despite the early promise, the morning is damp and sullen with the after-effects of wind and rain, but even as I climb the hill, the sunrise is fading into a grey day, the blue sky rapidly being obliterated by storm clouds roiling in from the Atlantic.

I get to the top field and sit on a stone, staring over at the ancient monument on the other side of the stream. I will have to visit it eventually, to measure it and mark it on the map, but it's on Savage land, and I no longer have childhood confidence to bolster me. I crossed here many times to meet with Ben Savage, in our secret place, but after the recent torrential downpour, the water is too frantic for my liking. I'll go another day, when I've got my bearings and discovered the courage. Historically, our two families don't get on, and I'm wary of exacerbating what is – after Ben's death – a somewhat sensitive issue.

I close my eyes and lift my face to soft falling rain, remembering how much I loved my home as I was growing up, and how much I had enjoyed Ben's expert tutelage during those illicit absences from school, because it was vibrant and real.

I open my eyes, and my heart does a strange sideways beat as I see him – or his ghost – standing like a statue on the other side of the torrent. It takes a moment to realise it's no ghost so must be one of Ben's brothers – so similar it's uncanny. He stares back at me, curiosity mixed with something else: irritation, dislike?

'Ginny Kingston,' he says flatly. 'I heard you came back.'

'This is my parents' farm. I'm allowed. Which one are you? Noah?'

'Ruari.'

The youngest of the five Savage brothers. Named after the red-haired king of Irish lore, though his hair is so dark it's almost black. Well, one of four brothers now that Ben is no longer in this world. Ruari was just a skinny lad when I left the school we both attended and has bulked out into the physique that characterises all the Savage boys: tall, broad-shouldered and solid with muscle. He has the same strong features, too: high cheekbones; thick, unruly hair; dark eyes. It's uncanny, disturbing. Yet Ben didn't have the aggressive stance, the arrogant set to the mouth, that Ruari is presently displaying. And why is he up here at this time in the morning? Did Ben mention that we used to meet here in the early morning sometimes, before everyone was up and about?

'Did you come up here looking for me?' I accuse.

'Why would I do that?'

Why indeed.

'It looked as if you were thinking of coming over to our side. Changed your mind?' he asks sarcastically. The stance, hands fisted on hips, an obvious challenge.

'The water's too high,' I say mildly.

He holds his hand out and gives a curl of the lip that isn't quite a grin. 'I'll make sure you don't fall in.'

'Thanks, but I'll pass. I'll visit when it's a bit less crowded.'

He takes a step forward, and for a second I think he's going to bound over the stream, using the big rock as a stepping stone.

I leap up like a startled rabbit, and his expression morphs into one of surprise. 'You're afraid of me? What do you think I'm going to do, Ginny?'

'I don't know,' I say honestly, answering both questions. 'But I don't trust any of you an inch.' *Savage by name, Savage by nature,* Dad said darkly. *You don't want to tangle with those boys.* 'So, what are you doing up here, anyway? Stalking me? I guess everyone knows I'm back.'

'Don't be daft. Father asked me to find his fencing tools. He left them up here a few days back and forgot to pick them up.'

He bends to pick up a galvanised bucket by his feet; the fencing tools, no doubt. Dad does the same: puts tools for the job in hand in a bucket and forgets where he left it. The farm is dotted with buckets of implements rotting in rust-coloured rainwater.

I hesitate, then say, 'I'm sorry Ben died. But it wasn't my fault.'

'When you left Roone Bay, he was lost. He wasn't the same, after. You destroyed him, and you destroyed my family at the same time.'

I'm still stunned by the accusation, when he adds, more quietly, 'I'd like to know why you upped and left without a word. Ben wouldn't tell us. Then he died, and your family clammed up and shut us out.'

'Nothing happened,' I say shortly. 'I just moved to a different school.'

We're standing just yards apart, but the storm water tumbling and roaring between us counts the years that have passed since then.

In a sudden flurry of driving rain, I hunch into my hood and turn to walk quickly back down the hill. I feel Ruari's eyes boring into me and glance back, just once, vaguely afraid that he'd leaped the stream and was following. He's still standing, a silent statue in the drenching rain, somehow diminished by loss and confusion. For a moment, again, I could have mistaken him for Ben. The constant reminder is just what I don't need.

As I take off my muddy wellingtons and dripping coat to leave in the porch, I hear Mam riddling the range. There's a familiar clang as the big kettle drops onto the hotplate. It will soon be followed by the scent of bacon frying. *Sure, working men need their bellies properly filled.*

'Ah there you are,' Mam says as I enter. 'You were out early enough for the larks.'

'I just went for a stroll up the hill.'

'In this weather?'

'It wasn't raining when I left. Are the boys up already?'

She laughs. 'Already, is it? Micheal has the cows brought in and your father's halfway through milking. Jimmy will be up for breakfast. He's after bringing the timber for the shed.'

It was a nuisance to us when we were young that our names sounded so similar, who could tell Jimmy from Ginny when it was shouted? Mam didn't think of that when she named him James, but even she stopped calling me Genevieve. *It sounded romantic when you were born*, she told me, laughing, *but it's too much of a mouthful altogether!*

'I'm just going up to change,' I tell Mam. My jeans are wet from the knees down, and I have a bit of paperwork to catch up on.

'I'll call you when breakfast is ready.'

But I don't get much work done.

The past is crowding in on me, as I knew it would, but I push it back relentlessly, thinking about the presentation I'll do in a couple of days. I've done it before in other areas. The presentation itself is not a bother to me, but the location is. I left

Roone Bay under a cloud of suspicion, and my return must have set tongues wagging.

I rise and peer out of the low window at the sleeting rain before clumping noisily down the uncarpeted stairs, thinking irrationally that Ruari, in just a shirt and jeans, must have been soaked through and freezing by the time he got home.

GINNY

The church hall in Roone Bay – an austere and unprepossessing space – is packed. I suspect my presentation has brought everyone out, either through curiosity or the fact that entertainment in rural areas is in short supply. It also provides a venue for social interaction, gossip *par extraordinaire*. The noise of the local grapevine at work is overwhelming. I have to call out several times before it begins to fade, and shushing noises are hissed like waves around the room. When an almost uncanny stillness has descended, I start.

'Welcome, everyone. I'm so glad you could make it. I'm Ginny Kingston as some of you already know.'

I smile professionally, and my eyes rove, encompassing everyone. I'm startled by a glimpse of Ruari leaning on the wall at the back of the room, and my voice catches briefly before I continue. 'I went to school with some of you, and I can even see my first schoolteacher here. Back then I didn't expect our roles to be one day reversed.'

There's a smattering of laughter.

'My family have lived here for years, of course, part of the farming community, while I left to study archaeology in Galway...'

The talk I give in Roone Bay is the same one I've used for the past two years in different halls in different towns. Part of my present job description is to educate people about our ancient Irish past, to impress upon country folk the importance of not literally bulldozing the old monuments out of existence. Many of the ancient ring forts, no more than mounds of raised earth, which were noted on the early Ordnance Survey, can no longer be found because they've been ploughed flat, and a few years ago, a prehistoric standing stone marked with ogham script was discovered being used as a lintel in a pigsty. Didn't that start a bother that bounced around the hallowed halls of Irish universities!

Even as I continue with my introduction, I'm aware of Ruari assessing me with that slightly superior expression I recall from the other day. Maturity sits well on him. When I was a child, the Savage boys would run like a pack of wild animals, untamed, always in some kind of trouble or the other and some-what exciting for all that. They were always having scraps with my two brothers. With the boys it usually ended in cut lips, bruises and scrapes that quickly healed, but when I became a teenager, the status quo changed. I still carry the hurt inside me, like a canker. Seeing Ruari standing there, at the back of the room, the mocking curl of his lips, brings everything rushing back.

He was in my year through school when the *bother* happened. That's what my family call the incident that changed the course of my whole life: a bother. Then Ruari had been tall and skinny. Now he's several inches taller than those around him. His shoulders have broadened, and his skin-tight T-shirt betrays ropes of muscle. His resemblance to his lost older brother is uncanny: Ben, forever welded to my past. Leaning casually with his hands stuffed in his jeans pockets,

Ruari exudes confidence, and I don't doubt he came specifically to discomfit me.

I tear my eyes away and carry on.

'You probably know, from the literature scattered around, that I'm part of a team of archaeologists tasked with logging our Irish national monuments on a national database. Now, that probably sounds pretty exciting, but on the whole it's really not. It's about documenting Ireland's prehistoric past before it gets lost forever. I'm talking about standing stones, tomb structures and raths – those circular mounds of earth you might call ring forts or fairy forts – along with the contemporaneous underground structures, sort of man-made caves or bolt holes, called souterrains. I want to stress that archaeologists are not treasure hunters, though I'd be pretty excited if a hoard of gold turned up on my watch!'

I pause to allow the audience to laugh, to feel included.

'There's a lot of gold in Ireland, of course. The Romans were rather fond of the stuff and came trawling around Ireland to find out where it came from. Luckily their brutal empire fell apart before they got around to subsuming this little island. We truly don't know which kings – or thieves – buried the unbelievable weight of gold artefacts that have been discovered in Ireland. Most of these finds aren't discovered through archaeology, though; they're mostly accidental finds, discovered when digging foundations for roads, railways and buildings.'

A gloomy evening light is falling through the window, boding ill for the weather tomorrow. Well, the only reason Ireland can boast of its forty shades of green is the seemingly endless rain, which, of course, makes the good days all the more precious.

'Every such discovery, of course, is an indication of someone else's *mis*fortune, which is exactly where that word comes from. I want you to think about that. Treasures discovered in our time speak of battles and slaughter and death in the past for those who never came back to claim their buried wealth. These were real people. Men and women and children. People who lived and loved and laughed and cried, just as we do today. Men who lost wives in childbirth. Women who lost sons and husbands in some long-forgotten war.'

My voice hovers for a moment as I emotionally connect with my own words. These ancient, forgotten people were possibly my ancestors.

'But gold artefacts, while beautiful and ultimately priceless, are not the endgame for archaeologists. What we truly seek is to understand how people used to live. What were their homes like? How was their society structured? What tools did they use? And the most ephemeral concept of all, what beliefs did they hold, and what gods did they worship? Some of these questions can never be answered, but the more we find out, the nearer we come to an understanding.'

I pause, and it seems the room pauses with me.

I'm totally consumed by the past while my present wafts away in weeks and years and lost opportunities. To me, the past is a vast jigsaw puzzle missing vital pieces, and even though some pieces will never be found, I can't stop searching for them.

I take a breath and continue.

'Right! That's enough about gold! The Irish national monuments we're in the process of cataloguing are the mystical marks carved into rocks on bleak hillsides, the standing stones outlined against the sky, the wind-scoured wedge tombs, and the raths that are sprinkled over Ireland in the thousands. This is where you lovely people come in. I have a ten-week window in which to complete this task around Roone Bay before I move on, and it would really help if you would inform me of monuments that lie on your land, because you know your landscape better than anyone...'

I take a sip of water as I finish then ask, 'Are there any questions?'

A hand goes up. 'If you find gold on our land, who owns it?'
The room erupts into laughter.

'Ireland owns it,' I answer with a smile, 'but you would get a percentage of the value, which would be considerable.'

When the questions peter out, I point people towards the tables piled with biscuits, cartons of milk and huge urns of tea. I mingle and chat, jotting down locations, names and telephone numbers. Some of these potential sites, I know from experience, will turn out to be natural landscape features, especially here, where icesheets scoured the rocks bare a little over ten thousand years ago and carried the debris southward as it retreated, dumping the piles of stones in long moraines that we now call hills. I don't lay claim to being a geologist, but archaeology does require a little knowledge of the substance one is digging in. But there's always the possibility, the secret excitement, of a yet uncharted discovery.

From my childhood, I vaguely recognise one older lady who comes up to me after my talk. She's thin as a whippet and wearing outdated clothes. She has a no-nonsense manner of speaking. 'Ginny, how are ye? I'm Jane Weddows. I know your mother, of course.'

I hold my hand out. 'Jane, pleased to meet you. I'll remember you to my mam.'

'Since my husband died, I'm working at the Big House for Noel O'Donovan,' she says, almost apologetically, 'as his house-keeper, d'ye see? She'll know that. Noel is mad keen for the old times, and I'm to tell you he's sorry to have missed your talk, but he had a prior engagement. He wonders would it be possible for you to visit him at his home tomorrow afternoon, around 2 p.m.?'

Why not start at the top and work down? I think with amusement. Noel is the local 'big nob', mentioned with a kind of reverence, him owning the prestigious old Roone Manor and all. He's kind of a local hero, I guess. He was born in Roone Bay, the son of a small farmer. When his young wife tragically died in the 1920s, in childbirth the story goes, he sold up and left for America like so many other young people. But he was the only one from Roone Bay who rolled home again with a self-made fortune.

'Sure, I will,' I agree. 'I don't have anything planned for tomorrow.'

'You know where, of course.'

I nod, and she gives a faint smile. I guess everyone knows where Noel lives. You can't exactly miss it.

She carries on, 'There's a fairy mound up behind the Big House, and he's up for showing it to you himself.'

She means a rath, of course. I recall playing there as a child. We also played in the ruin of Roone Manor, despite being told it was dangerous. When Noel returned to Roone Bay, he apparently bought it on a whim. Over the years, the building gradually evolved from an ivy-clad wreck back into the stately home it had been once before. A lot of local craftsmen worked on the building and there was a big divide amongst those who were grateful for the work and those who resented working for him. There was a lot of gossip, of course, about why he'd do something like that and how much it cost, but Mam said it was up to him what he did with his money and the auld gossips were just jealous.

The audience drifts away in groups, and eventually the hall is abandoned to the ladies who are wiping down the kitchen area. I pack up my notes, thank them and step out into a warm summer's night. There was a soft rain earlier, so the air is moist, and the midges are out in force. It feels good to be home for a while, though, despite my misgivings. My job takes me to various wild, wet and windy locations over the hills of Ireland, but I still feel a deep sense of connection with Roone Bay. My family have lived nearby for several generations. I was born here, went to school here, and spent my childhood splashing in the bogs and streams. I breathe in the clear air, with its hint of sea salt on the breeze.

Being back in Roone Bay is a nostalgia trip but I never wanted the farming life, and the small-town gossip-mill is irritating. On the whole, I'm a private kind of person, living in my own space. I can socialise when I need to, but I never bonded to the wider local community, unlike Mam, who knows everyone within a fifty-mile radius. For my present purposes, though, local gossip is something I intend to encourage.

'What happened between you and Ben?'

Ruari's voice comes out of the shadows, making me jump. I swivel. He walks into the light to stand intimidatingly close, towering over me. I take an involuntary step back before recovering my equilibrium. 'It's water under the bridge, Ruari. Just move on, like I had to.'

'You left us with a pile of grief to cope with. Don't you feel at all guilty about that?'

Despite his size, there's something vulnerable about him. Something that makes me want to reach out and hug him like a child, but I say, 'I have nothing to feel guilty about.'

'Our loss? Your family giving us the cold shoulder even though we're neighbours? Perhaps it would be best if you just went back to your university, your barren academic life, and leave us ignorant culchies to our cows.'

Anger flares. 'I never called anyone a culchie in my life. My family are farmers, too, in case you've forgotten. Don't you dare put words in my mouth, Ruari Savage!'

The fury behind my words is almost palpable, but it hides the anguish of past mistakes. Did I really sound like a frustrated old maid when I was giving the talk? It's how I see myself sometimes as my solitary future stretches ahead.

'I'll be here for ten weeks,' I add. 'And whether you like it or not, I have the legal right to walk on your father's land and visit the rath on your north hill.'

I try to stop myself from crowing my small triumph, but where the Savage family is concerned, I can't seem to bite my tongue.

'Well, you'd better mind yourself, then,' he rejoins in a deceptively mild voice. His smile has a predatory quality, like a wolf that scents prey on the breeze.

He turns and disappears into the evening as silently as he arrived, damn him. I'm annoyed with myself for feeling intimidated, which was no doubt his intention. Cornelius and Jenny Savage's four living sons all take after their father. They're built like Vikings, and it's not difficult to imagine them with their hair grown long and woven into plaits, screaming into battle, wielding swords. I shudder and quickly slump into my Cortina.

I wonder at myself. Ruari exudes a kind of feral attraction that's almost compulsive; like staring into the hypnotic eyes of a python even while common sense tells you all he wants to do is squeeze you to death. Jagged shards of poignantly embedded memory remain. I had been attracted to Ben – not as a prospective lover but with the hero-worship of an impressionable young girl to a spiritual guide, a guru. He was far too old for me to see him as a potential lover or husband. When I realised that was what he had been envisaging, I was shocked. His determination had ended up frighteningly forceful; and later, God forgive me, when Mam told me he drove his tractor onto a steep incline and it rolled over, crushing him, I'd felt more relief than sorrow. I'd hoped that with his death my fear would fade, but it hasn't. The legacy he left me with will be with me for the rest of my life.

I'm sorry for his family, of course. For anyone to lose a son or brother is no small deal. But sympathy can only go so far. I don't belong here any longer. Benjamin Savage stole this place from me, and I resent him for that.

My family have been at odds with the Savages for several generations, and my experience with Ben has probably added another layer of antipathy that will last another generation. I don't know what started the original feud. I'm convinced that some dreadful secret is sandwiched between the two farms, over and above the issue over the boundary, but it was so long in the past the details are no doubt lost to obscurity.

The event that has my curiosity fired, though, and the real reason for my choosing to take this assignment, is the mystery of what happened to Davan and Molly, my grandmother's brother and William Savage's only daughter, who simply vanished back in the early 1920s. Some thought they eloped, but if so, where did they go? They seem to have simply vanished from the face of the earth, but I suspect someone around here knows something, and if I'm to find out, it needs to be soon, before the whole of that generation is erased by time. I've always been intrigued, but with this present assignment, I have a real excuse to go knocking on doors, asking the old ones about the past. Maybe enough time has passed for the secrets to be whispered out loud. These families have lived alongside mine for generations, and one thing I know about my fellow countrymen: they do love to gossip!

3

GINNY

I'm human enough to be curious as well as flattered by Noel O'Donovan's invitation; it's like visiting royalty. Mam must feel the same way, because before I leave, she starts to provide all sorts of instructions about what to wear and how to behave, which makes me laugh. 'Mam, I'm going like I am. I'll have my wellington boots in the car for the uphill trek. If he doesn't like it, that's up to him.'

I'm pleased I did that, because as I drive up and park in front of the house, Jane Weddows comes around the side and invites me in through the kitchen door. I find Noel sitting in a rocking chair by the range in slippers and a tattered jumper. He has a massive dog at his feet. He jumps up as I come in, as spritely an old man as I've ever seen, and shakes my hand.

'Ginny,' he says. 'Thank you for coming. Come on to the table, now. Jane has just made scones. You have to have one, or it's me will beat the brunt of her disapproval.'

'Never mind him,' Jane sniffs, slapping a clean mug on the table. 'It's up to ye, but there's tay fresh in the pot.'

'Mr O'Donovan,' I start.

'Oh, goodness, call me Noel, or you'll make me feel old!'

I laugh, instantly at ease. 'Noel it is, then. Jane said you wanted to show me the rath up above the house. I recall playing there as a child. We thought it was very daring to go onto the raths, inhabited as they are by fairies and the like.'

'Ah, well now, don't be too cynical. I've seen them myself, dancing in the moonlight.'

We share a grin, and I reach for a scone. As I cut it open, it steams slightly, wafting out a heavenly scent. I slather on butter, which instantly begins to melt.

'Of course, we Irish are a superstitious lot,' he says. 'Add that to a love of the blarney and you get some interesting tales. They're what keep the wheels of legend turning, don't you think? We have a fine history of storytelling, and who's to say what's real and what's not, eh?'

'My grandpa was a great one for the tall tales,' I say. 'I miss him, you know. My mam and dad are just so rooted in the real world. No imagination.'

The dog stares intently as I lick the leaking butter from my fingers. A trail of drool starts to hang from her pointed jaw.

'Lanky, keep your eyes to yourself,' Noel says firmly, and with a heavy sigh, the dog sinks its head on its paws. 'You'd think we never feed her. So, tell me about your work.'

Between bites, I provide a precis of what I said last night, adding, 'Of course, I had to add a bit of blarney about treasure troves, for those who had come out for some entertainment.'

'Ah, yes. Entertainment is in short supply in the arse end of Ireland.'

I splutter, snorting out a spray of crumbs, and put my hand across my mouth, grinning. 'Sorry.'

'Not a bother. I heard all the talk was about gold waiting to be found. Strange they didn't come to America with me. The streets there were paved with the stuff, which is how I afforded this mausoleum.'

'So I heard,' I say with an equally straight face.

He laughs, rising. 'You've finished, then? Shall we go up the hill?'

'I'd love to. My wellingtons are in the car.'

'Mine are in the mud room. I'll meet you around the side.'

He's waiting by the kitchen door when I walk back.

'Follow me,' he says and marches through an overgrown garden to a small gate that leads on to the scraggy hillside. The deerhound bounces off on her long legs. Despite her size, her brindled coat blends in with the backdrop and in seconds she's no more than a shadow in the distance. The hill behind the old house is steep, stepped with rocks and running with small rills of water. I thought I was fit, but I find myself struggling to keep up.

Noel says over his shoulder, 'Of course, all this water is run-off. We saw a fair bit of rain last week. I think we're due for some sun, according to the forecast.'

'That would be welcome,' I comment, then reserve my breath for the climb.

On the left is a wide swathe of forestry, and a little to the right I see the rath. It's nothing more than a raised circle of earth tacked on to the hillside, scoured by the weather. Superstition and time have covered the abandoned rath with stunted trees and gorse, leaving it otherwise untouched by human intervention for several hundred years. Once it would have housed a dwelling of some kind, and would possibly have been hedged or fenced for protection against wolves and marauding bands of landless men.

When we're level with the rath, I lean my hands on my knees, breathing hard. Noel looks as if he's been for a walk in the park, but he does have much longer legs than me. 'I walk a lot,' he says, watching me struggle. 'With the dog, you understand.'

'So I gather. And I thought I was fit!' I take a deep breath and struggle over the boggy ground to the edge of the rath, which is unremarkable in the extreme. There's a small rise of maybe half a metre, though it might have been eroded over time. There's a faint depression that indicates the possibility of a ditch around the outside. The gorse presently makes it impenetrable. 'You've explored it?'

'Of course,' he says. 'I took a billhook to the gorse when I first bought the land, just to see what was what, you understand. I didn't find treasure.' He throws a fleeting smile. 'No sign of a souterrain, either, though I expect it must have had one at one stage.'

'They didn't always have one,' I comment.

'I think you're wrong. Even if the souterrain was never found, I think there would have been one near every rath. It was a hard life back then, and anyone who worked the land would have wanted to keep their chattels, women and children safe.'

He's probably right, but as an archaeologist I have to stick to protocol: if we can't find evidence, then we can't make assumptions. Though, I do prefer the oft-quoted phrase *absence of evidence should not be taken as evidence of absence.* Human nature being what it is, I suspect the tribes indulged in the occasional bit of kidnapping and murder: stealing girls for wives and slaughtering the male competition.

'You've thought a lot about the past, then?' I ask.

'It's all I do these days. I walk. I think. I'm planning my memoir, too, but not so much about Ireland's past. Mostly about my time in America and about the horses, you know. That's what people want to read about.'

'Mam said you own a racehorse?'

He grins. 'Several. Still do. In England and America. I put a little bet on now and again and go over to England for the Epsom Derby most years. The Queen invites me personally.'

I laugh. 'Right. I should measure the rath and put it on the map.'

'I'll save you the bother. It's thirty feet across, near enough. A single bank, with no notable features.'

'Oh. Okay.'

I wonder why we walked up the hill if he could have told me this below, when he turns to face the Atlantic. 'There she is,' he says softly. 'The little patch of wet that kept me from my homeland for such a very long time.'

I hear pathos in his voice and guess that life must have been desperate for him to have left. I hope he puts that sentiment in his memoir when he comes to write it. That's really what people will want to read about after he's gone.

The day is clear, the Atlantic a smooth swathe of grey curving to the horizon beneath a thin veil of cloud. I assume he's thinking of his own emigration, but he startles me with his next words. 'I remember you as a teenager,' he remarks.

'You do?' I'm surprised.

'You were the anomaly in this rural place, the academic achiever, of whom we breed so few.'

I recall Noel, of course, as a distant, almost godlike figure who stood aloft from us mere mortals. Times have changed, though. Back then, children held all adults in a kind of awe, especially people in positions of responsibility, like teachers, bank managers and police. The hierarchy was stronger, some-how: don't speak until you're spoken to, don't question an adult, just do as you're told.

He smiles distantly. 'I came from around here, as you prob-ably know. It was all changed when I came back, of course. So many people simply gone; empty spaces where whole families had been, the houses gone to wrecks. I had a pair of shoes to my name by then. But it was also oddly the same; the landscape remained, and the sons and daughters of people I used to know, with the same names, living in the same houses.'

'That must have been strange.'

'It was strange enough. But I had the wish to die in my

homeland, you see, not on the foreign shore. I knew your great-grandparents, Patrick and Maureen. Lovely people, they were. I was just a teenager when young Davan went missing. And that pretty Molly Savage, of course. She was beautiful, even then, and vivacious. We all thought she'd go off to America and become a film star or something. It was a strange one, that. People say they eloped, but I don't know.' He shakes his head. 'There were other whispers, that her father had killed them and buried them on his land.' His grin is that of a little boy. 'William Savage had an ungodly temper on him. But me? I don't know at all. I love a good mystery, but I guess we'll never know the truth.'

'It's bugged me,' I admit. 'I think that's the real reason I came back to Roone Bay. I've known about Davan's disappearance since I was little, and later, Ben told me there was a rumour in his family that Molly might have had a child by Davan. If there is anyone left alive who knows the truth, they'll be gone soon. If I'm going to find out, it's now or never.'

'Ah, yes, I heard about Molly being sent away, but as for having a child' – he shakes his head – 'I don't know what happened to it, if she did. They were usually sent to religious houses, nunneries. I wonder if there would be any records?'

'How would we find out?'

'Ask the old ones where a girl from Roone Bay might have been sent. I suspect some of them know from experience even if they wouldn't say as much.'

'It takes two to make a child. It bothers me that it's always the girl who is seen as the bad one, and the child is abandoned by the family, never acknowledged.' I grimace.

'It was the way of the church, of course.'

'It's not much different now.'

'Sad, but true. I knew Ben, too, of course. He did some work for me, clearing the grounds with the tractor, when I was planning the garden.'

I say nothing, but as his eyes catch mine, I realise this is the real reason he'd invited me over. I'm a little annoyed. Why can't the past just be the past?

He carries on, 'You knew Ben was a bit, ah, volatile?'

'Mam told me he could be unpredictable, especially if he'd had a drop taken. I didn't believe her, not really. Dad said the whole family were bad to the core, taking after William, but Ben seemed sound enough. I liked walking the country with him. He knew so much. I thought we were being clever and sneaky, but' – I grimace again – 'it turned out that everyone knew I was seeing him. I was innocent about how my friendship with him would be seen.'

He laughs. 'You can't keep anything secret in Roone Bay. Gossip is what keeps most people alive. Unfortunately, not everyone knows everything, girleen,' he adds gently. 'I have a bit of a liking for Ben's mam, Jenny Savage as she is now. It's the horsey connection, d'ye see? We met in England many years ago, when I came over from America for the racing. Jenny was a young woman, then, taking the showjumping scene by storm. She rode my prize mare for me, getting her to new levels. Utterly beautiful, she was.'

I think he's talking about his prize mare, until he carries on. 'That was, until she had that awful fall that put paid to her career. They all said she'd be an invalid for the rest of her life, but she battled through and learned to walk again. A couple of years later, she came to the races in Killarney, bringing a horse she'd trained. She met Connie Savage there and married him. It was one of those love-at-first-sight events, she says. And maybe she's not wrong, seeing as they're still together, thirty years on. They lived there, in Killarney, for several years, then moved to Roone Bay to manage the farm after Connie's father died. Jenny never went back to England. She's able to ride again, but not professionally. She feels very guilty about what happened to Ben.'

'What do you mean, what happened?'

My irritation recedes. I thought he was going to talk about my relationship with Ben, but this is something else.

'Well, from an early age, Ben took after his mother, with the love of horses, you see. She encouraged him and taught him herself. All the boys learned to ride, but he was passionate about it, as she was. He followed in her footsteps all right.' There's a wealth of words in the pause. 'He took a bad fall when he was about eleven. He hit his head on a rock and was in a coma for several days before coming out of it. He started to get better and they thought he would recover, but he was never the same, after. He lost the ability to mix with people and had wild mood swings. She was a bit precious about him, as you can imagine; taught him at home while he was recovering.'

'I didn't know. Everyone assumed he'd been born like that. Mam said he took after William, with his temper.'

'Well, people invent what they don't know. Jenny felt incredibly guilty, which is probably why she never told anyone about the accident. She taught Ben to be careful with his temper and that worked so long as he stayed away from the drink, which meant he couldn't join in most of the social events in town. He still loved the horses, though, and being out in the wild. I think he loved the outdoors more than he loved people.'

'He did,' I agree.

He nods. 'I don't mean to intrude, but I thought you should know the truth.'

'They blame me for his death.'

He casts clear grey eyes on me. 'Who does?'

'His family. Because he was upset when I left.'

'I doubt it. They would have understood. Ben was an accident waiting to happen, you see. It's just a shame you fell in love with him and you too young to know that he could be, ah, volatile.'

'I didn't love him, not in the way everyone seems to think. I just enjoyed being with him, because of his empathy with the environment. He made me love the land, not just for farming, like my family, but for the earth itself.'

He nods. 'That would be Ben, all right. Well, anyway, he took it hard when you left Roone Bay. If Ben's family blame anyone, they blame themselves for not seeing what was happening until it was too late.'

They don't know what really happened, though. Mam and Dad were adamant about that. Best for my future if I simply moved away, out of Ben's sphere of influence. I was sixteen at the time and didn't really have a lot of say in the matter.

4

GINNY

Being home stirs up good memories as well as bad ones. I lie there thinking about the past, before rising. My sister Sarah, five years my senior, very much my protective big sister as we were growing up, is now married and lives near Clonakilty. My younger brother, Jimmy, is gone from the home, too. He doesn't care for farm work and went to be a plumber, but comes at the flick of a tail when the family need his help. He married a local girl last year. They rent a house in Roone Bay, and a baby is, according to Jimmy, rising in the oven. I'm slightly jealous, because I long to have a child of my own, but that would mean settling down, and I haven't yet found a man who makes me want to do that.

Micheal, my big brother, is still here. He's a born farmer if there ever was one. He says I took to the academic life because I didn't like getting wet and dirty, but I'd like to see him coping with the sleet and hail I've experienced out on the hills, searching for the past. The truth is, I'm not made for the farming lifecycle, which is the same each year, even down to unexpected disasters – unexpected only in that they are different each time. The moment Dad thinks everything is sorted, a roof needs replacing, a tractor breaks down or there's a new epidemic sweeping a trail of destruction through the stock.

My father believes that land is an inheritance to be safe-guarded for the next generation. I think Micheal feels the same way, but I found it draining. The continual yearly battle against the environment is what makes a lot of farmers give up, let the land out or sell it rather than struggle on in poverty. Times have changed since Dad's youth, and there are plenty today who sell up their inheritance for an easier life in the city.

I was always a dreamer with bigger aspirations than tilling soil.

Often, as a child, I'd go missing for hours and Mam would worry, only to find me on a bank, dabbling my feet in the stream, or lying in the hayloft, lost in some book. She used to ruffle my hair and say, *It's your brain that's the problem; it just constantly needs topping up, like the boys' stomachs.* Well, I guess she's right. I've always been curious about everything around me. The landscape, the flowers, the wildlife. I'm even curious about farming, but from an academic point of view rather than a lifestyle choice. That's why I was so taken with Ben. His inherent empathy with the land and its inhabitants was fiercely engaging, far more so than anything I gleaned at school or from my own family.

Sarah left to marry an architect, and is happy enough being a full-time wife and mother. Micheal and Jimmy left school so fast there were skid marks on the lino. But me? I got good grades, and when I told my parents I wanted to go to university to study archaeology, they were shocked and awed. I would be the first in this family to get a degree. Education was no longer the domain of boys alone, and I wanted it.

My obsession with the past is undeniably Grampy Danny's fault. He was a great one for the auld story at the fireside. Back in the 1930s, he married into the farm that had been inherited by my grandmother, then Sally O'Brien, when her older brother, Davan, disappeared with Molly Savage, which was something of a mystery as they were never seen or heard from again. That's how the O'Briens' farm became known as Kingstons'.

Grandma Sally apparently had three sisters, Evie, Clodagh and Mary, but I never met them, and once Grampy Danny and Grandma Sally died, Mam lost touch with them, except for sending Christmas cards. When the Christmas cards stopped arriving back, she stopped sending, assuming they'd passed on.

I find the story about Davan both romantic and sad. Did it bother the runaway couple that they never contacted their families, even to say that they were alive and well? Grandma said her parents grieved for Davan to the day they died. She thought something must have happened to the young couple. Murdered, or lost at sea, maybe, which was not unusual in the time. She thought that Davan was just too sensitive to be so horrible as to not contact them if he'd been able.

Grampy told us William Savage was to blame for the young couple running off, which wouldn't at all surprise me, given what I heard. I'd love to have asked my great-grandfather, Patrick, but he died before I was born, and when I was only about five, Great-Grandma Maureen passed unexpectedly in the night, taking her empty grief for her missing son with her.

I have good memories of Grampy Danny, who lived with us on the farm until he died a few years back and Dad took over his chair by the fire. My siblings and I used to stare at him, wide-eyed in the evening light, as he carefully tended to his pipe, cleaning the bowl, pressing down the tobacco firmly before lighting the spill from the range, moving the flame to the bowl and puffing heavily to envelop us in a cloud of sweet-acrid smoke. It's amazing we didn't all get cancer, but we knew nothing of that, then.

He didn't tell us fairy tales, like Mam did when we were going to sleep, but stories of old Ireland. We were enthralled by the sweeping, bold tales that mingled history and fantasy. He told us about the immortal Queen Maeve, Fergus the Horse (so called for the size of his manly attribute, which made us giggle), and Cú Chulainn, the legendary hero. The characters came alive in the flickering light of the oil lamps, and we thought them heroic. It was only as I grew older that I realised they were largely tragic.

Cú Chulainn sought eternal glory so died young, immortalised by the number of men he slaughtered; Maeve was greedy and caused a war by stealing what she couldn't buy; Fergus lost his kingdom through coveting a woman. And Bricriu the druid was the spider lurking behind his web of deceit, poisoning everyone with his sly words. But they were grand tales all the same, with hints of magic and a strong thread of fate.

It was Grampy Danny who made me realise that those faintly insubstantial people from history, half-remembered through the mist of time, had once been alive, with all their warts and wrinkles.

My area of expertise – if you can call it that, because the more I learn, the more I realise I don't know – is rooted in Ireland's real historic past, rather than the history Grampy had created for us out of myth and superstition. That past is not so far removed if you count back in generations. .

The romance glossing the old stories, of course, conceals a horrifically hard life. The eternal conflict between tribes; the death, rape and pillage; and the hardship, hunger and cold. There's no real attraction in the concept of living in an age where families lived in fear of their neighbours and could be enslaved or slaughtered at the whim of some minor king. The verbal history invests the stories with charm, but it's underscored by human avarice, and that has never changed.

'Ginny?' Mam calls from the foot of the stairs, interrupting my musings.

When I get down, she's standing before the range clutching

the handle of a large cast-iron frying pan which is sizzling with bacon and black pudding. There's a pan of spuds simmering at the back, and a kettle on the boil. The radio is burbling on in the background, keeping Mam company. She turns it off as a car draws up; Jimmy, no doubt.

'Jimmy love,' Mam greets as he breezes in.

'Hi, Mam,' Jimmy says, pecking her on the cheek before turning to me. 'Heard you'd be here for a while, Ginny. Work, like?'

'Well, that and to see yous all,' I say, slipping into my childhood vernacular.

'Sure! So, we'll have some craic later?'

Jimmy is always up for a pint and a lark. 'Maybe later, so. I need to get some work under my belt first.'

'Work!' he snorts, rolling his eyes. Like Dad, he thinks walking around on the hills and writing up reports doesn't constitute real work.

Dad and Micheal then bring a whiff of the farm into the house as they fling open the door. I don't mind the smell of hay and the other farm odours that are engrained into their clothes; it's kind of comforting, the scent of home. The kitchen is flagged with stone, easily swept. Mam isn't too bothered about a bit of dirt on a dry day, but today the mud is thickly clinging to their wellingtons.

'Boots!' she screeches, shaking her head and rolling her eyes before they've taken two steps inside the door. I can almost hear her inner dialogue. *Men! When will they ever learn?*

Back out they go, laughing, to the little porch that Dad built around the front door when I was a child. The muddy boots are pulled off and lined up next to mine, under the bench seat. The men of the house pad back in their thick home-knitted socks. Dad busses Mum on the cheek, and my brother Micheal throws me a quick grin. It's as if I'd never gone away at all.

In Grampy Danny's day, our farmhouse had been a single-storey cottage with just the big kitchen and two tiny bedrooms, but over the years it was built upward and outward, so now boasts four living areas plus the bathroom, and four bedrooms upstairs. We have a dining room, a scullery-cum-utility area, and a posh room whose only purpose seems to be for impressing special guests and hosting religious visitations – of which, to my knowledge, there has only ever been one, and I had moved out by then. We pretty much live in the big kitchen, with its cast-iron range which dominates the end wall – Dad refuses to have it upgraded – and the tall pine dresser on the right, cluttered with old jugs and trinkets from our childhood. This morning, we gather as a family around the pine table which is so wide and solid it must have been constructed inside the room. It's worn smooth by generations of elbows.

The only one absent from our family nucleus now is my sister, Sarah. I sometimes drive over to stay with her, and I love her three children, particularly the middle one, Ivy, who I briefly held in my arms when she was newborn. Sarah's husband, between his other design projects, built them a brand-new house. *No old farmhouse for my wife,* he said. *Wouldn't be a good advertisement for an architect!* Mam tells people, *Like a palace it is, with electric hot water and a shower, God help us!* But like all such projects, it's not quite finished and probably never will be.

Mam serves up plates of bacon and black pudding, and fills our mugs with tea, bitter and strong from being on the hob. I tuck in with relish. I don't normally cook breakfast for myself, so it's a rare treat. There's a low murmur of dialogue over the clattering of cutlery on crockery. Dad asks me about my work; Micheal tells me about his plans for the farm and hints about a new girl he's seeing; and Mam chips in with a few titbits of local gossip, which, in her eyes, is news. The world beyond Roone Bay can have wars and tsunamis, and she will tut-tut and shake her head then tell us about the pig that escaped from the butcher's knife and took to the hills, and which they still haven't managed to capture.

'So, where will you be after walking now, with this work of yours?' Dad asks. He's proud of me but wonders how someone can pay a body to go traipsing around the hillsides looking at stones. They were both at the talk I gave down in the church hall, preening with pride, so hopefully they understand what I'm about, even if the *why* of it escapes them.

'I might start with Mrs O'Leary – that would be Young Jane. She said I was to go and check out the rath up the hill behind her house, and asked would I maybe pop in to see Old Jane in passing, because she doesn't get many visitors.'

Mam rolls her eyes. 'Well, if you get away from her prattle long enough to go up the hill, it would be a wonder.'

Old Jane, as they call her, as opposed to Young Jane, her daughter-in-law, does like to talk. But I'm quite happy about that. If I can get her started on *back in the day*, I might be able to drive her thoughts towards Great-Granddad Patrick and his arch-enemy, William Savage. Maybe she'll hint at what happened to cause the rift between our two families. I won't feel guilty about this. If Grampy Danny had come clean with me years back, I wouldn't need to creep around picking up my family's past as gossip from neighbours.

5

GINNY

The O'Leary property is up a long, narrow road that winds up the hillside. It's one of the oldest farms in the area and has never been upgraded. The floor of Old Jane's cottage is made of packed earth, and the windows, once just holes in the wall with shutters for the night or bad storms, now have home-made frames fitted with glass that doesn't open. The roof slates are so old they're porous, and her grandson is forever on the roof with his slate-ripper, heaving out the copper nails to slip a new slate in, securing it with a twist of lead. She's nearing the end of her days, and when she's gone, her son, who had built himself a new home alongside, will no doubt re-roof the house with galvanised iron and use it as a winter shelter for his animals. Such is the way of things in Ireland.

The rath is on the right as I drive up and, like many of its kind, has been left to become overgrown, the circle of trees hemmed in with gorse and brambles. I can see why local lore has turned them into fairy circles, magic or haunted spaces. I've brought my wellingtons and a pair of pruning shears, to see if I can clamber through the tangle. I doubt I'll find anything of interest, but I'll need access in order to assess the height and breadth of the mound, and see if there's any sign of a depression that might turn out to be a souterrain.

As I knock on the door and let myself in, Old Jane is already shuffling to the range to lift the kettle of boiling water. 'There you are,' she says. 'Sate yourself down, now, and I'll just wet the pot. You'll take a cup.'

It isn't a question.

'Thank you. I'll take a cup if it's handy.'

She busies herself, and I hold my breath as she struggles to the table with a chipped teapot, its glaze crazed from years of boiling water. To refuse a cup of tea would be a severe insult, so I try not to look too closely at the mugs, either, which are stained a dark brown inside. I wonder what it feels like to be nearly a hundred years old. She lived through two world wars and the fight for independence, but it has all sailed past, leaving her staring into the ancient face of God.

Old Jane has a pair of thick-lensed glasses hanging from her nose, but even with those, Mam said, she can hardly see. But that's how it is with the old. At least cataracts haven't left her blind, and as she's into her nineties, she'll see sunlight until she dies. Young Jane, who's in her seventies, brings her a dinner over every evening. Mam once asked her if she would put the auld one in a home, for her own safety. *Sure, and she's family*, she answered, surprised. *She's not a bother – why would we be putting her in a home, now?*

The old woman still washes at the outside tap, summer or winter, and if her clothes could do with a bit more washing, well, I guess her family are letting her leave the world with her dignity and pride intact.

'That's grand, so!' I say when the tea's been poured and she's settled back in her rocking chair. 'You're well? And how are John and Jane, and all the grandchildren? And Mam tells me you have great-grandchildren now!'

'I have,' she says proudly. 'There were nine of my own,

three still walking this earth, praise be; three died as weans, of course, and one from polio. And then there's poor Seamus who fell under the wagon.'

Seamus had been legendary for his drinking. The story goes, Jane found his poor donkey and cart standing outside one morning. She drove it back down towards the town and found Seamus cold as a coffin nail. He had fallen off the cart in a drunken stupor, and his own wagon had crushed him. Apparently, it was the best wake the townland had ever known as every drinker for miles came to wake him in style.

She was counting on her fingers. 'Now, Bridie had Stephen, Finbarr, James, John, Michael...'

There followed a list of names: the children who had lived to marry; the thirty-five grandchildren they had produced; and three great-grandchildren so far, more no doubt in the process of production.

'Wow,' I say, meaning her memory. 'That's impressive!'

'I might be pushing a hundred but still have my nob on,' she says, grinning, tapping her head with a finger.

'So,' I say, hooking her back into the past, 'you must have known my great-grandfather, Patrick O'Brien, back in the day.'

'Sure, I knew Patrick. A real gentleman, he was, and his wife, Maureen, was the sweetest woman alive. It was bad luck for her, I tell you, when her lad, young Davan it was, ran off with Willy Savage's girl, them leaving nothing behind but the dust from their heels. That Molly was ever a wild piece, running around the fields with those brothers of hers, all of them taking after their father and him with the divil of a temper! Sure, I could tell you some stories! Devastated, Mairead was, when her only girleen ran off, and never a word after. She wasted like a wraith, in church praying so much her knees must have grown calluses and her gone within five years. Black William surely lost his senses the day Molly disappeared and was never the same after. Sure, didn't they both dote on the girl?'

She shakes her head with the memories.

'They called him Black William?'

'Oh, sure they did. For his temper, which his father had before him.'

'And was that what caused the bad blood between William Savage and my great-grandfather Patrick?'

She shakes her head. 'Sure, no one knows what was in the daft donkey's nob, but he hated Patrick with a passion before. If he'd not carried a grudge, maybe young Davan could have courted Molly in the proper way instead of sneaking away with her, and the whole thing wouldn't have turned out the way it did. But you can't change a fool, so.'

I'm sure she means William, not Molly or Davan.

I'm about to push a little, but as sudden as a switch turning off, the old lady's head falls forward, and she's asleep. I carefully remove the cup from her slack hands, tip the tar-like tea outside and put the mugs on the table.

I make my way to the rath in my wellington boots. The rain has stopped, but the ground is marshy, scattered with tumps of rush and bog cotton. The rath has nothing remarkable to offer, but I pace it for the circumference, which will provide a rough measurement, and will confirm it on the map when I get back.

Old Jane O'Leary hasn't told me anything I hadn't already heard, except that William Savage was known as Black William, which was not surprising and also not very useful. I'm sure she has more stories tucked away, though, so maybe I'll come back on some pretext or other and try to wheedle them out of her; not that she would mind another chance to talk about the past. When you get to Jane's age, the past is more important than the future, which will soon trundle on without her.

. . .

I peruse my well-used map. Its paper is aged to yellow, its folds falling apart, just the cloth backing holding it together. There's another rath marked, just a couple of miles away, so I traipse to another farmhouse, by the side of a small lake, and knock on the door. I explain what I'm doing, and the woman of the house says, 'Work away, girrul, no bother, work away!'

I swallow a tiny trickle of relief. The attitudes from one farm to the next swing wildly, with reasons that sometimes defy rationale. To many, the raths are as sacred as churches and a body shouldn't put a step in them; to some, they're a blessed nuisance, an ugly wart on the flat green field. Those farmers would as soon remove the stones and trees and plough it flat to gain extra grassland for their cows, and I know some have done just that. Some farmers are outwardly aggressive and don't invite strangers to walk on their land at all; some invite me in with tea and cakes. But they all have one thing in common. Where farms are concerned, country folk don't give half an ear to the law, including my parents. *What do those politicians, sitting on their fat backsides way up in Dublin, know about farming, anyway?*

I squelch up a marshy field to the rath and wonder if the land was always this boggy, and if so, why someone, years back, chose to live here. This rath has a tall bank, which means it must have been impressive when it was built, in the early mediaeval period, according to 'experts'. I believe raths have been here far longer. Wolves roamed Ireland well before the Middle Ages, and isolated homesteads needed to protect their cattle and children. I suspect the man-made pans of earth had once been ringed with fences or thorny hedges of gorse and hawthorn, and were probably surrounded by deep ditches.

This rath is rather larger than the one behind Jane's house but has no view of the surrounding countryside, just the valley in which it's situated, and the lake below. I pace and measure and check the ground for evidence of a souterrain. I find nothing of note and make my way back down the hill.

I'm negotiating my careful way down towards the main road when I hit a pothole and the car jumps. My hands fly off the steering wheel, and the car slithers sideways into the drain, which is presently running with a fast stream of water. I try to drive out, but the road has been weathered ragged at the verges, so my Cortina is perched on its underbelly, the wheels gaily spitting mud, taking me nowhere. I sit for a moment, frustrated, then sigh and clamber out again. I put my wellingtons back on and trudge back up to the farm.

The same woman opens the door. Her brows rise as I explain why I'm back. 'It was waiting to happen,' she says, rolling her eyes. 'I've been telling Jack to get the track fixed, but will he? Not a bother, he says, and does nothing. He's just gone away out in the tractor now, and I'd be all day looking for him. Just phone the garage and get one of the lads to come and pull you out.' She looks down at my muddy boots and grimaces. 'Wait here a moment – I'll do it.'

I hear her talking, briefly, in the hallway, and she's back. 'Someone will be here within twenty minutes. Will ye come in and wait?'

'Thank you so much, but I'll wait down by the car if you don't mind, so he doesn't have to come looking for me.'

'Okay, so. God be with you, girrul.'

'And you, too.'

I have a reasonably fatalistic view of breakdowns, unforeseen events and the weather, which tend to fall in tandem. A bit of wet won't do me any harm, and presently I'm not a million miles from home. I could walk if I had to. I clamber up to perch on the top of a gate to watch and wait for the truck to arrive.

There's a slight wind, but thankfully the rain is holding off. There's a good view of the valley from here. Roone Bay will be just over the far ridge, and behind that the Atlantic. I'm tempted to visit America one day, following in the footsteps of so many Irish, though Europe holds more attraction for me, historically. The Gaelic tribes, now universally known as Celtic, migrated to England from the continent and on to Ireland, leaving a trail of artefacts behind them.

There's a faint wisp of mist over the valley, and in the distance, I hear a tractor chugging along. Other than that, the land is quiet, filled with the sounds of nature. The birds are busy tending eggs or rearing their young. I hear the annoyed croaking of a rook, the regular squeaky-gate huffing of a great tit, and somewhere behind me a robin is singing loudly, claiming his territory, warning off potential intruders. It was Ben who told me that robins, those cute little birds on Christmas cards, will fight to the death when their territory is invaded.

I love this land of ours, its eternally damp air rich with the tattered hints of ancient magic, its rocky escarpments reaching out of bogs and mires. I sink into quiet contemplation. Between patches of blue, the lowered storm clouds bulge darkly over the hills, and a blustering wind sends their shadows scudding over the fields in the valley, momentarily obliterating the bright yellow specks of gorse. I feel privileged to have a job that takes me to the wild, uninhabited places.

At the first splatter of rain, I hear the growling of a big motor, and over the unkempt hedge see the top of a tow truck heading my way. The person driving it knows the road, because he pulls into a gateway on the corner and backs up towards my car with an ease I'm envious of. I'm okay driving forward, but reversing sends my brain haywire and I go all over the road, probably to the amusement of any man watching. I'm the woman driver men like to joke about.

The truck stops a couple of feet forward of my Cortina, the driver's door opens and Ruari jumps down. My heart does a little skip and beat. Ruari naturally exudes that casual outdoor-rugged look that actors and models strive to emulate. He's so like Ben it's scary, but as he turns his smug expression to me, I see he's nothing like Ben at all.

6

GINNY

The shock of seeing Ruari get out of the breakdown truck hits me like a belt in the middle. Ruari thinks he knows about my relationship with Ben, but he hasn't a clue, really. I'm no longer a callow child, innocent in the ways of the world. I'm not afraid of Ruari in the physical sense, but the wide grin he aims at me isn't because he's pleased to see me; it's because he's enjoying my discomfort. The farmer's wife, up above, must have told him who he was coming to rescue. It's a shame she didn't tell me who was coming to do the rescuing so that I could be mentally prepared.

I jump down from the gate, which isn't a good move, because I'm so much shorter than him. He plants a hand on one hip, which is hitched higher than the other, his whole stance confrontational. 'Ginny Kingston,' he says, drawling the name out. 'We meet again. You seem to be in a bit of a bother.'

'I think it's fairly obvious,' I say dryly. 'Will you help, or are you just going to gloat?'

'Help comes at a price,' he answers, and I wonder if he's going to go all macho on me.

'Fine,' I say shortly. 'I'll leave the car here and walk.'

His tight grin morphs into one of speculation before he grabs a hook from the bed of his truck and touches a switch that winds a motor. He leads a tow rope from the back of the vehicle, bends and clamps it to something under the front of my stranded car and goes back to the truck to press the operating button. My car slowly clambers out of the ditch while he follows its progress, leaning casually against his truck, giving me the opportunity to stare. How is it possible that I feel so physically attracted to him at the same time as being angry at his whole family?

When it stops, he drives his truck forward a little, then opens my car door and pulls on the brake. I walk over and scowl at the damage. The car is scratched and scored down the left side. With what I do, it's inevitable. I'm not precious about it. The car is just a means of getting from one barely accessible place to another.

'Thanks,' I say curtly. 'What do I owe you? I'll call in at the garage, later, to settle up.'

But he crouches down and points at a spreading stain on the road. 'It's losing oil. You're not driving anywhere. I'll take it back and put it on the ramp, find out what damage you've done.'

'I didn't *do* it,' I say with childish petulance. 'The road was thick with mud. There was no traction at all.'

He presses the motor again, and the front of the car rises, reaching for the back of the truck.

'You should get a four-wheel drive with bigger tyres.'

He's right, but having a job I love is offset by a fairly minimal wage. I can't afford a four-wheel-drive vehicle.

At that moment, the threatening cloud decides to offload its burden, and rain cuts across the land with the rush of an approaching train. Ruari opens the driver's door of his truck and yells, 'Well, are you coming, or do you prefer to walk?'

I scoot around the other side. My waterproofs are inaccessible, flung on the back seat of my car, and by the time I've climbed up into the truck and slammed the door behind me, I'm probably looking like a half-drowned cat. Thank goodness the heavens hadn't opened as I'd been traipsing around the rath above.

The truck has a bench seat, and I squeeze as close to the door as possible, leaving a wide gap between us. Ruari gives that predatory baring of teeth again. He knows I'm wary and is enjoying his feeling of superiority. He drives slowly and carefully down the long, winding boreen until we hit the road in the valley, where he puts his foot down and heads for Roone Bay at a steady lick, the big wheels gliding over the pitted road, my poor car bouncing along behind. The rain lashes and the windscreen wipers hammer in unison.

'So, about that price,' he muses, passing a sidelong glance.

'I can settle at the garage.'

'It's not about money. I want to know what happened between you and Ben.'

'It was years ago. Done and dusted.'

I do have sympathy, though. I can't conceive what it must have been like for him, still a teenager, to lose his larger-than-life big brother. Despite everything, Ben had that indefinable presence, a kind of magnetism that I'd found irresistible as a young and impressionable schoolgirl. When I heard he'd died, it was surreal, almost unimaginable, as if a part of the landscape had suddenly disappeared. Ruari has that sense of presence, too, but I'm no longer young and certainly not as naïve as I had been back then.

'Well?' he says. He's not giving up. The road rumbles beneath us. 'I just want to understand,' he insists. 'You broke his heart, you know.'

That's a good one. He broke mine, but more than that, he nearly broke me. It was my family who saved me, brought me back from the depths of a breakdown that verged on suicidal.

At my silence, Ruari elaborates. 'After you left, he was more volatile than usual. He told Mam and Dad you were going to marry him. Mam said maybe you thought to inherit the farm then thought better of it.'

I gasp with indignation, and angry tears spring. 'She thought I'd marry for an inheritance? It was Brigid's mam who was after marrying her off for money, and Ben knew that!'

'That was never going to happen. We all knew what she was about. So why did you agree to marry him and then run off?'

'I didn't. I told Ben over and over that I was just a friend, I didn't want to marry, and I didn't want the damn farm. I didn't want to get stuck in Roone Bay for the rest of my life. Ben was older than me, besides. I was just sixteen. I thought I was so grown-up, but I was just a child. I thought of him like a teacher or something.'

'Ben was only in his early twenties. He loved you. He was never the same after you upped and left without a word,' Ruari says, mildly enough, but I see the pain written there.

'It was his fault I left. He scared me.'

His brow furrows. 'He wouldn't have hurt you.'

He really believes that. 'Perhaps you didn't know him as well as you think you did.'

'What's that supposed to mean?'

'He was dangerous,' I snap, my hands clenching on my lap. 'You should have warned me. Your parents should have warned me!'

My vehemence writes confusion over his features. 'What did he do?'

There are some things best left unsaid, and Ruari is trying to crack open doors I don't want to step through. 'Stop the truck. Let me out. I want to walk.'

'We're nearly there.'

'Stop the damn truck!'

I reach for the handle, and he swerves the vehicle to the

verge and brakes while leaning across me to grab the door pull. His arm presses me back to the seat, his face altogether too close to mine. I can see the stubble on his chin, the fear on his face. 'What on earth?' he says. 'You could have killed yourself!'

'Why would you care?'

He slides back to his own side of the truck and grips the steering wheel with both hands. I slash my hand across my face, annoyed that anger makes me cry.

'I'm sorry. I shouldn't have... Something happened between you and Ben, didn't it? Why can't you tell me?'

'Nothing happened,' I lie.

His eyes tag mine again. 'You didn't just up and leave Roone Bay for nothing. We didn't know where you'd gone, and your parents wouldn't speak to mine. They cut Mam dead when she tried. We just wanted to understand. Ben pined for you, Ginny. He grieved for you as if you had died. Later, I heard you'd gone to university in Galway, but he was gone by then. Dead,' he added, as if I didn't know what he meant.

'I'm sorry for your loss,' I parrot automatically.

His face hardens.

'I mean it. I'd be sorry that any young man died like that. It must have been hard for your family. But it wasn't my fault. I didn't want to marry Ben. You know that. If he thought we were going to set up home on the farm and play happy families, he was telling himself a lie. I told him no, over and over. I should have walked away sooner. I know that now, but I was a *child*. I was just enjoying his company, his knowledge of the country-side. I thought we were friends.'

Ruari is frowning, as if I'm telling him something he didn't know. Well, he probably didn't. I guess Ben only told his family about me after I'd gone, and what he told them was only his version of the truth. It's a shame he didn't say something to them sooner, so they could have warned me. But then, I didn't tell my family I was seeing him, either, because I knew they wouldn't like it.

With less aggression in his voice, Ruari said, 'He didn't want any other girl, just you.'

'Well, that wasn't my fault, was it? Sure, I loved being with him. We had a connection, but it was about nature, the magic of the landscape. I loved him like a *brother*. He knew I was going on to university, that I was always going to leave Roone Bay. I tried to make him understand that I wasn't ready to settle down, be a wife and mother. If it makes you feel better, go ahead and blame me. But he got possessive, so much that my parents sent me to stay with my sister in Clon. I lost my home. I had to move schools. It was traumatic.'

Ruari seems to be mulling this over, then senses that I've calmed down and I'm not going to jump out. He puts the vehicle in gear. We drive in brittle silence for a while, enemies thrown together by circumstance.

He pulls up at the garage, and I can see on his face that he doesn't want to remember his dead brother as the bad guy, but he believes me. I know now, after speaking to Noel, that Ben had been damaged in some way by his accident, even if it wasn't obvious to me at the time. That must have been hard on his family. I don't doubt Ruari's family knew that he became violent when his will was crossed; whereas I learned the hard way, but I'm not going to tell him that.

'That's why I left and didn't tell him where I was going,' I say softly. 'Because he wouldn't take no for an answer. He would have followed.'

Ruari jumps down and says, as if he hadn't heard my words, 'I'll give you a call about the car. We have a loaner you can borrow.'

'That would be useful,' I agree in a small voice.

He waves towards the office. 'Go in and say I said it. Jennie will give you the keys.'

'I need my waterproofs from the car.'

He opens the back door of my car and props it with his shoulder to reach in and grab my things. The door, hanging at a weird angle, slams hard as he lets go. He stalks into the mechanics' bay, not looking back, leaving my Cortina dangling off the back of his truck.

I stare after his receding figure. I doubt he realises just how arrogant he is, how conceited in his opinion. But then, he doesn't know what really happened between me and his brother, so he's filled the blanks with a story of his own making, just as everyone else has.

Maybe I've made him rethink just a little.

I go into the office and claim the keys to the loaner. I don't recognise the fresh-faced girl behind the counter, but there's something in her eyes that tells me she's privy to the gossip. I drive home, wondering if I wouldn't have been better off taking the job in Kerry, after all, but the past has kept me away from my family for too long. If skeletons are exposed by my presence, well, perhaps it's time.

Mam exclaims when she sees me pull up in the loaner, but I explain what happened, that I've probably punctured the sump on a rock, that the car is in the garage.

'So, who came and towed you back?' Something in her voice speaks of an added worry.

'Ruari Savage.'

There's no surprise on her face. 'And was he, ah, all right?'

I sigh. He's a Savage, after all, and there's history between us. 'It was a bit of a shock, but he was okay.'

She nods. 'I should have warned you that he owns McCarthy's. He started there as a mechanic after you left, and bought out Eoghan a couple of years back.'

It would have been useful to know he owned the garage, but

if I'd been forewarned, I would have had time to worry while I was waiting. When I go to collect my car, maybe I'll just be dealing with the office staff. There's no reason I should need to speak to Ruari again.

'That Ruari has quite the look of Benjamin about him, now,' Mam says, fishing.

'He does, but he's not the same at all. Did you know Ben wasn't born that way? He had a riding accident when he was a child.'

Mam's brows rise in surprise. 'But, sure, why didn't we know about that?'

'I guess Jenny Savage felt guilty, thought it was her fault.'

'Well now, that's strange news!'

I almost smile. I can see that piece of gossip spreading on the grapevine as soon as Mam hits the supermarket. But it won't do Jenny Savage any harm. Quite the opposite, in fact. Some secrets are best exposed, because they grow legs in the darkness.

'What do you know about the bad blood between our families, Mam? I mean what started it all?'

She stops what she's doing and grimaces. 'I don't know that far back. I just know what Father told me; that Davan got sweet on William Savage's girl and William got himself in a blather over it. William swore he'd kill Davan if he went anywhere near his daughter, so they must have met in secret. She was the only one, you see. All the rest were boys. Mairead, William's wife, you know, well, she'd been a beauty in her time, by all accounts, and the girl took after her.'

'So, Davan and Molly met and fell in love despite William.'

'That's what I heard. But they had no choice, did they? Young love is like the rain. It falls where it will, and you can't stop it for wanting.' She stills, and a dreamy look crosses her face. 'It was like that with your dad and me. Do you recall that song Grampy used to sing? *Just to see him is to love him...* It was like that, I guess.'

But I think about Davan and Molly standing on opposite sides of the stream, as I had with Ruari just a few days back. Had that been how they met? Had he jumped the stones, laughing, and held Molly's hand as they sneaked into their secret trysting place, maybe in the same rath where I'd spent time with Ben? Had Molly truly been sent away to have her child in secret, which was one of the rumours I'd heard? If she did, I wonder what became of the child.

7

EVIE, 1923

After the disappearance of Molly and Davan, Evie went back home and told her astonished husband everything that had transpired. She didn't want to believe that Davan could have eloped, but the young couple's continued absence seemed to speak for itself.

'He couldn't have taken her if she hadn't wanted to go,' she argued to her husband. She found the idea of her brother carrying a reluctant and screaming Molly off over his shoulder faintly ludicrous. 'He could barely lift a feather after the beating he got in prison, besides.'

'You told me the first thing he was after asking when he got back from prison was about the chit,' her husband reminded her. 'He said, *Was she well? Was the baby well?* So, he knew she was in the family way and believed he was the father. If he did go to make an honest woman of her when he got out, despite William's foul temper, it has to be admired.' He hugged his wife close and rested his chin on her head. 'It's strange he left no word, though. But after all, there's nothing to be done until we know where they are.'

His words reminded Evie of the missing baby. It had never

been admitted by the Savages, but she knew it to be true. And Davan's words, when he returned, confirmed it. Why else would Molly have left home for several months and returned pale and wan. It was one of those *secrets* that everyone had hinted at in sly asides, without actually saying the words out loud. As the Savages never told anyone where she had been sent – somewhere within County Cork, she didn't doubt – no one knew whether her baby had been born alive, or what had happened to it. But, in fact, no one really wanted to know, including her own parents. They totally understood why such a sin should be discreetly pushed aside and forgotten, Molly being unwed and all. They had a standing in the community to consider.

As word spread that Davan and Molly had stolen away while the God-fearing community were at their prayers, there were those who didn't blame them. Not only was Molly the only daughter of a controlling father with an unpleasant manner and a mother who wouldn't stand up for her, the girl also had seven brothers, all of whom seemed more inclined towards a fight than dialogue. She really hadn't so much been protected as stifled, because what youth in his right mind was going to risk her brothers' fists by trying to know her?

Evie wished it hadn't been her brother.

She remained doubtful about the elopement, though. It simply wasn't Davan's nature to leave his mother and father wondering. Even if he had eloped with Molly, he would surely have sent word, when tempers had cooled, to say they were safely married. If he had, indeed, stolen Molly from her domineering father, she didn't doubt that he would have made an honest woman of her.

If she hadn't, with her own eyes, seen William ride up to their house in a blather, she might even have suspected William of covering his back after doing Davan harm. But he wouldn't have harmed his own precious daughter, and she was gone, too. William might be short on temper, but without a doubt he doted on that girl.

Evie's parents waited a long time to receive a letter from their son, maybe letting the family know the couple had gone to England, or even America or Australia, but the letter never arrived. No trace of the young couple was ever found. It was as if they had vanished into thin air or been stolen by the fairies.

Over the following months, it was the possibility of the baby's existence, though, that consumed the childless Evie. It was Davan's child, too. It occurred to her that if Molly and Davan had eloped, they might well have tried to find their baby and take it with them, wherever they were going – if, indeed, it had survived. There was, of course, the possibility that the child was still in the hands of the nuns or sold out to America, but what if Davan and Molly had collected it and were maybe living happily somewhere as a family? If Evie could find out where the baby had been born, she might discover, at least, whether Molly and Davan had collected the child, which meant she could at least tell her parents Davan was alive.

She posed the idea tentatively to her husband over several weeks. *And what if you find the child?* he argued. *What then?* Evie was also troubled by that thought. If she discovered the child, did that mean Davan and Molly were not in this world any longer? She was sure that Davan, soft touch that he was, would turn every stone to find his child if he were able.

Evie knew her husband agreed to her search reluctantly, humouring her with good-natured devotion. She suspected he assumed she would fail in her task and might yet produce a child of her own, which would put an end to the nonsense; that she remained childless was not due to lack of effort on his part. But Evie had her own thoughts. The child might be a bastard, but if she found it, she was going to bring it home and bring it up as her own. Her husband might demur, but in time he would come to accept her decision. And if Davan one day reappeared, he would be devastated if his family had not made every effort to find the child. She would do this for him, she decided, blinding herself to the fact that her decision was partially rooted in her desperate need for a family.

8

MOLLY, 1921

Through historic tradition or habit, Molly's family sat on the left-hand side of the church, Davan's on the right. If they each managed to secure the aisle end of the row, whenever there was a rustling shift from bench to kneeler, they were able to exchange brief sidelong glances at each other. If their parents or siblings snagged the aisle seats, of course, they had to be more circumspect and look towards the altar from which the priest was giving forth.

Molly's brothers would sit stony-faced through the whole two hours, just the gripping and ungripping of their big hands betraying frustration that the farm was left wanting for their labour. There were never enough light hours in the day to finish the self-regulated, necessary chores that kept the animals and the land healthy and profitable, and to endure this endless lecturing twice a week was a chore worse than any the farm could provide.

Molly enjoyed the sermons, because they were mostly about being good and kind. They lent an air of community spirit and contentment to her young life. She wasn't drawn to the church as a vocation, of course. She had no hankering to take the vows and become a nun, being too invested in the great outside world, where the streams and wild places called out to her and made her run off to explore, much to her mother's exasperation. She was devout, though. She believed fervently in God and His everlasting grace and loved the overwhelming atmosphere of peace that pervaded the church, especially when it was filled with people who could be anything but peaceful beyond its walls.

The church was a gloomy, squat building, made of black and grey blocks. It towered somewhat menacingly over the surrounding countryside. It had been built quickly, within a couple of years, once the penal laws had been abolished, sometime in the middle of the last century. Inside it offered the strangest feeling of space. The ceiling rose right into the roof, which was latticed with exposed beams, and the windows, built tall and thin between pillars of blockwork, added to Molly's feeling of being a small speck in God's wonderful universe. The priests guarded the few precious church accoutrements with a passion, but for Molly they were of less interest than the pigeons that occasionally whirred overhead during the sermons.

She loved most to listen to the newly appointed priest, Father Mooney, whose sermons were less fiery than those of old Father McCloud. He was a new breed of priest, she understood, not filled with the brimstone fires of hell but with a gentler mission to keep God's sacred word simply because it was the truth, and the truth didn't need to be blasted at people like shot from a musket.

Molly's young life had been one of love and security. She was the only girl in a family of boys and had arrived late, when her mother had given up hope of a daughter. She was treasured, looked after by all of them with – if she were to be honest – a little too much protection. They were always fussing about where she was and who she was with as if she didn't have her own mind. There were altogether too many rules, especially for a girl! If she wanted to find a little freedom, she had to run and hide, and it was on one of those occasions she discovered the man she was going to marry. The love of her life.

Davan.

And that was the problem.

When spats blew up between the families who dwelled in the townland, her mother would shake her head and say, *People will be people; it will all blow over with the next wind.* But it was a bit of a disconnected statement, because her father's hatred of Davan's family endured despite the priest's preaching. But Molly knew her father had good in his heart, and was pleased to kneel with him every evening to say the rosary and remember that Jesus died on the cross to save everyone from the dark side of evil.

She tried to convince herself that her father would want her to be happy, but for a girl, love wasn't often a consideration. Her father would choose her husband for her own good. No one took into consideration the fact that she had her own mind and knew love when it fluttered down one day through the gnarled oaks on the old fairy fort on North Hill, in their topmost field. She wasn't supposed to go onto it, of course. No one was. It was sacred, not because of Jesus and God's angels, but because of the legends, the fairies and old, forbidden magic. Despite the church and the priests, the old ways permeated their lives with hints of a world long gone, a world of battles and castles, heroes and kings, spells and curses.

Gorse had been allowed to grow rampant around the trees that surrounded the hidden grove, but her father's goats had eaten their way in, and she followed. They had made a winding path, like a maze, and with care a body could avoid the wicked prickles and be like the princess in the fairy tale, surrounded by a hedge of thorns.

The rath was just a circle of earth, really, like a dinner plate stuck on the side of the hill. She had been threatened with dire tales of the little people if she ventured onto it, but discovered none, though she had waited quietly for the longest time. But it was her quiet, secret place, away from the endless tasks provided by her mother.

Right in the middle, there was a secluded clearing where the grass was cropped short by hares or deer, where a big rock stood sentinel. Behind the rock, the earth had collapsed into a chamber she liked to imagine was the entrance to the other-world where fairies still dwelled. She knew, really, that it had been carved out by people in the olden days, though for what reason she had no idea.

Primroses gathered in the glade in the spring, followed by bluebells, and when summer came, slender white toadstools would spring up almost overnight. These she steered clear of, as her mother said they were deadly poisonous. On a fine day, she could lie quietly, staring up at the little patch of blue sky visible between the fresh new leaves that were gently twinkling in the rays of sun, and imagine that the earth had tilted, so she was looking down at the sky from a great height.

It was on one of these days, watching the fluffy clouds drift by, that she experienced the strangest feeling of being watched. It wasn't the first time. Once she had turned her head slowly to find a deer staring curiously. It stood frozen for a moment, then bounded away as noiselessly as it had arrived. How something so big could live in the countryside around them, yet remain hidden and mysterious, Molly couldn't fathom. But so it was. They could be a nuisance, spoiling crops, and secretly culling them provided meat for the family in lean times. Though she didn't want to think about it, Molly wasn't silly enough to mind about the killing; it was part of farming life. But to see a live deer, its astonished bulbous eyes rimmed with lashes a girl would be pleased to own, was a kind of magic. Another day there had been a hare, sitting tall on its sturdy back legs, its long ears pricked high before it stamped its foot and bounced into the undergrowth. And always there was the bright call of small birds singing.

But this time she turned her head, and there was young Davan O'Brien sitting a few yards away on a fallen log, watching her. She felt a trickle of fear run through her belly. Not for herself, of course. Davan seemed like a nice boy, but she was forbidden to speak to him. Her father hated his father because he'd moved the stream and stolen some of her father's land. At least, that was what her father said, though she didn't see how O'Brien could have done that. But her brothers had decided to hate Davan for it, too. If they knew he was here, trespassing, they would surely hurt him badly, teach him a lesson. Davan was the O'Briens' only son, which made her father sneer with righteous pride at having produced a clutch of sons before Molly had arrived – as if girls weren't important!

Startled, she rolled and jumped to her feet, brushing the dry earth and mulch from her dress, feeling the heat rising to her cheeks. She balanced on her toes like the hare, ready to run.

'Don't disappear on me,' Davan said softly. 'You looked so beautiful lying there; I wasn't sure for a moment if you were real. I wondered if the fairies had opened the secret door and crept into our world.'

She snorted dismissively, as if she didn't believe in them herself.

He gave a lopsided smile. 'Well, I was happy to sit and watch for a while, anyway. Did you see the robin that came? I thought for a moment he was going to hop onto your hand.'

'He does, sometimes,' she said shyly. 'When I bring crusts and I'm very quiet and still.'

She felt the blush rising higher and lowered her head in shame. She was in her old working clothes and stout boots, her apron muddied, and the hem of her dress ripped by the gorse. As she reached up to pat her hair into shape, she felt leaves and bits of dirt. Her mother would be ashamed. She was nearly fifteen and was supposed to act with some decorum, practising, she supposed, for the day when the world would start to see her as a young woman, not a child.

'Here, let me,' he said. Two strides and he was beside her, his fingers gently untangling a twig. He handed it to her with a flourish. 'This can be a keepsake. Put it by your pillow to remind you of me.'

Her eyes lifted. He was at least a head taller than herself, sturdy and pleasing to look at, despite the hard work she knew he did on the farm. His clothes were ragged, though his thick locks of dark hair were neatly brushed. Despite the sisters that had come before and after him, he would one day inherit the farm that her father said, sneeringly, was nothing but fifty acres of scrub. But Molly didn't care about that. She was attracted by the gentle touch of his hand, the slight curve of his lips, the hazel eyes hooded under dark curling lashes.

It was as if her own eyes had been opened, and she really saw him for the first time. She felt the stirrings of womanhood rise in her breast. Maybe he really saw her for the first time in that moment, too, because he bent his head, quick as a sparrow, and pecked a kiss right on her lips. She squeaked and jumped back, her hand to her mouth. Kissing wasn't allowed! Not at all it wasn't!

He grinned. 'I couldn't help myself. Don't worry. I'm not going to hurt you.'

Well, of course not. It hadn't occurred to her for a moment that he would. 'I'd best be on,' she said hesitantly but didn't move.

'Will I see you here again?' he asked. 'Do you mind if I come here sometimes?'

'Maybe, but I'll not tell Father.'

His lip quirked. 'That would be best. But you're brave, yourself. Aren't you afraid of the sprites and the little folk?'

She smiled a little in return. 'Not at all. And Mam can't find me, here, for the chores.'

He laughs. 'And I come here to be free of the nagging of all my sisters!'

She giggled. 'They don't nag.'

'Sure, they do. They wear the life from me with their *Davan, will ye just do this, Davan, will ye just do that,* all the time.' His face attained a sad expression. 'You have no idea how hard it is having four sisters.'

'Get away!' She found herself echoing his breaking smile. He loved his sisters, obviously.

'So, I'd best be away,' she said. 'My mam will be after me for the water.'

'When we marry,' he said, 'you won't have to fetch the water. We'll have an indoor faucet, like they have at the priory.'

'Get away!' she exclaimed, embarrassment stealing the words from her. Married! Why, that possibility seemed like a lifetime away, and her just a girl, with a couple of years yet before men might come courting. And what a daft idea, water running into the house. Wouldn't the house get wet? Yet she skipped home light in the head, her heart blossoming with the newly awakened needs of a young woman.

She found her eyes drifting to the skyline many times over the next few months, and whenever she was able, she made her way to the rath. Her mother grew exasperated with her, wondering where she was, and what was she thinking, daydreaming when there was work to be done.

But sometimes, rarely, Davan would escape his family and find her there. Over time, that stolen peck of a kiss blossomed into a deep and reciprocated kiss, their bodies pressed together as close as their minds. She was going to marry Davan. Though it was never mentioned again, they both knew it. They were in tune with each other in a way she had never been in tune with another person –

not her parents nor her brothers. He wasn't like her brothers, who were all brash and loud like her father. He was gentle and brought her presents: a ribbon for her hair and tiny treasures discovered in the woods: acorns, bluebells and a dead bird that they wept over together, even while spreading its wings and marvelling at the beauty of its perfect creation. She didn't need him to voice the words to know that he loved her as deeply as she loved him.

9

GINNY

The next day, the clouds have blown over and the sun has started to evaporate the water. I stand at the kitchen door, shivering slightly in the early morning, still wrapped in the warmth of sleep, and see the world with fresh eyes. The beauty of it astounds me afresh.

There's a snake of mist following the river in the valley, and the fields are glittering with dew that's waiting to take off and burn in the hazy summer sun. Mornings like this seem to capture the spirit of the land, with all its tales of a magic that somehow got lost in the ancient past. I've tried to take photographs before now, but it's not my forte. The images never fulfil the beauty that lies in the memory.

I suppose my deep and abiding interest in the ancient landscape started because I grew up with it staring me in the face every morning, but it was certainly nurtured by Ben. His connection with the land was profound and emotional, and I couldn't help but absorb it. Then, somehow, that interest morphed into academic curiosity. Archaeology, to me, is a detective story, each tiny piece of information adding to the overarching knowledge of who once inhabited this landscape. I try to

bring them to life in my mind, but the reality eludes me. Why
did people undertake seemingly impossible tasks, like carrying
tons of stones up a hill to make it a metre taller? Why are the
stone circles there? Were they places of worship or meeting
places where policies were discussed, and information dissemi-
nated to the tribes? Why did they carve thousands of circular
patterns and grind 'cup marks' into the rocks? I've undertaken
physical experiments, and these things take hours and hours.
But the 'why' of it eludes modern thinking.

People have asked me how I can be so consumed by something that nature itself is making an effort to destroy, but that
would be an equally difficult question to answer. Why does one
person want to swim the Channel or climb a mountain? Why
does another have a skill with painting or creating things with
fabric? Some things lie so deep in the psyche, the genes and in
the tiny experiences that lead us to the place we are now that
trying to unravel them would, in itself, lead to fairy-tale leaps of
the imagination.

All I know is that I love what I do, and yet I'm slightly
saddened that my stay here will be short. A week has flown by
almost unnoticed, and no doubt the rest will slide past me
before I've managed to dig my roots back into the soil.

Yawning, I make my way back indoors. Mam has the range
stoked, and another half hour will see the griddle hot for when
Dad and Micheal come in for breakfast, but I decide to head out
early. The loan car is better than mine. It doesn't grumble and
groan with the effort of waking. I turn the key, and the engine
fires instantly and settles to a slow tick-over. Well, I guess it
stands to reason it's looked after if not with love, then with
expertise.

Today I'm to meet Ryan Swinburn, an amateur archaeologist whose specific passion lies in the Mealagh Valley. I head
north, across an ancient, arched stone bridge, and take the
narrow road that winds up the yellow pass, through wild, boggy

land sprinkled randomly with rocks. I pass the occasional stone cottage, some still inhabited, some silent wrecks speaking of past tragedy. The rocky slopes might once have been dense with sessile oak, the skyline broken by the odd Scots pine, the lower landscape covered with vast swathes of deciduous forest, but not any longer. Centuries of population have seen the landscape largely deforested, meeting human needs: farmland, wood for houses and tools and warmth.

The Mealagh Valley is indeed special. Hidden deep in a cleft in the rocks, its habitation by ancient people makes sense. It's sheltered from the blasting winds and has clean, running water. It probably doesn't look much different now to how it had looked in the Megalithic Stone Age, several thousand years ago, when the tombs were constructed.

Several wedge tombs have been discovered there, and a little rock art. Ryan has been scouring the whole valley for several years and has apparently made another discovery to add to the mapped data. I have to admit to echoing his excitement. When I arrive, he's already here, waiting in a small parking area. He climbs out of his car to greet me; a tall, gaunt figure with a thick shock of white hair. He might be sixty or eighty; it would be hard to tell as his face is unlined and he moves with the ease of someone who leads an outdoor life.

'Ginny Kingston?'

Nodding, I hold out my hand, and he gives it a firm shake. 'Pleased to meet you, Ryan.'

I open the back of my car, and pull out my waterproofs and wellingtons.

'You've come prepared.'

'This *is* Ireland!'

With a laugh, he leads me down a small track, slick with mud, and we enter a different world. We don't have so many trees in the south of Ireland, and this woody valley, its ancient deciduous woodlands carved in two by the Mealagh River, is pure delight. The rain is holding off, but a faint mist is rising through the dripping trees – willow, alder, ash and birch – providing the feel of a tropical rainforest. It's dark and dank under the canopy, rich with fresh fern fronds and the scent of wet loam. Although I see patches of daylight through the canopy, it will be midday before the rays penetrate to the forest floor.

There's little talking to be had as we slide and scramble down the muddy slope, to where a small bridge has been constructed of rough-hewn timber. We cross the tributary stream that feeds a large boggy area and head further downhill.

Then Ryan leads me off to the right and up onto a small rocky escarpment that reaches out of the enclosed space. There, glistening darkly in daylight, is the capstone of the first wedge tomb. This one is already on the database, but actually being here sends a thrill through my body. I think of the ceremony and rites of death – unknown but imagined – that probably brought a whole tribe down these very slopes, thousands of years ago, reverently bearing the body of some esteemed clan member and laying it to rest. The tomb might once have been covered with turf, but if so, it's long gone, as are its contents, leaving the huge stones leaning against each other, outlined starkly against the sky.

'This one's been known about for years, of course,' I say.

'It has,' Ryan agrees, 'as are the two below. Can we sit for a moment? I need to catch my breath.'

'Sure.' I join him at the edge, and we sit facing south, our legs dangling over the edge of the small escarpment. The Atlantic, not so far from us, is hidden somewhere beyond the foothills. It's serene here, the silence only interrupted by the sounds of the stream and small birds, and a cow bellowing for her calf in the distance. A blackbird shoots out of the vegetation behind us with an alarmed call. Something came too near its nest, I'm thinking, where her eggs will soon be ready for the hatching.

Above us, in the lowered arc of the sky, a bird of prey is wheeling, its amazingly sharp eyes scanning the terrain below for unwary small animals or birds. I screw my eyes against the light. From the blunt shape of its wings, I guess it's a buzzard. I once saw a buzzard fold back its wings and dive to earth at an incredible speed before almost somersaulting a few feet from the ground, to rise with something dangling from its claws. It was both fascinating, beautiful and kind of appalling at the same time, but such is nature.

'The new tomb is down there.' Ryan points southward, bringing me back to earth, and my eyes follow along his line of sight. 'I've walked past it many times, it was so covered in vegetation. Trees, ferns, moss. Maybe it was the time of day, the light... but you know how it is. This one time I just knew the structure wasn't natural, and sure enough, when I started to clear around it, there it was!'

I understand his excitement. Though I've never been lucky enough to find a wedge tomb, I've discovered a few artefacts myself, the same way, through some underlying instinct that defies explanation. Maybe one day there will be no undiscovered artefacts left to find. But as technology improves, those we have found will be reanalysed, maybe even dated, further exposing the story of these long-dead burial places.

'Does make you wonder who it was and how they died,' he muses. 'Death is a strange old thing. One day we're here, with a whole life ahead of us, the next we're gone, along with all the things we spent so much time learning. A puff of wind, and one day we're just a name on a gravestone.'

I nod, feeling a pull of empathy for this man who spends his days tramping the hills, laying his hands on stones that keep their silent stories hidden. 'Ancient Irish stories are filled with long lineages, learned by heart. Generations of people must have known who was laid to rest here, but time steals everything in the end.'

'It does. A million years from now, I wonder if anything will have survived of our present concrete world, our homes and tower blocks.'

We sit, enjoying the peace and the sense that time has briefly stopped.

'I was at the churchyard the other day,' he says, 'paying my respects. You know Ben Savage was laid to rest there? The story is, you were sweet on him, once.' Ryan says this with a lift of the brows and not the least hint of embarrassment. Nothing is ever really secret in a small town.

'I wasn't sweet on him. That was just what people said.'

I guessed that Ben had been laid to rest with his forebears, in the same graveyard forever looking out to sea, but I have no intention of seeking it out.

He shakes his head. 'Sad old business, that.'

'I feel sorry for his family. Ben should have known better, driving the tractor on that slope.'

'There are some say he did. Despite everything, he knew the danger.'

My mind reels. 'You think he rolled the tractor on purpose?'

'I'm not saying one way or the other. The coroner decided it was an accident, which is why he was allowed to be buried by the church. But there was talk in the town, in case you didn't hear it already.'

'Thank you,' I say dryly.

We carry on and check that the various monuments we know about remain undisturbed – and I make a quick sketch of the newly discovered tomb and mark the location on my map. I'll phone my professor later. He'll be excited, though he rarely shows it, and will no doubt visit over the summer. When I started my degree, I assumed that Ireland, which is a tiny country, had long given up all its secrets, but ancient sites are being discovered all the time. There is a secret hope that someone might one day discover the ancient site that explains everything... the holy grail of the Stone Age researcher.

I somehow doubt it, though.

It's been a long day, and I'm physically exhausted by the time I'm driving home. But I'm mentally exhausted, too, by Ryan's exposé regarding Ben's death. Ruari said his brother was different after I left, depressed maybe, but if there was talk of suicide, my parents never mentioned it to me. Maybe they were shielding me from feeling guilty. Not that I would have felt guilty at all had I known.

If what Ryan said is even remotely true, Ben certainly had reason to feel remorse, even though his pursuit of me had become a compulsion or a sickness over which he had no control, which is plain sad. Ben was a troubled soul, but he knew right from wrong. If he did choose to end his own life, it would have been through guilt, not unrequited love.

I always thought the Savages blamed me in part for their eldest son's death, but from what I've recently learned, it was Mam who refused to speak to Jenny Savage after I left, propagating the long-standing bad blood between the two farms.

10

GINNY

Someone from the garage called Mam while I was out, to say my car is ready for collection. I'm hoping I'll just be able to sneak into the office, pay the invoice and drive away without having any encounters with Ruari Savage. He might own the garage, but fixing the car wasn't a favour; it was just business. I suppose I should be grateful, though. He could have been awkward, given our history.

Ruari thinks he knows what happened in the case of Ben vs Ginny and no doubt believes that Ben's death was at least partially my fault. After my talk with Ryan, I'm wondering whether he's right, but I'm not going to enlighten him.

I don't doubt Ben's family is still grieving, but in Ireland one doesn't speak ill of the dead; there are too many emotions at stake. I think one of the worst kinds of trauma is to lose a young relative. It's not the right order of things. That kind of grief stays with a person their whole life, and sometimes, prompted by some emotional trigger, the shrouded mists of time part to allow the grief a brief airing before closing again. Me coming back must be bringing it all closer to their minds.

．　．　．

I head out early the next morning in a torrential downpour, extreme, even for Ireland. As I'm driving, the windscreen wipers are barely quick enough to leave glimpses of the dark tarmac, so I wonder whether to go and visit Sarah after all while I wait for this weather front to pass through. I'll give her a ring, find out what her plans are. I haven't seen the children for a couple of months, which is too long, all things considered.

The rain eases off a little as I drive into Roone Bay. The roll-down doors of the mechanics' bay are half-lowered against the weather. The lights are on inside so someone is working. I don't know if it's Ruari, but I hope not. My Cortina, which looks suspiciously clean, is parked to one side. Someone has washed off the mud that had been smeared over the passenger side, maybe to check the damage. I park the loaner beside it and, shielding my face from the sharp spits of rain, walk quickly to the office.

The girl in the office grins when I query the cleanliness of my car. 'It's just part of the service,' she says. 'Ruari started it when he bought out Eoghan. He said it would bring return custom. No one likes washing their own car.'

She pushes an invoice over the counter and turns to pull my keys from a row of cup hooks on the back wall. The invoice is tiny, for just a couple of hours of work. I'm confused. 'Didn't he have to buy parts? Isn't there a charge for the rescue?'

The door behind opens, and Ruari fills the space, making the office seem uncomfortably small. He answers for the girl. 'I've got a breaker out back. I just took the sump cover off it and put it on yours.'

'But you should charge me, surely?'

'I told you my price.'

The office girl is agog. Her eyes flash between Ruari and me, her surprise and curiosity not so well hidden. I suspect she's wondering quite what kind of a deal Ruari has worked out with me. She's young enough to maybe not know about my history with Ruari's brother, and old enough to possibly be fascinated by Ruari's somewhat charismatic persona. I feel heat rise in my cheeks. It would be hard to find words to explain why he is so attractive, but that unknown quality in men has been the downfall of many a woman, and I'm not going to succumb to it.

'Have you got time to come for a drive with me?' he asks. 'I said you need to buy a better vehicle. Someone I know has a working Land Rover for sale, cheap. I've been doing the maintenance on it the past few years, so even though it looks battered, I know it's sound.'

'I don't think—'

'And while we're up on the farm, there's a portal tomb that's not on the old map. A potential portal tomb,' he amends.

It would be impossible for a layman to be sure that a pile of large rocks was, in fact, once a tomb. Some Megalithic tombs have collapsed over the years, and sometimes random deposits of huge stones left by the ice sheet thousands of years ago can be deceptive. It would take an expert to know. But excitement rises, and I ask, 'Which farm? Where?'

'We'll take the truck. The road up to the farm isn't so good.'

The cool assessment on his face suggests that he knows I'm hooked. He's resorting to blackmail, but I can't resist. He walks out to the truck, and I follow.

He fires it up, sets off and after a few minutes says, 'So, what did happen?'

'Leave it alone. I don't want to start digging up memories I've spent years trying to bury.'

'It's not ancient history,' he says mildly, changing gear to take a sharp bend. 'I was eighteen when Ben died, and losing my brother wasn't something I could just get over. It's still with me. I know he had his faults, but I idolised him. I'd really like to know what happened, because he changed, almost overnight, when you left.'

I sigh. He's nothing if not persistent. 'It's quite simple. Mam was worried. She told me I had to stop seeing him, because there was gossip. I had no idea people were talking about us. My relationship with him really was quite innocent; on my part, anyway.'

'So, what pushed him over the edge?'

I flash him a curious glance. 'You think he killed himself?'

'I don't know. But he certainly wasn't thinking right when he drove out onto that slope.'

'I'm sorry he died. What more can I say?'

'You could tell me the truth.'

'I have. He made more of our friendship than he should. I found him interesting, that's all. None of my school mates even knew what philosophy meant, but Ben was deep, somehow.' I turn in the seat to give him the full benefit of my words. 'We got on really well. Don't you get it, Ruari? When he realised I really meant it – that I didn't want to be with him – he became demanding, intimidating. After I left home, I was too scared to even come back to visit my family, not until—' I take a deep breath before ending the sentence, but I can't just stop, because it's hanging in the air. 'Until I knew he wasn't going to be here any longer.'

He's silent for a long while. Where Ben would have argued, kept on and on at me, I see Ruari taking in my words, tasting them, thinking about them. He was the same age as me when all this was going on. Maybe he recalls himself as being a child at the time and me as a young woman.

'I was a child, too,' I say softly, just in case he hadn't got it.

He drives maybe eight miles along the Bantry road before turning inland, heading up a small winding road that's little more than the width of the vehicle. There's a bank on the right and a drop on the left, a barren wasteland of stumps where the Forestry has been harvesting spruce. I'm glad I'm not driving as the road has been eroded into bad potholes in places. Ruari drives carefully but confidently, trundling up the track in a low gear, the big motor quietly purring. He's right that a four-wheel drive would give me a bit more confidence on these rutted tracks and would probably be a lot safer. I had never considered getting an old Land Rover, though. I'd always assumed that kind of vehicle was a status symbol for macho male drivers. But they had been designed to work on rugged terrain, and people didn't call Land Rovers the *poor man's tractor*, in a kind of derogatory fashion, for nothing.

Ruari turns through a pair of impressive stone-built gateposts. At the end of the drive, it's a culture shock to find an impressive modern home. It has a steep roof inset with gabled windows, a glassed-in front porch and on the side a double garage. It isn't a poor man's dwelling. The walls are lipstick pink, the front door and window surrounds a violent splash of dark red.

Ruari pops out an infectious grin. 'Not what you expected?'

'No,' I agree, grinning back, despite myself.

He beeps a ratatat on the horn, and we wait until the front door opens. 'Come on in,' a woman yells in a cockney accent, beckoning frantically.

We jump out and run to the door. Even in that short space of time, our hair and noses are dripping rain onto the mat. Ruari indicates our shoes. She shakes her head and laughs. 'It's all part of being in Ireland, ain't it?'

She's a large woman, her size accentuated by a kaftan in shades of violent purple and orange. She's wearing pink fluffy mules. 'George is out in the stable with the 'orses,' she says. 'I'll give him a bell, and he'll be here in a jiffy. Meantime, I'll get the kettle on.'

She really does mean a bell, I realise, as she reaches up to a rope by the door and gives it a hefty tug. A large brass bell mounted on the side wall clangs loudly, the reverberations following us into a large, modern kitchen area fitted out in oak, with a long marble breakfast bar the other side of the working area. We perch on tall stools while she busies herself with water and milk and mugs.

'Joannie, this is Ginny I told you about,' Ruari says.

'I guessed, sweetie. I saw the advert for the talk, down in the post office. Can't say I'm too bothered about a few old stones, but each to their own, eh?'

'So, who found the tomb?' I ask.

'Oh, that would be the contractors. They were clearing some gorse from the top field, to make a track up the hill, for the pony trekking, know what I mean? And one of the guys said it might be old, so everything came to a halt. I thought he should just push the stones out of the way – I mean, no one would ever know – but George says he can find another route up the hill and if it's old, he can charge people to see it.'

She has no idea that my mouth is hanging open behind her back. Ruari shakes his head at me. The back door slams, probably taken by the wind, and a well-built, middle-aged man bursts in, shaking water from an expensive Barbour coat. 'Cor, if it ain't raining cats and frogs,' he says sourly. 'I told the missus this was a mistake. We coulda gone to California, but no, the missus wants to come to Ireland 'cos her gran came from here, see?'

'What, from Roone Bay?' Ruari asks Joannie curiously.

She shakes her head. 'Up in Kerry, around Glenbeigh, she thinks. I know Ireland's wet, darling, but bugger me, I didn't expect this kind of wet.'

'This ain't just wet, Joannie love,' George says, shivering. 'I'm bloomin' waterlogged.'

'Well, it wasn't me what decided, whatever he says,' Joannie tells us. 'It was George what wanted to come here because of Noel O'Donovan and his plans for a racecourse, what isn't even going to happen now. But he likes to blame me. I said it would come to nuffink.'

'There's time yet. And we can always up sticks and head for the sun, love,' George says, 'if that's what you really want.'

'You've put a load of work into getting this business up and running. I'm not going to be accused of scuppering it. I'm sure you'll do that all by yourself in the end!'

She gives a belly laugh as he leans over to give her a hug and a kiss. 'That's me girl,' he says.

Despite my horror at Joannie's complete disregard for Irish antiquities, I'm amused by the couple's obviously loving relationship.

'So, are you two connected?' George asks, glancing from me to Ruari.

I flush a little. 'It's just business,' I say quickly. 'Ruari came to my talk, then rescued me when my car slid into a ditch. He told me about the Land Rover you have for sale and also your potential archaeological find, and offered to bring me here.'

'Ah, so you'll be going up in this?' He inclined his head towards the window.

Ruari points out of the window at a tiny patch of blue sky fighting through the black clouds. 'It'll stop in a few minutes,' he says.

George looks sceptical. 'Well, if you say so.'

Joannie pours hot water onto teabags, then pushes the mugs towards us. We swirl the teabags, throw them into the nearest available receptacle and add our own milk. No genteel graces here, despite the almost ostentatious surroundings.

I was wondering how this middle-aged couple had been able to buy a plot of land big enough to run a pony-trekking outfit and build a brand-new house, when George enlightens me. He's standing by his wife the other side of the breakfast bar, when he puts a comfortable arm around her shoulders and squeezes, directing his words to me. 'The missus were a model,' he says proudly. 'Cor, she were a stunner! She did features, like, with them skimpy mini dresses. Tall, she was, with a tiny waist and huge—'

'George!'

He looks at her, unabashed. 'Well, it's what first attracted me, sweetheart, you know it was, seeing as I first saw them in a girly mag.' He turns back to his guests. 'But she ain't no fool. Didn't squander it on flash cars and flash guys. Lived with her mum, she did, and saved for when she met the man of her dreams, and that's me, it is!'

'Yer great lummox,' she says fondly.

'She gave it all up for me.'

'I gave it up because things started to droop, yer lummox. I would have been modelling those all-in-one corsets soon enough... Well, darned if the boy ain't right! Looks like the rain's stopped.'

'Might be a good time to head up the track,' Ruari says, 'before it starts again.'

'I'll run you up in the Land Rover. Then that bombshell you've found can get a handle on it, like.'

His wink as he speaks deflates the possibility of anger, and I laugh with him, realising it was meant as a compliment. 'No one's ever called me that before,' I say.

'You haven't lived, girl, you haven't lived.'

We quickly down the dregs of tea and pull on our water-proofs. The Land Rover's cab – scruffy and bashed about – has just one long bench seat, and I end up crammed awkwardly between the two men as doors are slammed hard. I'm moulded embarrassingly to Ruari's thigh on one side, and I'm sure George's hand flitting over my knee as he changes gear isn't accidental.

Once the low range has clunked into position, the engine seems to roar as we trundle at a slow crawl up an incline surely not meant for vehicles. I'm not one to panic, but I'm holding on to the front ledge on the verge of doing exactly that when he turns in a sliding skid towards the left, and I see the mound of dying gorse glistening gently in the damp air.

'I'll burn that when we get a patch of sun,' George says. 'That stuff don't rot down. Even when you think it's safe, the thorns snag you like a bunch of piranhas as you pass.'

He pulls to a halt, and Ruari, who seems as uncomfortable as me at the close proximity, leaps out. I shuffle along the seat and slip to the ground.

'She's a great ride,' George says, thankfully staring at the Land Rover, though he looks a bit dubious. 'Got bigger tyres than usual. Keeps you a bit higher off the ground and uses less fuel,' he adds hopefully.

I squelch along a small path to the stones George is indicating and have to catch my breath. I'm pretty sure Ruari's right, that this is a portal tomb. My breath shortens: only two portal tombs have been discovered in West Cork, and this might be another! There's a distinctive row of upright stones, over four metres in length; a court, maybe, leading to some larger stones supporting a huge stone that could only be a capstone.

'Oh, wow,' I say in wonder.

'Is it a portal tomb?' Ruari asks.

'Maybe. It could be a wedge tomb. Sometimes, when the sides have fallen, it's hard to tell, but even so it's significant.' I turn to George. 'I'll need to call it in officially, but it would be really useful if you could remove the pile of gorse rather than burn it so close to the stone. I'll get someone from the university to come over and verify it.'

'Are sightseers allowed to just walk up here? Can I charge people?'

'It will be declared a national monument, but as it's your land, it's up to you how to sort out access. As I see it, you can charge people to park on your land, maybe down by your house, but you can't charge them to view the monument. Most people would put up an honesty box to support the management of paths and parking.'

'A car park is going to cost an arm and a leg,' he grumbles.

'Sure is,' I say cheerfully.

I like the idea of some monuments being left as found, but as George and Joannie don't seem like the sort of people to allow a cash cow to escape, I add, 'It would be a good idea not to do anything until the experts have checked the site over. They can put you straight about the legalities, too.'

When I've taken a couple of photographs, we head back down to the house. Ruari makes apologies and says he has to get back to work, and adds, 'So, what do you think about the Land Rover?'

'Sounds brilliant, but I can't afford it.'

'You don't know how much he wants for it.'

'I still can't afford it.'

'But you'd like it?'

'Ruari!' I laugh. 'Wanting and having are two different things.'

He flashes me a grin. 'My parents used to say the same thing. You should laugh more often. It suits you.'

At that my laughter dies. I used to laugh a lot with Ben.

Back at the garage, I slip into my own car and drive home, knowing I'll never have to speak to Ruari again. I'm not quite sure why that bothers me.

11

GINNY

'Sarah's after asking if you'll be driving over to see her and the family,' Mam says.

'I was thinking I would. The weather doesn't look as if it's going to improve any time soon.'

'It can change in an hour but, sure, isn't it bad enough now? It bothers me, you traipsing those hills when it's like this. What if you fall and break a leg?'

'I always let someone know where I am, so don't be fretting!'

'So, will you ring her?'

'I suppose.'

It's not as if I don't want to visit my sister and her family, and them only an hour from here, but I need to get my head into the right space first. Sarah is older than me. She married Thomas at eighteen and had Patrick, named for Great-Grandpa. Then came Ivy, and Ellen was kind of an accident, though she wouldn't put it that way.

With his fancy clothes and impressive office, Thomas must be making a good living. I was surprised at Sarah's choice of a husband when I met him, us coming from generations of farming folk. I don't quite feel at ease with him now, what with his blarney and cracking jokes all the time. I can't understand how she puts up with it, but each to their own, as Mam would say. He's kind, Sarah loves him to bits, and he's great with the children. She's lucky, I guess.

I once dreamed of finding the perfect partner, a man who could love me to distraction, like those in the romances I'd devoured with my schoolfriend, Brigid, as a young teenager. But life taught me to be wary of protestations of love. The few men who have interested me more than fleetingly wanted too much, too quickly, scaring me with their overwhelming *need* for sex, which isn't love at all. I'm not a stranger to sex, but without an emotional connection, it's just an animal function. I've been called frigid, before now, and that's a sure way of knowing the guy in question is the wrong one. Men seem to have a strange disconnect, wanting casual sex but expecting to marry a woman who hasn't thrown it around, so to speak.

Well, how about me feeling the same way about a guy?

I like to think I'm saving myself for the right person, but maybe I'm just scared to commit, which is what Sarah says. She tells me I can't use Ben as an excuse to hold people at arm's length forever. She's right, but it would take a fairly determined man to climb over the emotional wall I've built up, and I haven't found him yet.

I'm a bit envious of her, if I'm honest. I would dearly love a home of my own and a family to come home to. When Ivy was born, I held her in my arms in the hospital long enough to experience an unexpected rush of maternal emotion which, combined with the baby's absolute trust, would be hard to separate into identifiable strands. It shocked me. From an early age, I'd maintained that I didn't want the ties of a family but at that moment realised I was wrong. I did want those things, after all. As Sarah walked away home with her new baby, I felt bereft, unfulfilled.

I pull myself away from maudlin possibilities and make

three telephone calls to people I've never met before, all of whom seem to know about me and my strange task: why on earth would the government want to know about all the old stones and fairy forts? It's weird, so it is!

I decide to check out some raths on the hills overlooking Bantry Bay, despite the ominous black clouds sailing down from the north and the spit of rain in the air. I zip up into my wet weather gear and set out. A bitter north wind has picked up, and the temperature has plummeted, so maybe I'll be going to see Sarah sooner than I thought.

The first visit is on land owned by Freddy Mason. His son, Luke, who must be into his forties, walks up with me, ostensibly to show me around but more likely through curiosity. He's hugged deep into a stockman's waxed coat and wears a home-knitted woolly hat pulled down over his ears. As we scramble up the steep slope, slipping on the wet rocks, our boots sinking into pockets of bog, he asks keen questions about the people who used to live there, which I'm happy to answer to the extent of the knowledge we have to date, which is little enough.

'A lot of it's educated guesswork,' I tell him. 'We find the remnants of their physical presence, but the people themselves – their day-to-day lives, their beliefs, their stories – are lost in the mists of time. The only way we'll ever really know is if someone invents a time machine!'

'Call Doctor Who,' he jokes.

I've heard of the ongoing series, seen adverts, but never watched it – it sounds pretty daft to me. Some doddery old fool racing around time in a telephone kiosk! My parents invested in a television a few years back – for the news, Dad said – but recently I've caught him watching horse racing and John Wayne westerns. I don't blame him. Getting old is a rare trick, he says, rubbing his knees for the pain.

'So, you're interested in the people who made the rath?' I ask as we trudge uphill, battling the wind.

'I wasn't,' he admits. 'But I was curious when I saw the notice for your talk and went along to listen. You were good. You held everyone in Roone Bay quiet for an hour, and that's got to be a miracle.'

I laugh but experience a little tingle of pleasure, knowing that I've made even one of the farmers interested in the heritage on their land. 'I think the young these days are more interested in discos than the past.'

'But you're not?' he says, casting a straight glance. 'It's where the young go to find partners, these days, isn't it?'

'I don't see how,' I reason, 'when the music is so loud you can't have a conversation.'

'Young men don't want to *talk* to girls,' he jokes, making me laugh again.

He's right, I suppose. Gone are the days when girls had to be chaperoned, but Irish culture is still very much led by the Catholic Church, and unmarried mothers are still treated as if they're criminals. As Mam says, women have ever been trapped between the devil and the deep blue sea. Men want to sow their wild oats, but if a girl gets pregnant, it's her own fault – even when it's not.

But Luke is talking about the rath, above.

'It was just part of the landscape when I was growing up,' he says, 'like gorse and stones and fields and cattle. The only reason my dad hasn't flattened it is the superstition that's trickled down through the years.' He casts an amused sidelong grin as he adds, 'My parents don't believe in all that nonsense, of course, but they aren't willing to get cursed finding out they're wrong!'

And that sums up a good many country folk, I think.

When we reach the rath, it becomes obvious why it's there, on the brow of the hill. It commands a sweeping view of Bantry

Bay, with all its tiny inlets, and to the left, another rath is clearly visible on the brow of the next hill. Raths aren't usually discovered in such close proximity, nor are they on the hilltops where they reap the full vengeance of the Atlantic weather. Maybe these were different: forts or lookouts. Vikings and, later, African slave traders were known to have landed along this coast, so it would have been in the interests of all who lived here to keep a weather eye on the sea. It's possible that an early warning would have been signalled along the hilltops with fire.

We measure the rath as the rain sweeps in and the clouds deliver a torrential downpour. Even as we're scurrying back down the hill, small streams are forming in the gullies as the rain, too heavy to sink into the already sodden ground, rushes from the hill.

At the farmhouse door, Luke shouts over the noise of the rain, 'Come on in and dry off.'

We rush into a hallway, dripping water, laughing like teenagers. He pulls his wellingtons off, and I follow.

'Can I get you a cuppa before you head?' he asks as I follow him into the kitchen.

He's plugging in an electric kettle as he's speaking, and I suddenly get that horrible, uneasy feeling at being alone with a man I don't know at all.

'Mam and Dad'll be back soon. They want to meet you,' he says, and I feel daft for worrying. I'm wondering why they want to meet me, when he adds, 'We're kind of distant relatives, you know.'

My brows rise in question.

'Go and hog the range and get warm,' he invites, then explains, as I do just that, 'Mam was telling me, after the talk, that her grandmother was Maureen O'Brien's sister.'

I have to think back for the relationship to gel in my mind. Maureen was the wife of Patrick O'Brien, my great-grandfather, and Davan was his son.

'Going back that far,' I say, laughing, 'I'm probably related to half of Roone Bay!'

'Yes, but that was a strange one, wasn't it? About Davan and Molly, I mean. My grandmother said she never believed the story about him running off. She said it was more likely that William Savage killed his own daughter in a rage and probably killed Davan, too, when he got out of prison. She said they're probably buried on the farm somewhere.'

William murdering his own daughter seems a bit of a stretch, but, 'Prison?' I query, startled by that new piece of information.

'She said William called the magistrate on Davan because he'd been courting his Molly and her being underage, and what with the bother between the families. He was given a term in jail. I expect there are records up at Cork, if you want to check it out.'

I'm fascinated. I'd never heard of this from my own family, but time in prison is a stigma to law-abiding folk, maybe even more so back then, when my parents were young. Perhaps Grampy Danny and Grandma Sally never told them. But they would have heard the gossip all the same. 'That was a horrible thing for him to do.'

'Maybe. I'm thinking that Davan must have done more than just courting for that to happen,' Luke says. 'If William found out his Molly was with child, and her being just fifteen or so, I can see why he would have lost his temper.'

It's possible. Young girls have been *getting into trouble* since the dawn of civilisation. 'Do you know how old Davan was when he was courting Molly?'

He shakes his head then glances out of the window. 'Oh, here they are. Mam'll be pleased she didn't miss you.'

I hadn't heard the car arrive, for the overwhelming sound of the rain beating on the window. Luke's parents rush in from the downpour as we did and shake their coats before hanging them at the side of the range. They're both wiry as whippets, probably from long years working the land.

'Ginny, dear,' Mrs Mason says, squeezing my hand and presenting an overly friendly air kiss. She's obviously determined to stretch the boundaries of our distant familial connection. 'I hope Luke's been treating you well?'

'Sure, he has.' I point to the mug of tea on the table and the open tin of biscuits. 'Luckily we finished as the heavens opened on us. I think the stone circle to the east is on your land, too? Maybe I could come back another day and check that? It was pointless staying up there in this downpour.'

'You're welcome any time, Ginny love,' she agrees. 'If we're not here, just makes yourself at home. You wouldn't think it was summer, would you? I suppose Luke told you we're family?'

I give a tight smile. 'Three generations ago. I had no idea.'

Luke's father nods at me, then disappears into another room as his wife settles herself by the fire, holding her hands out for warmth. 'So, I want to know everything!' she says.

I suspect she's fishing for personal information, which irritates me. 'Luke says you were at the talk in Roone Bay. I don't know what more I can add.'

'Oh.'

She sounds a bit put out, so I quickly add, 'Luke was just telling me about Davan O'Brien being in prison. I didn't know that.'

'Oh, sure, he was. The whole town knew it. It was a scandal, sure enough. But in fact, there weren't so many who thought it was right, him being just a biteen lad himself, you know. William didn't win himself any love by that action. His poor wife, Mairead, had so much to put up with.' She shakes her head. 'Such a temper he had on him. I wouldn't have put it past him to have given his daughter a good thrashing, too. Not that I ever heard he did,' she adds hastily. 'But for the rest of her life, Mairead blamed her husband for her daughter disappearing.

Sure, Davan would have married the girl in due course if William hadn't been so pig-headed.'

'Apparently there was talk that William murdered Molly and buried her on his land somewhere.'

She flushes slightly. 'Well, talk's cheap, so it is.'

At his mother's comment, Luke raises a brow at me, and gives his head a minuscule shake. I get it. The gossip that's whispered behind doors isn't meant to be broadcast. The rift between our two families, mine and the Savages, was created so long ago it's become folklore. How can people be so – what was it she said? – pig-headed. The feud should have been buried long before poor Davan and Molly got caught in the backlash.

We chatter for a little while, and I make my excuses. 'My mam will be worrying where I am and am I all right.'

'We could ring her if you want to stay and chat?'

'No, please, it's fine, but I should go now. I have a lot of notes to catch up on.'

'Sure, and won't ye be back soon?'

'I will,' I agree. 'When the weather breaks, I'll come and look up that stone circle that's over the brow of the hill.'

'And mind ye pop in for a cuppa.'

I escape thankfully from what was setting up to be a third degree. I sensed that Mrs Mason was more interested in recent happenings than the distant past, and was itching to ask me why I'd run out on Ben Savage before he had that dreadful accident. But I'm not going to discuss that with strangers, even those who claim to be family.

Luke sees me to the door. 'Come any time to catch the other rath and the stone circle,' he says, and whispers with a wink, 'and don't be worrying about knocking at the door.'

I smile gratefully and rush out to the car with my waterproof over my head. I drive home thinking all the while about Davan and Molly being in love and Molly's father going ballistic because of some long-forgotten slight. Or perhaps it was because she was underage and maybe even pregnant. I doubt we'll ever learn the truth of that.

But it's easy enough to work out how they'd managed to meet each other behind their respective parents' backs. The rath on the Savages' land is just out of sight of their farmhouse. Davan could easily have carved a secret path through the gorse, if the wild goats hadn't done it for him.

When I get home, as the weather hasn't produced the promised sunshine, I put off my hillside trek and phone Sarah. She's fine for me to visit the next day and stay as long as I want.

12

DAVAN, 1921

Davan was turning the newly scythed grass in the small meadow when his father came to him, saying in a worried voice, 'Mickey Roark is at the house, asking after you. Son, why would the police be after looking for you? What have you done?'

'Nothing, Dada,' he said. He stood, spiked the long, thin tines of the hayfork into the soft ground and stretched his back. He closed his eyes briefly, letting the sun catch his face. It had been a warm week; thanks be to God. It meant the hay could likely be lifted the next day if it continued. There were some years when rain blasted in from the Atlantic on the back of storm winds and the cut grass went mouldy on the field. That was bad news for the approaching winter, when the cattle were in the sheds, in calf, desperate for the feeding. 'Let's go and see what he wants. It will be something daft, I'm sure. Don't worry yourself at all.'

Davan picked up his precious sketchbook and pencil from the gatepost where they rested, and walked back towards the house. His father eyed him suspiciously, and he smiled inwardly, but the evidence of his labour lay on the turned grass steaming in the sunshine. Though he was set to inherit the farm, he was aware that his whole family were puzzled by his dreaming ways. He loved to draw and was good at it. He didn't have any real hankering to be an artist, though. He liked the farm, the freedom of the outside life, even though it was hard sometimes. He simply liked to sketch the things that drifted past his eyes. There were times his pencil would be creating a wren, a cow, a flower, or some tiny, exquisite thing like a stone or a snail while his mind wandered to the birds flying high above.

Why would you draw a snail? his father once asked, exasperated.

Sure, isn't it one of God's creatures? Davan had replied.

He was the only one who saw the beauty in such things, and would be capturing them with his pencil while the cows bellowed impatiently to be milked and let out into fresh pasture. His family wondered where that need had come from and – they had to admit – that skill, and shook their heads; but when the mood struck him – a flash of sunlight, the tilt of a head – he simply had to draw it.

Davan marched happily back to the house beside his father. He was tall and sturdy, but lately he seemed taller than Dada, who seemed to have bowed like a branch over the years of labouring on the land that had been in his family for as long as they'd known.

His parents had survived through some hard times, including the Great War, the Irish War of Independence and the Easter Rising, in which one of his cousins had died. Isolated as Ireland had been, the times had brought hardship on its heels, keeping the poor struggling, as always. But Davan's young life had been safe in the knowledge that his family owned the land they farmed, and evictions were a thing of the past. It was a good era to be living in Ireland, a young country on the verge of a new dawn. He was contented in his life, and once Molly was his wife, his happiness would be complete.

The sergeant, Mickey Roark, seemed to overwhelm the

small kitchen in which his mother and his two yet unwed sisters were working. He was a big man with a ruddy face and an impressive pair of dark, bushy sideburns, as was the fashion. Known for his love of a good pint, his stomach bulged above a tightly cinched belt. His two accompanying officers stood behind him, poker-faced. Davan had known them since school, but they didn't greet him with their usual cheery smiles. His own smile of greeting faded into confusion as he asked, 'Lads, what can I do for yous?'

Mickey cleared his throat and held out an official-looking document. 'Davan Savage, I'm charged with arresting you for the rape of a minor.'

'What?' he exclaimed, the flush of health fading from his face.

'Molly O'Brien's father is laying this charge against you. Do you deny it?'

The enticing scent of bread was wafting from the oven at the side of the fire. His family had frozen like statues, their faces gaping with shock. It was a surreal moment.

'Why would he say something like that?' he asked in wonder. He knew who they meant, but Molly loved him, of that he had no doubt. It certainly hadn't been rape, and they had made vows to be wed.

'The girl told the priest, apparently.' The sergeant sounded almost apologetic. 'Molly asked the priest to marry her. It seems she's in the family way, and her a minor not yet fifteen.'

Daft as it seemed, he had never thought of her being with child. Despite the sergeant's presence, a smile of satisfaction creased his cheeks. He was to be a father!

'Davan, what have you done?' his mother wailed, screwing her apron in her hands.

'Hush, woman,' his father told her and turned to Davan. 'Tell them there's been a mistake made.'

'No. Tell Mr Savage I will marry Molly,' Davan said. 'It will make everything right. He'll understand.'

'I think Mr Savage in not a man to listen to reason,' the sergeant said dryly. 'According to the law, a man having relations with a minor is statutory rape, for which there is normally a term of imprisonment. William Savage is arranging for Molly to be sent away.'

'Sent away? Why would he do that?'

The sergeant flushed. 'So the nuns can look after her.'

Davan was silent for a moment, then he said, 'No, he mustn't do that. I love Molly. Sure, I'll marry her. Why would he want her to become a nun? What would happen to my child?'

'There will be no child,' Mickey said with a hint of sadness. 'I'm sorry, Davan, but I have to do my duty.'

'But...' Davan faltered, confused.

His mother wailed again and brought her apron up to her mouth, stifling her sobs.

The constable held out the handcuffs. 'It will come before the magistrate, but for now I have to take you into custody.'

'No, Mickey, don't do this,' Davan argued. He turned to his father. 'Go and speak to William. Tell him I'll make this right. I always intended to make it right.'

He recognised the consequences of his actions, and marriage was, quite simply, the obvious answer. He didn't understand why William wouldn't agree to that.

'I will,' his father agreed doubtfully.

'Men!' his mother interjected, turning angrily to her husband, her face damp. 'Didn't I tell ye years back to let him take a yard of land and put an end to the nonsense? Your father was pig-headed about it, and you take after the stubborn old fool! And about a biteen of land that's of no matter? Now see what ye have done?'

'It's a matter of honour,' Davan's father said stiffly. 'Women don't understand these things. If I'd done that, it would have been all around the townland. I would have been a laughing stock.' He compressed his lips. He didn't like being told off by his own wife in front of the constabulary and his own kin, but he knew he couldn't meet the challenge. 'I'll speak to William, but he won't be listening to any proposals from me.'

Mickey nodded in agreement. 'That's a fact. He won't be after giving any consent for the marriage, either. He said he won't be after having an O'Brien bastard born into his house.'

'A bastard?' Davan said, in wonder. The child he and his lovely Molly had made between them? No. It was a child of love, so it was. Surely her father would see that. 'Her father cannot mean that? Not when I'll marry her and make everything as it should be. And that's all over a wee strip of land?'

He knew about the land fracas, of course, but up to now he had seen it as no more than a spat that provided entertainment to the community when the two farmers inadvertently passed each other in town. It had been going on for generations, since before his grandfather's day, and neither man would give way. *There are none so stubborn as donkeys and men*, his mother had been known to mutter under her breath, rolling her eyes.

Davan turned to his parents now, tears in his eyes. 'If her family won't keep her, will we take in Molly and bring our child up here? It will all come out right in the end, you'll see. We'll be married as soon as we can and make our confessions.'

'Maybe,' his mother said doubtfully, 'but the priest—'

'God will surely forgive us, even if the clergy don't.'

The sergeant interrupted before she was able to make the arguments to her husband. 'Her father has the saying of it,' he stated, 'and that's the end of the matter.'

Why is this happening? Davan thought. God would surely understand that love was not something one chose. It had come down like an angel spreading its glory around them, bathing them in its beauty. The hours he had spent with Molly in the magical serenity of their secret place had not seemed like sin. Not at all. She had encouraged his tentative yearnings, and they had been together in mind as well as body. He had never been with a woman before, and they had coupled with naïve pleasure. To be sure, he had not expected a baby to come so soon, perhaps believing that God would not send a child to her until they were married. But they were created for each other, their minds reaching out through the continuous daily cycle of chores that demanded their time.

Together they lifted each other's lives and hopes beyond the boundaries of their farming backgrounds. Davan's pencil had captured Molly's exuberance for life, as poetry and songs she had heard just once in school came tumbling out, the words of long-dead poets cleverly expressing what they were unable to express themselves.

Davan's family were caring and hard-working, and never understood his nature the way Molly did. She spoke her dreams out loud, about having a house together, which she would paint yellow, like spring primroses.

Yellow! he had asked in wonder. *Who paints a house?*

We will, she answered, lying on her back, perusing the tiny flower against the overcast sky before turning her face to his. It had been a promise for the future.

'Where's the sense in all this?' Davan said in frustration, to no one in particular. 'What's wrong with her father?'

His own father surprised him by standing up to his enemy's actions. 'The chit should never have been so brazen. If it was one of my girls, I'd do the same.'

'She's not brazen,' Davan corrected softly. 'She's sweet and charming and innocent, and I love her. Maybe it shouldn't have happened, but it did. She's the best thing that ever happened to me. She's the candle that lights my soul, the sunshine in my darkest day. I will marry her; if not now, then as soon as I may,'

Davan said, confounding his parents by quoting the words Molly had spoken to him.

'Come on, lad,' Mickey said, not unkindly.

Davan's mother and sisters huddled closer together. Davan's actions were going to impact on his family in more ways than one. His father was in agreement with his neighbour, for the first time in their lives, but it wouldn't resolve the long-standing feud; it would serve to rekindle its dying embers.

'God help us all,' Davan's mother whispered.

Mickey Roark was clearly embarrassed by his task, eager to be gone. He unclipped the handcuffs from his belt and handed them to his junior officers. Davan's two erstwhile school mates put them on him, and Davan stared back over his shoulder at his stunned family as he allowed himself to be shepherded to the waiting cart. It was unreal. He would go along with it without complaining, though, because the solution to the problem was obvious, so the whole misunderstanding would soon be sorted.

13

GINNY

The drive to Clonakilty is slow, the windscreen wipers betraying flashing wet strips of tarmac as fast as the rain obliterates them. A couple of times I hit potholes without even seeing them and find myself praying that I don't meet some idiot driving too fast the other way. I arrive at Sarah's house in good time, though, and run to the door with my coat over my head. She must have been waiting for me. The door opens as I reach for the latch, and I almost fall through into her waiting arms.

'Ginny,' she shrieks above the noise, hugging me.

'Yep, that's me,' I say with a grin as we disengage.

We give each other appraising glances. Age is subtly making its mark; a new thread of white in the hair, new lines on her face. We have strong physical similarities, so I wonder if she's seeing the same changes in me. Age doesn't sit as well on women as it does on men. We seem to shrivel to wrinkled prunes while men grow distinguished.

As always, we deal with the present and don't spout platitudes about a past that could have been different. I'm lucky to have the support and love of a close family. I've seen too many families fall apart through small disagreements that somehow escalate into huge conflicts.

'Come on into the kitchen. Ivy's been bothering me something dreadful asking when you'd be arriving.'

'Isn't she at school?'

'It's Saturday?' She shakes her head. 'Same old Ginny. Your head so far into the past you don't even know what day of the week it is! You'll be staying over for a couple of days?'

'If the weather doesn't take a turn for the better. And if you don't mind.'

'Mind? Ye eejit!' She bustles me through, calling, 'Ivy, Auntie Ginny is here!'

Ivy rushes up to hug me. She's eleven, now, with dark hair, clear skin and enquiring blue eyes. She's a little more reserved and studious than her brother, Patrick, who is nearly two years older than her. We enjoy a brief moment of silent communication before settling around the kitchen table.

'No Pat?' I ask.

'No, he's out with his father, checking some new-fangled car that's on display in Cork. He wants to be a racing driver now, but I'm hoping he'll settle for mechanic.'

Ivy states authoritatively, 'He wants to drive cars, Mam, not fix them. You know that.'

'Well, maybe he could drive a bus or a taxi, then I wouldn't be so worried.'

'He's not going to do that!"

Her tone has the belligerence of a girl who thinks she knows what life is all about. She probably sees Sarah and me as old women. Children always believe their parents were born old and don't have all the memories of being young. I remember thinking that myself. But it's those very memories, with all the joys, cruelties, random happenings and unintended consequences that change the course of one's life in an instant, which make us overprotect our children. As I grew older, the age gap between myself and my parents lessened, and we became more like friends. I'm hoping the same will happen with Ivy and Sarah.

'And Ellen?' I ask.

'She's catching a nap.' Sarah looks at her watch. 'She'll be an hour or so, yet. How strange it is to have another wean after all this time. I really thought I was done with all that! Ivy, what have you forgotten?'

'Oh! We made you a cake,' Ivy recalls and rushes to fetch it from the press. It's generously iced and covered in sugar sprinkles.

'What's this for? It's not my birthday!'

'No, but once you phoned, Ivy wanted to, and she decorated it herself,' Sarah tells me. 'She said the rain would bring you over, and wasn't she right?'

Again, there's a meeting of eyes and flash of unspoken communication between myself and Sarah, which makes my heart lurch with self-pity. I might have a child of my own if I'd chosen a different path, but I guess I'm not mother material. There's still time, of course, though I'm sure I'll do the same now as I did in the past: reject the possibility of a stable relationship in favour of personal freedom. I'm younger than Sarah by a few years, but my lifestyle is too random to accommodate a home and children, even if I had a husband, which isn't on my horizon, anyway.

Sarah makes us a cuppa, and Ivy cuts the cake very carefully and shares the slices out. I'm not a great fan of cake, and it's very sweet, but I make happy munching noises, and her eyes sparkle with pleasure.

I'm probably not good wife material, either. It was my own choice, to invest in a somewhat academic pursuit above choosing a family home and the somewhat limiting boundaries of motherhood, but sometimes I get torn between wanting the best of both worlds. I just have to make do with being an auntie; that I can do well!

'I brought presents,' I finally say, snagging the last crumbs of cake with a wet finger. 'We'll have to wait for the rain to stop, though.'

'Auntie Ginny!' she moans.

'Okay, well maybe you can dodge the raindrops and bring the purple bag in from the car.'

'When you've finished your cake,' Sarah adds.

Ivy stuffs the remains in her mouth with little adherence to manners and jumps up, scraping her chair on the tiled floor, making me wince.

'How are you doing?' Sarah asks seriously as the kitchen door slams behind her. 'Really, I mean.'

'Well,' I say. 'Honestly, I thought it would be difficult, but it's not so bad.'

'It's early days,' she says darkly.

'The past is the past.'

'You know that's not true. Not in Roone Bay. The past will be there to haunt us until we're all laid in our graves, and then some! Mam told me that Ruari came to your talk.'

I'm startled. 'I didn't know she saw him.'

'She didn't. Brigid's mam took delight in telling her. That auld biddy has a mouth on her.'

'I saw her there. She has to be in the thick of the gossip.'

'She's a poisonous tattle monger.'

'And she doesn't like me, particularly.'

Sarah sniffs with amusement.

The rift between myself and my one-time schoolfriend Brigid was an open sore in her mother's mind. Brigid told her I'd stolen Ben away from her, and her mother had taken up the reins of the galloping horse, making out that I'd deliberately wrecked Brigid's future. After Ben died, Mam said Brigid made a real exhibition of her grief. I suspect it was to attract attention rather than real grief – though, if Ruari wasn't taken in, he's probably not the only one.

How people fool themselves, I think. The need for wealth can become obsessive and lead to all sorts of complications. One would suppose age and maturity would make people realise that, but grudges and blame can settle like immoveable rocks in the mind. And when a story is told enough times, don't people find themselves sucked into believing it?

Ivy comes hurtling back in, shaking her hair like a damp dog, her eyes gleaming with anticipation. I laugh out loud. 'Go on – open it, before you burst.'

I don't actually like shopping for myself. My own wardrobe gets replenished from necessity, but I do love shopping for the children. I suspect they get regular trips into Cork city, but there's nothing like being spoiled with presents, especially if it's things they wouldn't have thought to buy for themselves – or things their sensible mother wouldn't approve of. I've bought Ivy a book about fashion, pop stars and make-up, a couple of novels, and some girly fripperies: clothes and things for her hair. For Patrick I bought a tiny working steam engine, which wasn't at all cheap, but which I'm sure he'll treasure long after Ivy's presents have been lost to the winds.

My sister and I don't stop talking for an hour, about Mam and Dad, the boys, and my return to Roone Bay. Meantime, Ellen wakes and is engrossed in the activity toy I bought her. Later, when Thomas and Patrick arrive home, they lean, heads together, and get the little steam engine working. It makes hissing, chugging noises and seems to wind up slowly to full steam. We watch in wonder as the little pistons work away, and the big wheel begins to spin. Next, I'll have to buy him something that works off it, I realise, as the novelty of watching a static engine soon palls.

Later, as we sit around the kitchen table, the gentle clatter of cutlery on plates and the easy chit-chat make me a little nostalgic for the past. Thomas does his best to be the life and soul of the party, and irritates me a few times with his inane quips, but I dutifully laugh along with Sarah, who seems to genuinely find them amusing. I drift a little at times, between feeling close with this family and being a stranger, watching from the outside.

The children go to bed, and we settle in front of the TV to watch *Bewitched*, a daft series about this woman called Samantha who is secretly a witch. I try to wiggle my nose the way she does, but my face doesn't seem to work that way. Sarah and Tom snuggle together on the sofa, then make their excuses of tiredness and head off upstairs.

I pull back the living-room curtains and stare out into the night. The house is on the outskirts of Clonakilty, facing a rural valley rather than the town. The rain has eased, but the cloud base must still be low as I can't see the moon or stars. The almost-complete darkness is dotted with small twinkles of light from distant farmhouses. Fifty years ago, the vista would have been endless dark.

The door behind me opens silently, and Ivy comes in, in her pyjamas and dressing gown. 'I couldn't sleep,' she says hesitantly.

I indicate the sofa that's been vacated. 'Come and have a cuddle and tell me something secret.'

She giggles. 'If I tell you, it won't be a secret any longer.'

I smile. It's a family joke, handed down from my mam. 'So, I could tell you a story.'

'Please. I love your stories.'

'They're my great-grandpa Patrick's stories, really, and much older than that besides.'

'I know.'

She snuggles against me, and I put my arm around her. It's all I can do to stop myself from telling her my secret, but secrets once told aren't secrets any longer. 'Well, you know there was once a beautiful queen called Maeve?'

'Yes, and her husband was called Ailill, wasn't he?'

'He was. Well, Queen Maeve was supposed to be some kind of goddess. People thought she had magic powers.'

'But did she, really?'

'Maybe. It was long ago, when the fairy hills were still gateways to the otherworld, before the old gods faded away from Ireland. There were many heroes around at the time. Sort of half-gods, because they had one human parent and one god parent.'

'And heroines?'

'Not really. In the old stories, women with powers were usually witches or seers. But Maeve was different because she was a queen, you see. She was supposed to have lived somewhere in Connaught. She was, I think, a very fickle woman, not satisfied with her life, because whenever she got what she wanted, she discovered something she wanted more.'

'Like Una from school.'

'Naughty,' I say, but we giggle like schoolgirls, then I carry on and tell her the story of how she sent an army to steal a bull she coveted, which resulted in a war and thousands of lives lost.

I have a unique connection with Ivy, and although I haven't tried to influence her, I know she's going to follow in my footsteps in some way: go on to university, be interested in the more academic aspects of life, even if it's not archaeology. I have a brief worry that if I encourage her, she'll end up lonely like me, with no family to call my own.

Maybe, unlike me, she'll find a compromise and have the best of both worlds. Times have changed, even since my own childhood; it's more usual for women to combine work and home, though there's still a lot of men grumbling, saying women should stay at home and not steal their jobs. And still women get less money for doing the same work – doing it better, in some cases!

For me, home is an ephemeral concept, like water that keeps churning away downhill under the bridge of life. But nothing can turn the clock back, and as I sit here with Ivy, I know I wouldn't want it to. We mere humans sometimes make bad decisions, and sometimes others make them for us. We just have to cope with the consequences, because there's nothing else to be done. I'm eternally grateful to Sarah and Tom for allowing me to share their family when the need hits me.

The next day, Patrick and Ivy are off out to the swimming pool. They're competent in the water, so Sarah no longer feels the need to be with them. She hates swimming pools with their excessive need for chlorine, and this allows us space to catch up on things not meant for young ears. They depart, bickering about something trivial, after pleading for snack money as well as the entrance fee. It makes me smile. Sarah makes a play of being a hard taskmaster, and eventually I step in as the generous auntie and give them more than she would have. It's a game we all play. That's what aunts are for, isn't it? Like fairy godmothers who bring gifts, but without the wand.

'So, how is it going, back in the old house?' Sarah asks, when peace has descended and we're sitting at the kitchen table nursing mugs of coffee.

'Difficult,' I admit. 'I was worried about how I'd be treated. I'm sure the gossip is doing the rounds, but the people I've met so far are simply curious, fishing for detail.'

'And Ruari Savage? He was the middle one, wasn't he?'

I guess Mam has said something. 'No, the youngest. He was in my year at school. He's interested in the past, too.'

'What, he's pestering you about Ben?'

'Not really. He's interested in finding out what happened to Molly and Davan, though, the same as me. But listen...'

Interest lights her features as I tell her about meeting Noel

O'Donovan and finding out about Ben's childhood accident. She looks suitably pitying, probably thinking how she'd feel if it had been her own son. But her real interest lies in my visit to Roone Manor, and my brush with the famous horse breeder.

'But you went in the Big House? What was it like?'

'Well, I only saw the kitchen. Noel is just like this ordinary guy, not posh or anything. Mrs Weddows had scones made, then we walked up the hill behind his house to the rath. Remember playing there as a child?'

She laughs. 'And I dared you to go in! That was wicked cruel of me.'

'But I did, and I was more in fear of our mam finding out than being frightened of the little folk!'

We're silent for a moment, remembering the misty enjoyment of our childhood before she left to be married and I got friendly with Ben. If she'd still been there, I suspect I would have told her about my blossoming friendship. She would certainly have dobbed me out to mam, and the bother would never have happened.

I sigh. 'We can't change the past, sis.'

'No. But what about his family? And Ruari? You're not going to tell them what Ben did, are you?'

I put my hand across the table and squeeze hers. 'Of course not. Not after all this time.'

She looks relieved. But I will never forget the look on Ben's face before he ran, leaving me lying on the ground wetting the grass with my own blood. Unfortunately, that's the look that lives with me, because it was the last time I saw him.

'Well, one day you're going to find some man who lights your fires and all that fear will just evaporate.'

'Maybe,' I say lightly. And maybe not.

The incident left me with a fear of men in general, because I will never forget my absolute helplessness in the face of his anger. When Ben attacked me, I'd been a slight teenager, and yes, he hurt me. But the most damage he did was to my psyche. People see me as a confident and independent career woman, but when I'm alone with a guy, doubt creeps in, whispering that bad things can happen.

The rain keeps up its endless rattle on the windows for three more days, and on the fourth day, the storm breaks. The wind dies down, and the fitful sun tries to bludgeon its way through the clouds, so I make my excuses. We all hug and kiss, and I head back to Roone Bay, but being with Sarah and her family, the talk often turned to our childhood, bringing a rush of memory, good and bad. Making mistakes is all part of growing up, of course. No one can make your mistakes for you, and it takes luck to survive childhood mistakes intact.

14

GINNY, 1966

'Genevieve! Get out of that bed now!'

Ginny groaned. When her mam used her full, and somewhat peculiar, name, she knew she couldn't procrastinate any longer and slid out reluctantly. It was freezing in the bedroom, despite the range in the kitchen below, which should, in theory, send heat up through the bare floorboards. In her experience it didn't get that far. Her best friend's father had recently installed radiators into all rooms in their house and put insulation in the ceilings. *New-fangled nonsense*, her father said when she told him. He had grown up without heating and didn't see why his children shouldn't. It was an expense he wasn't prepared to pay for, and there would be the added cost of fuel. He wasn't made of money and, sure, wasn't it hard enough to keep the farm going already?

She threw her clothes on and ran downstairs to park herself in front of the range while the chill gradually receded.

'You had your head in a blessed romance book again,' her mam accused, cracking eggs into the pan with a deft flick of the wrist.

'No, I didn't,' Ginny lied.

Her mam didn't understand that sinking into a fictional world gave rise to all the possibilities she was missing out on while living in the isolation of a farm, with just boring old Roone Bay near enough for shopping excursions. It was just a tiny backwater town with its one of everything: church, library, school and shop. She loved the farm and her parents and school, of course, but longed for the excitement of the city – the whole world! She was aching to leave school, go places and find her own real-life romance. She'd talked with her friends about this, and they all agreed that life was waiting out there, if they could only escape to find it. Her sister, Sarah, being several years older, recently married, had escaped but only down the road to Clonakilty, which – though it wasn't a thriving metropolis – at least had a whole row of shops.

Ginny liked visiting Sarah and her new husband. Even if he wasn't exactly the epitome of a knight in shining armour, he was nice. He seemed like a man of the world, with his endless ribbing and jokes, and if he hadn't provided Sarah with a castle, he had at least provided her with a good home, which she was presently kitting out with a nursery. And it had central heating!

'So, will ye be coming home with Brigid's mam?'

'Sure, Mam. Me and Brigid will be off to the library after school, and her mam is going to drop me back home before teatime.'

'Okay, so.'

Eggs and toast were plonked in front of her while her mam carried on and made sandwiches for lunch. After hastily consuming her breakfast, earning a quick comment from her mam – *Sure, don't ye gobble better than a goose?* – she heard the beep of a car horn, and Brigid's mam was outside to pick her up. It was an arrangement that suited all the parents. Ginny's mam didn't drive, and her own dad could pick both girls up when Brigid's mam needed to be somewhere else. Ginny liked going in with Brigid as they could sit in the back seat and compare notes on the latest

Mills and Boon romance Brigid had borrowed from the library. Her mam wasn't so daft about it as her own mam. When they were discussing the hero, Brigid's mam would sometimes fly a ribald comment over her shoulder that sent the girls into fits of giggles.

Her own mam wanted her to do well at school and was pleased when she saw Ginny reading books for schoolwork. *Sure, why would ye want to read cheap romances? Haven't ye more brains than half of Roone Bay?*

Didn't her mam realise that although she was good on the academic stuff, wasn't she a young woman, too, with needs? Reading romances was the nearest she was going to get to understanding about real men. The boys at school weren't real men in the eyes of the girls. Brigid had once kissed Jimmy Nolan behind the library, not that he ever took anything useful out of its hallowed doorway. He'd been after leaving school as soon as he could to help his dad on the boats. It had been a real proper snog, Brigid informed their peer group.

Later, Ginny snogged him, too. She told everyone it was fab and basked in the light of their jealousy for a few weeks. In reality, him stuffing his tongue into her mouth had been shocking rather than pleasant, nearly making her vomit. The men in the romance stories didn't do that. She hid her distaste, though, Jimmy being almost idolised because he was the best-looking boy around; romantic possibilities in Roone Bay being kind of limited.

They were both sixteen now, and the long summer break was just a few weeks away, after which everything would change. Brigid would be gone to work, and Ginny would be one of the few remaining at school with academic aspirations. Brigid's mam, who was giving her a lift home, was in a hurry after school and left her off at the foot of the small lane up to the farm. She slammed the door and waved goodbye. It wasn't raining, and she enjoyed being outside, listening to the birds, sometimes wandering on the hills long enough for her mam to nearly be sending out search parties.

'Ginny Kingston,' a man's voice behind her said.

She jumped and turned, and there was Benjamin Savage, leaning his arms on the top of a gate. She knew who he was. Everyone did. Mam and Dad said she wasn't to talk to any of the Savage boys, but sure, they weren't here to tell her off, and didn't Micheal say they were sound altogether?

He leaped over the gate in a single bound, one strong hand grasping the top bar, his long legs scrunching and stretching like an athlete. She was suitably impressed.

'It's a grand day,' he said. 'Can I walk ye up to the house?'

'You aren't working?'

'I was. But I can take a break on my own farm.'

He wasn't potential boyfriend material, of course, being so much older than herself, but he looked quite well in a worn checked shirt and the jeans that clung tightly to the carved muscles of his thighs before flaring over his boots in the current fashion. He had a sort of rugged, outdoor cleanliness about him, his home-cut dark hair parted to one side, leading into the extended sideburns.

The Savage boys were handsome lads altogether, their aquiline faces providing an air of sophistication. They had straight noses and deep smile-lines either side of generous mouths – *made for kissing*, Brigid had whispered. The older Savage boys all had a way with themselves, made big and confident like their father. Ruari, the youngest, who was in her class, and Noah, in the year above her, had yet to attain their full size but would no doubt spring up the way of their older brothers in due course.

'I saw Brigid's mam drop ye off and waited in behind the

hedge,' he admitted after a moment of silence. 'Brigid's mam is after pushing her at me.'

'I heard,' I say with a complicit grin.

He kept pace with her easily on the rutted drive.

'But you're all right. Will I carry your bag up the hill?'

'Ye can,' she agreed, preening slightly at the compliment.

He gave a sidelong glance. 'I've been watching yous for a while now.'

'Ye have?'

'Sure I have. You've turned into a fine girrul, so. You like the fields. I've seen you up in the rath.' She flushed faintly, and he grinned. 'Sure, I won't tell anyone. I've been wanting to get to know you better.'

That made her feel as if she was walking on air. A good-looking lad, interested in her? Sure, she'd had the curse for several years, and her breasts had formed small and neat, which her mam said was a blessing, but which she lifted with handkerchiefs inside her bra. Her mam complained that she should be careful because she could be taken for older.

'If I was to come a-courting, then, would ye maybe mind?' Ben asked.

She laughed at his naivety. 'I'm too young, of course, Ben Savage. I have two more years of school, yet, then university.'

'Why would you want to be going to university?'

'Because I want to get a good job. I have no intention of working in the shop in Roone Bay, like Brigid.'

'Fair comment,' he agreed. 'But if you married me, you wouldn't have to work at all, seeing as I'm going to inherit a farm.'

She stopped, turned to face him and put her hands on her hips, echoing her mam's words, usually said with a kind of stoic frustration. 'Benjamin Savage! As if being a farmer's wife isn't a full-time job! But I'm not going to tie myself down to this place, farm or no farm. If I do marry, and I'm not saying it's going to happen at all, I want someone who wears a suit and has a city job.'

'Mam will buy me a suit?' he suggested hopefully with a practised gormless expression.

She laughed out loud. 'She will not!'

'She will, for the wedding.'

'I'm too young!' she repeated.

'Then I'll come a-romancing.'

She liked the way he said *romancing*, which was old-fashioned, suggestive of violets and chocolate, rather than a quick snog behind the bike sheds, but it wasn't going to happen. She shook her head, laughing. 'Benjamin Savage, just give over, will you?'

'Okay, then maybe we could just be friends.'

'Friends, okay. Now I have to get home, or Mam will be after sending out a search party.'

She turned to walk quickly on, and he matched her, step for step. Actually, it would be kind of nice to have another friend. Brigid could be annoying at times, and wasn't she after leaving, anyway? *Sure, haven't I had enough learning already? I'm going to find me a rich man and have my own home.*

When they were near the last corner to the farmhouse, she stopped. 'You'd best be leaving me here, so Mam doesn't see.'

He handed her the bulging school bag, grinned and held out his little finger. 'Friends, then, pretty Ginny Kingston?'

She chain-linked, her little finger lost in his massive grip, and laughed. 'Friends, Benjamin.'

There was bad blood between her parents and the Savages, but she had a feeling neither of them quite recalled why. If she met with Ben in friendship, maybe it would go some way towards mending the rift. After all, Ruari and Noah Savage were in school with her, and they were just normal. Maybe she could find out from Ben the cause of the friction between the two families.

.   .   .

After that day, Ben appeared at odd times, when she was
walking home, or out and about on the farm. For a big man, he
was surprisingly stealthy. Like the deer that live on the hills, he
could be within a few feet of her, and she wouldn't see him until
he made himself known. As the summer drew high, Ginny
began to look forward to their illicit meetings. His knowledge of
the countryside, though, and all the creatures and plants that
inhabited it, was astonishing, and as their friendship consoli-
dated, Ginny listened and learned with the keen interest of a
pupil to an ancient professor.

He had a massive mental collection of folk history and was a
mine of information on local lore. He showed her things her
parents had no interest in: the Holy Well up on the hill that
people were supposed to walk around nine times and pray their
request to the Virgin Mary before drinking of its water. The
altar stone overlooking Roone Bay, where people had once gathered for mass when it was prohibited by law. The field where a
German plane had crashed during the war, killing the pilot and
a poor unsuspecting sheep. Bits of the plane were apparently
still hanging on the back wall of the local pub, not that she had
ever been in there.

He told her of the clearances during the famine, where
skeletons could sometimes be seen peeping out where the rain
washed away the soil; why Roone Manor had been abandoned
and then destroyed by the locals, and how Noel, the rich guy
who had bought Roone Manor, actually became rich by buying
a mare that had become a racing legend. Ben told her where the
birds nested, where the wildflowers grew and explained some
things about farming, which she found interesting from a purely
academic point of view, her father telling her what he was doing
but never why. Somehow, Ben became more like her brother

than her own brothers, who were always out and about, like ghosts in her peripheral vision.

After the long summer break, she would have to make a decision about what area to study in university. It was going to be something to do with history or anthropology, she thought. Ben's fascination with nature somehow swung her thoughts to her own Irish heritage, which lay in the very stones she walked upon, with its monuments and mystical legends, and in the townland names that had possibly survived for thousands of years, since Ireland had been a tribal landscape. She became engrossed in the ancient legends that had been scribed by monks and somehow survived the Viking raids. These included the tales Grampy Danny had regaled her with in those dark winter evenings, huddled around the kitchen range. Ben also knew the magical stories about Cú Chulainn, Queen Maeve and the unscrupulous Bricriu, because they were rooted in the ancient landscape around them.

'I want to go and see Newgrange, one day,' she told Ben after reading about the ancient site in the library. 'One day, when I can drive and have car of my own.'

'I'll take you.'

Ginny said, 'Ben Savage, will you stop joking around? You know I can't go anywhere with you. Where would we stay? And people would talk, besides.'

'Then marry me.'

'I've told you I'm not going to marry you. I'm going on to university. You could marry Brigid!'

'Her mam is still pushing her my way, for the farm, no doubt,' he said, with a sly grin.

'No, really?' She laughed. 'Well, the best of luck to the both of you! I won't marry anyone for a farm – or a house or a castle, for that matter. When I marry, it will be for love.'

'I love you.'

'Oh, Ben,' she said sadly.

15

GINNY

Mam must have heard me coming up the drive as she greets me at the door, wiping her hands on her apron. 'How's Sarah and the family? It would be nice if they visited soon.'

'Sarah said the same thing about you.'

'Eh, well. She knows I don't drive and your dad is always busy on the farm.'

'Dad needs to let Micheal have more responsibility.'

'Haven't I told him that myself, but will he ever listen?'

I answer her question as I dump my bag. 'Sarah's fine, the kids are wonderful, Thomas is still an annoying eejit, but Sarah loves him,' I add with a quick grin. 'They might come over in a couple of weeks' time and stay in the hotel in Roone Bay, because you don't have room here.'

Really, Tom likes to stay in a place that has hot running water, but I can't tell Mam that.

She perks up at the thought of the family visit, though. 'I'd best give the house a bit of a clean and bake some cakes for the weans.'

'Patrick and Ivy aren't weans any more, Mam.'

'They'll always be weans to me, love.' She gives me a hug. 'The same as you.'

'So, anything new or strange, seeing as how I've been away for three whole days?'

'The girl from McCarthy's phoned to say there's a Land Rover waiting for you to pick up. How can that be right?'

I grimace. 'Ruari said I needed one, and knew one that was for sale. He said it's a good vehicle, he knows because he's been maintaining it for some rich fella up the valley, but he didn't tell me how much it was going to cost and I didn't say I'd buy it. Whatever the cost, I don't have it.'

A worried expression slips onto her face. 'You've been talking to Ruari Savage?'

'Mam, it's okay. He's hurting over what happened, and I think he's holding out an olive branch.'

'Well, be careful,' she says, with a voice full of dire prediction. 'Ben seemed all right, too, don't forget.'

'Ruari isn't brain damaged. At least, I don't think so. I'll never trust anyone in that family, but they're hurting. It's nine years down the line since Ben died, but the family is still grieving.'

'Ye have a big heart, daughter.'

I hug her back. 'I got it from you, Mam. So, listen.'

I tell her about the huge house, with the woman in the pink fluffy slippers and ethnic kaftan, and the man himself setting up horse trekking up on the ridge for holidaymakers. Mam shakes her head, laughing with me. 'People coming here for holidays! Whatever next! It wouldn't have been known back in the day. Sure, times are changing. And where might ye be visiting today? Will ye be home for dinner?'

'I haven't made any plans. I need to look at the map and make some calls for tomorrow, but I'll nip down to the garage first. I'd better go down and tell them it's a mistake before I get on.'

. . .

The Land Rover is sitting on the forecourt when I arrive, and I sigh. It's tempting, of course. I go and stand on tiptoe to peer in through the old-fashioned cab window. Basic doesn't quite describe what I see: bare metalwork for a dashboard, a bench seat and little else. I would dearly love to have that vehicle, for the sheer practicality of it. As Ruari said, it would take me places that my poor Cortina can't go.

But wanting and having are worlds apart.

Ruari must have been watching from the mechanics' bay, because he slips out from underneath a car perched on a raised lift, wiping oily hands on a grimy rag.

I shrug helplessly. 'I told you; I can't afford it.'

'And you with a degree, flying around the countryside?'

'Doesn't mean I get a good salary,' I admit. 'In the world of academia, I'm on the bottom rung of the ladder.'

'So, let's go for a drive, anyway.'

'But I just said...'

'Humour me. You still haven't paid the price for the recovery of the Cortina.'

I flush. 'I don't know what you want me to say.'

'I just want the truth. I will keep asking. It's been a long time coming. One minute, Ben is alive and happy. Next, you've disappeared, Ben is sullen and withdrawn, and no one in your family will tell my family what really went down.'

'You want me to apologise? You want an admission of guilt? You'll be waiting a long time for that.' I can't help the snippy tone in my voice and the rigid anger that straightens my spine.

He stares down at me for a moment, then says quietly, 'I blamed you for a long time for Ben's death, but there's more, isn't there? I have it in the back of my skull that something bad happened. Can't you just tell me? I want closure. My whole family want closure. We're not monsters, you know.'

I wince slightly at the pleading tone. There was a time I thought Ben was a monster, but he was a troubled soul who paid the ultimate price for something he surely hadn't intended. It must have been so hard on his family.

Ruari walks around the Land Rover and holds the driver's door open in invitation. 'Please?'

I climb in a little reluctantly.

Ruari manoeuvres into the passenger seat and suddenly the vehicle doesn't seem so big. The sheer size and power of him has me wanting to scurry for safety. I push back the thought.

'You need to get the feel of the drive before we go off road,' Ruari says, knowing nothing of my thoughts.

'Off road?' My panicked glance briefly snags his eyes.

'There are a few farm tracks, drove roads, that we can practise on. If tractors can go on them, so can the Land Rover. Within reason, of course. You'll surprise yourself. You'll be fine. We'll take the road for a bit, but I'll just tell you what's what. This isn't like an ordinary car.'

His hand hovers over the two knobs by the gear change lever. I used to be fascinated by Ben's hands, the long fingers, darkened from being out in all weathers, the backs sprinkled with fine black hair. They had been so different from the blunt and knobbly hands my brothers inherited from my father. Ruari's hands are like Ben's, save for the fingertips engrained with oil. But Ruari is not Ben.

'It's in high range at the moment,' he reminds me, 'normal on-road driving. I'll explain the rest later. You can have four-wheel drive in high range, too, for when it's icy or muddy, but you don't need that today. It burns out the tyres. So, turn the key, then press the start button. That one, there.'

The vehicle roars into life, then calms to a steady, slow thumping. I pull away slowly, taking the Bantry road Ruari indicated, feeling ridiculously high in the cab. The vehicle rattles and clunks as though it wants to fall apart at any moment. Ruari seems relaxed enough, so I guess that's normal.

For a few miles, it feels as though I'm fighting the steering and the engine is over loud, then I relax into it and begin to see the attraction. From this height, instead of being hidden by ragged banks and verges, the scenery is a wide vista laid out like a map, rising to peaks in the misty distance. Then, rounding a corner, I gasp with surprise. The storm has cleared the air, and on a stretch of road I thought I knew, the Atlantic appears before us, sparkling with innocence under a curved horizon. The carved mouth of the bay is dotted with tiny islands and inlets. I gasp with surprise and laugh.

Ruari casts me a conspiratorial glance. 'It's amazing, isn't it? I never get over that view. You don't see it in an ordinary car. But up here we're like the Fomorian giants who once roamed these hills.'

Something plummets in my mind at the words, because Ben said that once, when we were standing on the top field, looking out over the valley. At the time, I'd imagined him as the gentle giant from old surveying his domain, and I find it almost impossible to reconcile the two images: the gentle guru he seemed to be as he lectured about the land and its history, whom I trusted as I would trust my father or brother, and the man who betrayed that trust, stealing my childhood from me in an instant.

I drive a little further and keep my eyes to the road as I ask, 'Why are you being nice to me? I mean, when I first gave that talk in the hall, I think you came specifically to frighten me. Maybe to drive me away.'

'I did. I'm sorry.' He grimaces and cogitates for a moment as the countryside trundles slowly by. 'I guess I wanted someone to blame. I came to your talk with the sole intention of hating you. But you were funny and passionate and warm, and I found I couldn't hate you after all. But I want to know what happened, and you're the only one who knows.'

I'm not the only one. My family all know the truth, and that's where it's going to stay, but I give him something to think about. 'Ben was charming and funny. He knew the landscape like no one else. He brought it alive for me. I loved him a little, then, like a best friend, like a brother.'

'Not like a lover.'

I return his sidelong glance. 'No. He's the reason I studied archaeology. I was going to take English before he enthused me with a love of the past. I didn't know about his accident back then. Noel O'Donovan told me.'

Ruari nods. 'There have been too many secrets, Ginny. He was a wonderful brother, but even I saw the angry side of him once or twice.'

He doesn't see my faint flush as I say, 'I was just sixteen, pretending to be so sophisticated, so grown up. He taught me so much about nature. I loved his company, but we were walking different paths. When Mam found out I'd been walking the hills with him, she told me there was gossip about us in the townland, and about a fight he'd been involved in after drinking down in the town. So I told him it had to end, I had to stop seeing him. He took it hard.'

I feel tears springing.

'There's a viewpoint just ahead. Pull in.'

I drive into the layby, and we both stare at the uncaring ocean reaching placidly into the curve of the bay. There's a sprinkling of lazy whitecaps twinkling in the sun. A small rowing boat sits calmly rocking on the tide, a day fisherman, maybe, hunched in the stern. Seagulls are wheeling over him, too far away for us to hear their cries.

Ruari waits.

I take a deep breath, swallow hard and manage to speak the words that were nearly choking me. 'He was determined to make me change my mind. He said I had to stay in Roone Bay and marry him and have his children. I was just sixteen. He kissed me. He seduced me, but I don't think I really knew what was happening. Girls weren't told things about that back then.'

'I'm sorry.'

I turn to face him. 'He made me pregnant.'

He's obviously shocked.

'You wanted to know why I left. That's why. Mam and Dad didn't want my future ruined. I couldn't keep the baby. I was too young to look after a child, of course. It's illegal to have abortions in Ireland, but they found out I could go to England...' I pause, letting the sentence hang, unfinished, and sigh. 'Ben didn't know that. He went to my dad after I'd gone, begging to know where I was, and even threatened him.'

'I'm sorry.'

'It didn't come to blows, but Dad said it was close – he was off-the-wall angry. I stayed with my sister, Sarah, for the two years it took to finish school. Then I went to university in Galway. When Ben died, I felt guilty, that perhaps in some way it was my fault for not putting a stop to it all sooner.'

Ruari is taking this in, in silence. He tips his head back briefly against the seat and closes his eyes for a long moment, before sitting up straight again and clearing his throat in a self-conscious manner. 'I'm sorry,' he says again. 'No wonder you don't want to know us.'

I shrug. 'So, now you know what happened.' It isn't all of it, sure, but he doesn't need to know the rest. 'I'm certain that Ben was just confused. Maybe he suffered from remorse, after, and maybe that's why he had the accident. But it wasn't my fault he died. You shouldn't have blamed me.'

We're there for a while, just watching the sea. The past is rolling through my mind like breakers on the shore, but I've presented Ruari with enough to occupy his thoughts.

He asks, finally, 'Why did you come back to Roone Bay? Really, I mean, not just for the job.'

He's not so daft, I think, and answer honestly. 'Because I was afraid of coming back. It was a bridge I needed to cross. I was afraid of your family. I thought the whole townland hated me, that everyone blamed me for Ben's death. Sometimes I even believed that and hated myself for it. It was hard carrying that weight around. It was stopping me from moving on. I came back to solve a mystery, if it's even possible, but also to face the past. And here we are.'

He sighs. 'And we were all so wrapped up in our own grief, we never stopped to think about how it affected you.'

'I had another reason for coming back, too,' I add, changing the subject. His brows lift in query. 'I want to find out what caused the rift between our two families. I want to know what happened to Davan O'Brien, who would have been my great-uncle, and your Molly Savage. My grandpa told me many stories, and they all had endings. But that one still hangs, unresolved. And it's real, not fiction. It's bothered me all my life, that lack of an ending.'

He shuffles in his seat, sitting up taller, as if thankful we've moved on to a different subject. 'You aren't the only one who'd like to know that. It has me and half of Roone Bay baffled, too. How they could disappear so utterly has confounded everyone who's tried to solve the puzzle. It's a mystery that vexes both our families, going back over four generations. Mam even trawled through shipping documents to see if they had gone abroad. Davan was your ancestor, Molly was mine, so I guess we both have a vested interest, but I can't tell you anything you don't already know.'

'I was told that your great-grandfather and mine already had a kind of feud going on before that. Have you any idea what it was about? My grandpa didn't know. He just said that William Savage had an unpredictable streak, and that was why Davan wasn't allowed to court his daughter. I think if they had let the young couple marry, the nonsense between the families would have been settled. But after that, whatever the bother had been before, that made a much bigger rift.'

'My family never talked much about the past,' Ruari says. 'Dad says you can't change the past, let it be, but I think he's wrong. It's more than just curiosity. Mysteries tend to stifle the future, because you're always left wondering. I'd like to know what your grandpa told you.'

'You know William had Davan sent to prison?'

'I knew that. Not a nice thing to have done.'

'No. Grandpa told me about Davan's experience in prison. It was horrific, apparently.'

'I'd like to hear about it.'

'Now?'

'If you don't mind.'

It feels kind of weird, sitting in a vehicle by the road verge, staring out over the battleship-grey sea, telling a story my grandpa told me, to a man I never wanted to speak to at all. The very daftness of it eases the tension between us.

DAVAN, 1921

Davan spent two weeks in the tiny cell in Roone Bay. His older sister, Evie, came in and whispered that Patrick had tried to speak to William but had been hounded off the property. Molly had been sent away to a convent, she didn't know where, to have the baby. Davan was distraught, but as his sister pointed out, even if they wanted to help, they could do nothing because Molly had to obey her father and they couldn't interfere. She said she would try to find out what was happening, but she didn't think anyone would tell her.

Davan learned nothing more, despite begging Mickey for news.

Eventually he was transported to Cork for trial. He was taken from the tiny holding cell in Roone Bay's police station to the prison in Cork, manacled like a common thief, and, indeed, his companion on the journey was a self-confessed, unrepentant, somewhat ebullient rogue who would no doubt finish his sentence and go straight out robbing again. He spent a month in Cork jail, worrying and wondering, and was finally brought before the judge in chains. There, the judge called him a degenerate and sentenced him to thirteen months.

Davan was shocked. 'But I love her! I want to marry her!' he yelled.

The prison officers beat him into silence, and the judge's distant voice ordered them to take him away.

After the prison gates clanged shut behind Davan, he underwent the indignity of a search, and his head was shaved to prevent the spread of lice. He was thrust into a tiny cell that already housed three men, who also held him down and searched him, despite his furious indignation, in case he had something worth stealing, but he hadn't even been allowed to bring his pencil and sketchbook with him.

His head still throbbing from the beating, he collapsed onto a plank bed hanging from the wall and passed out. When he awoke, he was disorientated and after trying to sit up, slumped back, fighting the urge to be sick. His head felt strange, and tentative exploration with his fingers discovered a raised, bloody weal. The three other men in the cell were sitting in a row on the opposite bunk, watching him. They were all older than himself, badly dressed, their thin bodies hardened by poverty.

'What kind o' baste are ye, a t'ief or somet'ing?' The man's thick Cork accent betrayed sympathy.

'Thief,' he admits on a hiccup of hysterical laughter. 'I stole a girl's heart. That was my crime. Her father called the coppers on me.'

'Ah, dat'l do da t'ing,' the voice said. 'Faders, eh? Mine was a right basta'd. Bate da living bejasus out'n all of us when he'd a drop o' da pure in him.'

Davan curled up facing the wall and cried.

How had it come to this? The other men didn't jeer. Perhaps they were quietly envious that he was able to allow himself that release.

At first, each night brought the judge's resounding pronunciations to his mind: 'You, sir, are a degenerate! How dare you raise your voice in this court? You have ruined a devout young girl's life and ruined her father's chances of seeing her settled in God's good grace. What good man will marry her now she is soiled? I'm giving you thirteen months to reflect on your crime. I advise you to use that time well, think upon what you have done and repent of your sins! May God forgive you, for the girl's family will not.'

The gavel banged loudly.

He had referred to her as 'the girl', not as Molly. To the judge, she had been just a faceless no one, no more important than an animal owned by her father. According to him, her father was the true victim; his name had been ridiculed, his honour violated.

During the day, he found his hours consumed by pointless tasks: oakum picking, the treadwheel, scrubbing floors, or on his knees in prayer in the crowded cell, which was the only way to avoid further punishment when the guards came around.

In the night, Davan turned his mind to Molly, and the wonderful unity they had discovered in body and mind. He was determined to keep his love for her untainted by this experience. It was difficult enough, in the circumstances, but the thirteen months, be they like thirteen years, would one day be over. He couldn't change what was happening to Molly, though guilt fell thickly upon him.

He should have waited until they were married.

Everyone knew what happened to *fallen girls*, but until this time, it had never occurred to him that *fallen* could simply mean loved. He hoped the nuns weren't treating her too harshly when he wasn't there to protect or defend her.

Evie had whispered that the baby would probably be given away. He hoped the nuns would find the baby a good home. It wrecked his sanity, trying to understand the concept that it was a sin for an unwed girl to bear a child, but it was fine for another woman – who perhaps couldn't have a child – to take that bastard child on. The world was surely mad. But one day they would create another child to fill the space where that tiny life should be in their hearts.

Despite her father and all her brothers, he would marry Molly. He would survive this prison term and pick up his life. He knew she would wait for him, if it were at all possible. If he couldn't make things right when he wanted to, he would do so as soon as he could. But the waiting drove him to distraction. Evie could give him no news of Molly. All he could do was hope that Molly remained staunch through her father's anger, as he had to. In the end, even if they had to elope, she would be his love to the end of time. This he knew.

Mentally he was strong, but the prison term was slowly destroying him physically. His body was wasting from sickness, too little food, too little sunshine and the heavy physical punishment. The prison was squalid, dark and damp, and the continual clanking of chains and doors was a constant reminder of where he was, even when he tried to close his eyes and dream. There was no nourishment in the insufficient food – porridge or bread and gruel – that was passed daily through the grate, and outside exercise was spasmodic and far too little.

At those times, he would simply stand in the courtyard, shut his mind from everything and stare up into the sky, seeking a sense of freedom. Would that he was a bird and could fly! He would fly to his Molly and take her and the child as far from this place as he could. He dreamed of taking a ship to Australia or America and starting a new life with her. There was no way the two of them could marry and stay in Roone Bay if he returned a felon, his skin yellow with the prison pallor.

Molly didn't come to him in prison, neither did he get any word from her, though he didn't doubt she would have tried.

Her family were obviously keeping her as much a prisoner in her home as he was a prisoner in this gaunt, cold tomb of a building. Between her father and her brothers, she would have no chance to slip a letter away, let alone come in person. His family did not visit, either. What with the farm work that fell to the hands of his parents and two unmarried sisters, he guessed they were having a tough time of it. His father, who had been at his farce of a trial, told Davan, with a brief hug around the shoulders, to simply count the days. Never fear, he would be there to fetch him home.

So, he counted the days.

But although every day was a day nearer to the time of his release, days had never seemed so long. Nor the weeks or months. On the farm, the year had passed in a rolling wave of seasonal chores, in the hay that survived the weather, the calves that were reared, the litter of pigs, the eggs that were hatched.

Contained in a tiny cell, he desperately missed the outdoor life he was used to. Some people said farming was hard, but it was not so hard as living each day with nothing useful to do, nothing to read, nothing to pass the time but thinking. As the months passed, the muscles earned by the continual labour of farming life degenerated. His face sank into lines more suited to an old man, and his teeth began to fall out. One of the men in his cell hanged himself. He was found in the morning, his ripped clothes tied to the grating that covered the tiny window. Davan had heard nothing, but the guards beat him for not shouting, as if he were complicit. He awoke and saw the man hanging there, and shared an almost emotionless glance with the man in the opposite bunk. They quietly envied him his choice of freedom.

But Davan didn't want to die. He wanted to see his Molly again, to pick up on life, not how it had been before, but how rich it would be once they could be legally together as man and wife, even if they had to travel to Australia to do it. He almost smiled with the vindication of such an act.

And so the long weary days passed into months.

On the eve of his release, Davan was stoically waiting for the doors to finally open when two guards came for him and he was brought to an empty cell and left on his own. Was this just how it happened? He didn't know and didn't care. On the morrow, his father would arrive to bring him back to his home and to Molly, his love.

But in a short while, the doors opened to admit two guards he had never seen before. They wore hard expressions, and a whisper of alarm made him rise and take an involuntary step back.

He was not wrong.

The guards pulled out their truncheons.

'Why?' Davan asked, holding his hands out as if to ward them off. He had no strength, no weapon.

'We was told to teach yous a lesson,' one guard said.

'Wasn't thirteen months enough?' Davan asked in wonder.

'Not for her faither.'

'So, William Savage is responsible for this?'

The man bared his black stubs of teeth in something approximating a smile. 'See, it's like this, young fella. Ye was told ta stay your side of the fence, and ye shoulda listened. And we was told ta let you know that if you go anywhere near the girl, next time will be the last time, get my meaning, fella?'

He tapped his nose in exaggerated slyness before kicking Davan in the side of the knee, sending him down with a cry of pain. Emaciated, and in no state to fight back, he writhed on the floor, spasmodically reacting to each blow, protecting his head with his arms. They kicked him and lashed out with their truncheons. The beating was vicious, not the first Davan had experienced in his year at prison, as the guards had learned how to hurt a man without actually killing him, a consideration for their own futures rather than any kind of concern for the men they abused.

He was finally hauled to his feet and shoved out through the prison door a day early, barely able to walk. He was frightened that he would be hauled back, maybe to the prison infirmary, that this brief sense of freedom was some kind of cruel trick. He hugged his arms tightly around his chest. He guessed some ribs had been broken as every breath was agony, and his head was ringing strangely. He turned his face towards home and set off at a slow hobble, staggering like a drunkard, fighting to keep his eyes open, determined to leave the prison well behind him. After less than a mile, he sank slowly to his knees. Darkness rose behind his eyelids, and he flopped face down onto the road, his last confused thoughts of Molly containing the surreal premonition that he would never see her again.

17

GINNY

After I've told Ruari what Grandpa had told me about Davan's prison experience, we drive on, both lost a little in our thoughts. We arrive at a small farm track leading up into the hills. He obviously knows the owners as no one comes out to shout at us. The past recedes as I concentrate on driving the Land Rover around bumpy fields and rutted tracks – the kind I would never have attempted in my Cortina – until I have the way of it. I must be grinning, because a soft smile penetrates Ruari's somewhat distant expression before he says, 'I should really be getting back to work.'

'Me, too.'

As we roar loudly back towards Roone Bay, he withdraws into himself, staring out of the window, probably pondering what I told him about Molly's own father, his great-grandfather, having Davan arrested. He had known the fact but not the detail.

When we get back to Roone Bay Motors, I clamber down from the cab and slam the door. Ruari exits with a little more decorum. I can't help thinking Land Rovers were designed for men.

'Take the Land Rover on. See how you get on with it,' he says.

I shake my head, saying ruefully, 'Thanks for letting me give it a go. It would be useful, but I still can't afford it.'

'Leave the Cortina with me. We'll call it quits.'

'No way!' I say, shocked. 'My car is on its last legs!'

'Call it an apology from my family.' His dark eyes, hooded against the light, assess me frankly. 'Is it okay if I tell them what you've told me?'

I wince, then nod. 'But no one else needs to know. I'd rather it wasn't broadcast that I was pregnant. Mam would be mortified. For the record, I don't believe Ben was a bad person. He was just confused. And now I know why, it helps a little.'

'Thank you for that. So,' he says after a pause, 'I'll have ownership of the Land Rover transferred to you. I'll leave it insured on the business until you tell me you've sorted it out. Take what you need out of the Cortina. If you let me have the documents, I'll put it for sale on the forecourt. Farms always want bangers for the kids to learn in.'

I'm almost stunned by the generosity. 'Thank you.'

Ruari turns suddenly, and I jump back. He looks shocked. 'What can I do to convince you that you don't have to be scared of me?'

It can't think of any answer to that, so, shaking his head, he walks slowly back into the mechanics' bay. From the set of his shoulders, knowledge of my schoolgirl pregnancy has given him a sideways knock, and he's probably wondering how to present that knowledge to his family.

It's easy to hate someone. Much less easy to forgive them or learn that what you thought you knew wasn't the case at all. I know, because it's taken me a good few years.

· · ·

Mam is surprised when I turn up in the Land Rover. 'I don't understand,' she says. 'I thought you couldn't afford it?'

'We came to an agreement. Ruari took the Cortina in exchange. So that I don't get stuck in any more ditches while I'm out and about on the hills.'

'But why on earth would he do that? Why would he be speaking to you at all?'

'He's been pushing to know about Ben and me. I told him about leaving because I was pregnant. I told him Ben seduced me.'

'Oh, Lord,' she says, closing her eyes briefly.

'He's not going to spread it around. It doesn't reflect well on Ben, after all. His family knew nothing of that. Nor did Ben, actually.'

'Not at all, he didn't. I wasn't going to be the one to tell people he'd got you with child, and you still at school.'

'Yes, but it left everyone thinking that Ben died for love of me.'

Mam sighs. 'Perhaps he did, the eejit.'

'Well, it made me look bad, anyway.'

'You didn't have to stay here and face the neighbours,' she grumbles.

'No,' I flash. 'I was a kid, and got sent away from my home and lost the child I wanted to keep!'

'It was for the best, love,' Mam reminds me gently. 'As you say, you were a child yourself. No way would you have coped. You'd have been stuck here at the house with no job, no income, no life. You would have ended up sour, resenting everyone. No, we made the right decision, all of us, together. You got to go to university; and – be honest – you love your job. Leave it at that, eh?'

I nod. Everything she says is true, if a person wants to be practical about things. But sometimes the loss of my child hurts so badly I cry – not when anyone can hear me, but when it wells up deep inside me in lonely places and I want to scream my grief to the world. And Mam's right; it was just a sensible and logical decision – until the day it happened. Then I was bereft.

And you can't go back from that kind of decision. I'm torn between wanting a family, if only I could find the right man, and being scared of getting pregnant again. How could I love another child when I was prepared to lose the first? It would be callous.

Can I ever forgive myself for what I did?

Four weeks into my assignment, I phone my professor and give him a progress report. He sounds pleased. This is happening all over the country, and he probably wants to come in first at the winning post. After that, I don't know what I'll do. There's talk of making it law to have an archaeologist present at building sites and roadworks. I'm not sure whether that will ever be practical, but when this job comes to an end, there are many opportunities in Ireland. The country is just waking up to the fact that it has a heritage of its own, something it can sell to the whole world, even if a lot of it is mythical blarney about a past none of us really knows much about.

I doubt I'll stay in Roone Bay, though. I have too much history here, and I'm not sure I will ever see the future through it. Coming here with my head held high was a hurdle I had to overcome, but when that's done, I want to walk away and live my life where memories don't haunt me in the shape of a younger brother who looks just like the man who betrayed my trust.

After my talk with Ruari, I feel a bit spaced out, going about my phone calls and my visits as if there's something left undone in the back of my mind. The Land Rover proves its worth as I drive up tiny rubble tracks to farms that barely scratch a living on the sides of mountains that grow more rocks than grass. I visit more raths, draw sketches, take measurements and mark them on the map. They're all known monuments, and in a way the job could be seen as tedious. But can't all jobs, on a day-to-day basis? At least I'm out in the open air, surveying the land, investing myself in the landscape in all its myriad forms.

One day, I arrive home grubby and wanting a bath, but Dad calls me into the kitchen and hands me something bound up in an old rag tied with string. I cast him an enquiring glance as I take it. 'What's that?'

'Davan's sketchbook.'

'What? You never told me about this before!'

'Your grandfather kept it safe, from way back. He was afraid that someone would put it on the fire. We found it after he died and didn't know what to do with it, but I thought you'd be interested, seeing as it's old.'

They really don't understand what age means in terms of archaeological dating, but a thrill of anticipation shivers through me. 'You've had this all this time and never thought to mention it?'

Dad shrugs. 'I kind of forgot it was there, in the cupboard, until your mam said you'd been asking about Davan and Molly, asking what do we know. But, as she said, we only know what Grandpa told us.'

I hold the package with gentle reverence. 'Did you look in it?'

'Grandpa showed it to me one time. I remember. There are pencil drawings. People and stuff. I'd be best on up the parlour to help with the cleaning up.'

'Thanks, Dad. I'd best clean up, too, before Mam sees me bringing my mud into the kitchen or gets me to help with the dinner.'

We both grin and go our separate ways.

After I've bathed and washed the mud out of my hair, I sit at the little table in my room, where I'd done my homework all those years ago. Then, pushing the typewriter back, I lay the precious find in front of it. I wonder why I hadn't known about it before now, but maybe Dad was waiting until I was old enough to be interested. Then, of course, all the bother happened and I left home. I try to unpick the knots on the hemp string, but it's already falling apart from age or moths or mould.

It would be a leap to call it a sketchbook. It's maybe just one or two larger sheets of thick paper cut into smaller squares pierced through and joined by a piece of fading green ribbon. There's a blank sheet of rough card as a cover, which I turn over carefully.

I gasp with astonishment. I almost want to cry at the beauty of the pictures. The tiny images, which adhere scrupulously to nature, have been drawn with such care by a sharpened pencil, I'm amazed. What talent! An oak leaf, a frog, a stone in water, a startled deer. Every scrap of space on the page has been used, filled in, as though the paper itself was too valuable to waste. That might well have been the case, in fact. I turn the pages one by one, stunned by Davan's ability to invest life into the objects he's portraying.

But the last page stands out above the others. It has a solitary image circled by a complex frieze of leaves. It's a girl's face, drawn with exquisite attention to detail. There is a hint of rough working clothes at the neckline and above it, a cross – perhaps silver – on a delicate chain. She is so real she seems to be looking right out of the page at me. The caption underneath simply reads: *Molly, mo chroí*.

'*Molly, my heart*; oh my God,' I breathe.

I cannot take my eyes off her for a long while. This beautiful girl, with a hint of mischief in her large eyes and a lilt of amusement on her lips, is the very girl Davan fell in love with all those years ago. I'm stunned. The image brings her desperate plight into greater clarity.

Grampy Danny said her parents had sent her to the nuns to have her child, and she came home scrubbed clean, as though it had never happened. I suspect she was lucky to be sent home at all; so many girls, through the moral code of the church, ended up mentally ill, institutionalised or even dead through lack of care.

How she must have mourned for her child. My sympathetic arms ache for her. The nuns might have sent the baby away to America, or if it had been a girl child – if it even survived – retained it to become a nun, to work for them. I have heard some stories from those times – almost unbelievable stories – about how the nuns treated unmarried women and their babies. There's still a stigma to being an unwed mother today, but it's not uncommon these days for families to clan together against convention in support of the 'fallen' girl, despite the rigid dictates of the Catholic Church. But how could her own family have done that to her, when Davan would have accepted the responsibility and would have married her?

After dinner, Mam and Dad and Micheal show interest in the drawings, and Mam exclaims over Molly's beauty, but they don't seem to recognise the depth of Davan's inherent artistic talent. I doubt for a moment he had any tutoring. In his day, school was to teach reading, writing and arithmetic. The poor weren't supposed to waste their time on art. Wherever that talent sprang from, it hasn't resurfaced in my generation. I hope he and Molly managed to escape somewhere and live their lives out as a married couple. Perhaps he was even able to make a living drawing. I'd like to think so, anyway.

Exhausted with my efforts over the last couple of weeks, I haven't made any plans but have absolutely no doubt what I should do next. Ruari seems as interested as I am in discovering what happened to the unlucky couple who had been so cruelly treated by William. No wonder they chose to run away. I'm sure his family have no image of Molly, so I suspect he'd be pleased to see it.

I drive down to the garage, but he's apparently out test-driving a car he's mended. I tell the girl I'll walk down to the quay and come back in half an hour. It's a nice day for another hurdle to cross. I don't doubt everyone in Roone Bay knows I'm back, now, and past gossip has grown new legs. To walk in the town as though I have a right to be there is to take my courage in both hands again. It wouldn't surprise me if I get a few spiteful comments thrown in my direction, even if people aren't willing to come right out and say things to my face.

I pass a couple of young people I don't know and buy chips at the little hatch on the quay, served by a lad who sounds foreign. Times are surely changing when foreigners choose to move into a land that people have been flocking to leave for the last two hundred years.

I sit with my feet dangling over the edge, staring moodily into the oily sheen of water lapping fitfully at the barrier. There are two fishing boats tied up at the quay, bumping gently against the tractor tyres that hang over the edge, and a couple of auld ones sitting mending nets, who glance at me with little interest. Perhaps my notoriety has finally ceased to interest anyone.

I suspect a quay has been here for hundreds of years, in one form or another, but the concrete that presently binds the giant stones can only be 120 years old at most. I wonder how they moved the stones. I am in awe of the ancients for many things. These days, we would use motorised vehicles, cranes and lorries to create such structures, but they moved stones weighing many tons with nothing but their own strength and engineering skill.

I sense movement behind me, and suddenly Ruari plonks himself beside me, a packet of chips in his hand. 'Jen said you'd be down here. Seems like a good day for it. She said you wanted to talk to me. I'm not taking the Land Rover back, if that's what it's about.'

He makes me smile and shake my head. For some reason, he seems keen to undo the damage of the last eleven years. What I don't know yet is why. We munch quietly, almost companionably, for a while. I find myself confused by him, mostly because he seems friendly and I'm looking for ulterior motives.

'Dad had an interesting snippet of a story about Molly,' he says, screwing the newspaper wrapping into a tight ball in his fist. 'Shall I tell you?'

My interest is piqued. I nod curiously.

'I can't promise to be as articulate as you, but he said that Molly went to the priest, assuming he'd help her. That was a little naïve, given the era. So, here goes.'

18

MOLLY, 1921

Molly visited the priest in his home, because she was troubled in a big way. On the doorstep, she told him she had fallen in love and needed his advice before she told her parents.

'Tell them what, my child?' the priest asked with a gentle smile, while stepping back in invitation. 'Come on in, why don't you? So, who's the lucky boy?'

'Davan O'Brien,' she said, blushing.

'Oh,' he said. It was common knowledge that there was bad blood between the Savages and the O'Briens, though no one seemed quite sure what started it. No one he had spoken to, since coming to Roone Bay, told the same story at all. Well, the Lord worked in mysterious ways, and was perhaps paving the way for the old disagreements to be settled. 'Well, Davan's a good boy, with a good family. There's no reason to suppose your family won't come around to the match, not at all.'

'I'm not so sure, Father,' she whispered, 'My father won't have any O'Brien set foot on his land. But Davan's a sound man altogether. He works hard and will be a good husband. It's just that – well, they will say I'm too young.'

The priest laughed. 'Well, young Molly, maybe you'll have

to learn a little patience. If he's as sweet on you as you are on him, in a year's time, he can court you to his heart's content and I'll see to it that your father won't say him nay!'

'I love him now, and he loves me,' she said desperately.

The priest heard the panic in her voice, for he asked, 'Did he tell you so himself?'

'He did.'

'It's not right that he spoke as much to you, and you being so young. He should have known better, Molly. Sweet girl, I know it's hard, but you need to put aside your childhood before you can ever really know what's in a man's mind. In a year, he might feel differently. By the time you're old enough, he might have married another.'

That wasn't the answer she was hoping for. She wanted the priest to understand that she was in love, so deeply in love it wasn't a question of changing her mind, or of Davan changing his, it was simply a matter of convincing everyone. 'He would not! We are in love, Father!' she said, in a rather stronger tone than she meant to use. 'We have made vows!'

'Promises can blow away on the wind, my child,' he answered in a troubled tone. 'And, of course, in this day and age, you may marry a man of your choice, but you are still a child, and children do not yet know their minds.'

'We do,' she said adamantly. 'Father, I want to know, will you marry us?'

There was a long silence, then he said, 'Molly, surely I will, when you are of age, and with your parents' consent.'

'Father, this cannot wait.' She paused, then added in a low voice, 'I'm with child. My baby must not be born out of wedlock.' She felt the blush rise from her breast to her cheeks.

'Oh, Molly,' he said, aghast. 'What have you done?'

It wasn't a question, she realised. He knew exactly what she'd done. What he meant was: what is going to happen now?

'It's not wrong if you love someone,' she said defiantly.

'But you aren't yet fifteen! And young Davan, dear God, what was he thinking? Your father will surely want justice.'

'It's not a crime if I consented,' she denied.

'But it is, by law!'

'But if you will marry us, everything will be put right.' It was the obvious answer, after all.

'I must talk to your parents.'

'No! You cannot! Davan and I should be married, before—' She gasped, putting her hand in front of her mouth. She had not spoken under the seal of the confessional, so the priest was free to use the information she had imparted in the way he thought fit. 'Father, no! I beg of you. If you won't marry us, give us time to find someone who will!'

From his resolute expression, she realised he would do what he thought was right. He would tell her parents. Well, maybe that was for the best. Once her parents knew, they would be able to persuade the priest to perform the ceremony. She didn't realise, until later, just how horribly wrong it was all going to go.

'Dada!' Molly cried, pulling at his arm. 'Stop it – I won't go!'

She turned to her mother, who was packing a small wicker shopping basket, scarcely able to speak for the tears and the hiccups that filled her throat. 'It's been decided.'

'But, Mam, I can stay here. Davan will marry me. Dada just has to give his consent. And even if the baby comes before we are married, God will understand that we will be joined in holy matrimony.'

Her mother's face looked even more haggard than usual as she supported her husband. 'The baby would be born out of wedlock, Molly! It will be a bastard even if you marry after. The neighbours would all know! We would bear the shame! How could you do this? And you, barely fifteen. Davan should not have... What he did was evil!'

'He's not evil, and I love him,' Molly cried. 'I won't be put
away in the convent! I won't!'

'You will do as your father tells you.' Tears ran down her
mother's face even as she dictated. Already her parents were
distancing themselves, saying 'your father' and 'your mother'
rather than the childhood diminutives.

'But, Mam, they will take my baby away!'

'They will. Then you will come home, and your father will
find a good man for you to marry. He might have to pay someone, of course, and that's not going to be easy.' She sits back and
thinks. 'We will say that you went to visit your aunt, in Cork, for
the education. And when you come back, I want no word on
your lips of babies and Davan.'

'I won't go.'

'You will get in the cart, if the boys have to put you there,'
her father butted in sourly. 'Father Mooney organised it. It will
be here soon. It's your own fault, anyway.'

'Davan will come and find me and bring me home,' she said
mutinously.

'No, he won't.'

Her father said it with such certainty, Molly's breath stilled.
A cold breath flooded her – made her light-headed. 'Dada, what
have you done?'

Her father glanced away, so her mother answered. 'Davan
will never come near you again, child. He ruined you. He
ruined all of us! You must forget him.'

Molly was aghast. 'No! You cannot mean it. You're thinking
about the neighbours, about yourself, not me and Davan?'

'We have to live here. How could we live with the shame?
And you, my only daughter.' At that her mother wailed into her
apron again, and Molly's distress turned to anger, because her
family cared more about what the neighbours would think than
about her own happiness. Everything she'd ever known about
her family was undone in that moment. Her parents would

send her away and let the nuns steal her precious child that had been conceived in love. Her brothers, who had treated her like a princess up to now, would force her into the cart if she resisted. They would stand by and allow it to save their own standing in the community.

'I hate you,' Molly said slowly, her very tone filled with the promise of a curse. 'I hate you all and will hate you to the day I die.'

Her mother looked horrified. 'Don't say that, Molleen, my sweet – you don't mean it. You'll be grateful in the end, you'll see.'

Molly's lip curled. The childhood endearment added fuel to the flames of her anger. 'If you make me go, and if our child – mine and Davan's – is lost to us, I will never speak another word to you or Dada until the day I die.'

When the cart came, Molly climbed in silently, her cheeks running with tears. It would have been embarrassing if her father had to call upon her brothers to perform that duty. There was an unknown man driving who nodded a greeting to her father but didn't so much as glance at his passenger as he clicked his tongue and bid the mare, 'Drive on!'

The black-clad nun in the back with her glared at her charge, no sympathy in her hard face.

19

GINNY

When Ruari has finished telling me about poor, naïve Molly going to the priest to ask for help, only to bring the might of Catholic moral disapproval down on herself, I feel sad for her all over again. All through the ages, men have imposed their will on their women, while often failing to restrain their own needs. Falling in love is a desire buried deep in a woman's psyche, but for men, sex is an imperative that overrides everything. The rules society imposes on the young are hard to reconcile with nature. Even my thoughts on the subject are confused, however, because Davan knew the score and should have waited until they were wed. I feel sorry for them both, though they are long dead.

There's a pill now that women can use to stop the arrival of babies, so maybe the tides have finally turned in favour of women. This pill isn't available in Ireland, though. I don't think the Catholic Church will ever relinquish its archaic stance on the subject. It will continue to let women die in agony rather than allow them the freedom to choose. Where does it say that in the Bible? I wonder.

Ruari shields his face from the sun with his hand and turns

his dark eyes on me. 'I'd best be getting back to work. What was it you wanted to see me about?'

'Did you know Davan was an artist?'

'Davan? No, was he?'

I had surprised him, but then who would have thought a poor farmer's son, at the beginning of the century in Ireland, would have even thought about drawing.

'Dad gave me an old sketchbook yesterday. It was Davan's, though it doesn't have his name on it anywhere. I didn't know about it before.'

'That's kind of weird.'

I know what he means; like a ghostly voice out of the past. 'Dad thought I was too young to be interested, then after the – ah – incident, I moved on and it kind of slipped his mind and got forgotten. It seems that Davan left it behind when he ran away with Molly. His parents held on to it all those years, waiting to be able to give it back to him. It came to my grandfather via his wife, Sally, who was Davan's youngest sister. Anyway, that's by the by. We have it.'

'Does it give us any clues as to where they went?'

'No.'

Ruari glances at his wristwatch. I can tell he's curious, but he's itching to get back to work. I heave myself to my feet, and Ruari jumps up like a real gentleman, taking my arm, maybe to make sure I don't fall into the cold water clawing at the quay, but it has quite the opposite effect. I snatch my arm back and stumble nearly to the edge before finding my balance.

My reaction startles him. 'Jesus, Ginny,' he says, stepping back, holding both hands out in supplication. 'I was only trying to help.'

'I don't like being touched,' I admit.

He rakes a hand through his hair, confused. 'Sorry, I won't do it again.'

'No, I'm sorry. I didn't mean to be rude.'

'So, we're both sorry,' he says, a wry expression on his lips. 'Where does that leave us?'

'Confused,' I say honestly. 'It's not a choice, you know.'

'No, I can see that.'

But I can see how he's thinking it through and wondering if my aversion to bodily contact is a direct reaction to my 'bother' with Ben. He would be right, in fact.

'So, this sketchbook. Is it significant in some way? Did you bring it with you?'

'No, I think it's too precious to be toted around in my back-pack. Actually,' I add, 'it's just as well I thought that, because it might well have gone in for a swim, just now.'

'True.'

Then we're both grinning and the moment has passed.

There's a brief pause, then Ruari says, 'Well, the very fact that you told me about it means you'd like to show it to me? I'd like that. But how do we manage that if you won't, ah, tote it around. I gather I'm not exactly welcome at your house.'

'Nor me at yours,' I say.

'Well, that's not exactly true.'

I glance at him in query. 'Your folk don't talk to my folk.'

'Because your folk don't talk to mine. My mam did try to speak to your parents after Ben died, but she was turned away.'

'I'd forgotten about that.'

We begin to walk back up the road, towards the garage, and he says, 'Well, you know, we have a choice. We can either keep this stupid feud going or be the generation that heals it. What do you say? Can I bring you up to the house?'

I feel a hot flush rising. How can I walk into his house, and him with a father and three brothers all bigger than himself? It's not just being touched that bothers me; it's being touched, even inadvertently, by men. I can't even let Dad or my brothers or Sarah's husband give me a friendly hug in greeting.

'I take it that's a no, then?'

'Maybe you could come up to ours?' I say.

'I will, if you talk to your parents and make it okay.'

I wonder, as I drive back up to the farm, whether that was the reason he was generous with the Land Rover. Perhaps he really does want to heal the multi-generational rift. I had assumed that Ben's death stoked the fires of animosity, but if Ruari's mam had come up to the farm prepared to talk, and my family turned her away, maybe it's not so cut and dried, after all.

I can understand why Mam turned her away, of course, but Ruari's right. Someone has to mediate the situation and end the daftness, the roots of which are so long in the past, neither family knows how it started or how to end it. Ben was certainly at fault where I was concerned, but if I hadn't had to be sneaky in seeing Ben when I was a schoolgirl, maybe things would have turned out differently.

I broach the subject at dinner that evening.

Micheal goes quiet and looks at his plate. Mam takes a quick inward breath, and my father shakes his head.

'Is that no?' I glare at them in turn. 'Is this going to go on for another generation? What happens when Micheal has children? Will they not be allowed to talk to the Savage children at school?'

'But they blame us for Ben's death,' Dad says warily.

'Do they? I just learned that Ben's mam came up to talk to you afterwards and Mam turned her away. Did it occur to you that maybe she was just wanting answers?'

'Love, we couldn't have told her, anyway,' Mam says.

No, she couldn't. Some things are best left unsaid. 'But still,' I mutter.

Micheal lifts his head. 'I agree with Ginny. I actually think Ruari's a decent guy. I say we invite him up and see if we can all manage to be civil, at least.'

I hear a faint hint of amusement in his voice and suspect he's talking to Ruari already. Or one of the brothers. They're of an age, after all.

I tackle him with this, later, out in the yard. 'I see them in the bar,' he admits. 'It nearly came to blows once, but we got over it. The problem is the parents. Mam and Dad bear deep grudges. You know they do. And it's because of you.'

He doesn't mean that the way it sounds. 'I guess it really is up to me, isn't it?'

'It is. Sis, it's time to get over stuff, you know?'

He puts his arm around me and gives me a hard hug. I freeze, and it's all I can do to not panic. Then he walks away quickly, not looking back. I shudder and hug myself tightly. Micheal has obviously decided to stop pussyfooting around me. He's telling me to grow up, move on. He's right. It's all in the mind. But knowing that doesn't actually help make it happen.

I phone Ruari at the garage.

It takes a minute before his voice comes on the line. 'Ginny. What can I do for you? Is the Land Rover going okay?'

'It's fine. Look, will you come up to the house for dinner tomorrow evening?'

There's a pause, and I'm almost sure I hear him gulp, before he says, 'Sure. Why not.'

'We eat at six. Come around five, and I'll show you the sketchbook.'

'I finish at five. It takes a bit to get cleaned up. Can I be there by half past?'

'Sure. Micheal and Jimmy will be there, too.'

'You know I'll bolt at the first sign of aggression.'

'Do, by all means,' I say politely, 'but I'll try to keep my temper in check.'

He laughs. 'I can see why Ben was taken with you.'

That wasn't, perhaps, the best thing to say in the circumstances, but I guess he's as worried about coming up to be in the house with my family as I would be to see his. Well, nearly, anyway. There would be five big, strong men in his house and only three in mine, none of them as daunting in size and stature as a single one of the Savage clan.

There's tension in the kitchen that evening as we wait for Ruari to arrive.

'He'll be the first Savage to set foot in this house since William came looking for his Davan,' Mam muses. 'Four generations back, that would be. According to Grandpa, William was in a right lather, screaming that Davan had stolen his daughter, and it turned out he was right, after all. But if I'd been his daughter, I think I'd have run away, too, after the way she was treated. By all accounts, after being sent away, the poor child came home bruised and half-starved, with all her hair falling out. The nuns could be ruthless when it came to unmarried mothers.'

'They still can,' I mutter.

'They just need a good rogering,' Jimmy says with a grin. 'That 'ud sort them out.'

'James Kingston! You mind your tongue,' Mam rebukes. 'We don't have that kind of language in this house!'

'I wonder what happened to her baby,' I say.

There's a silence.

At that moment, the rumble of a heavy motor is heard heading up the drive. All of us freeze, as if waiting for a giant anvil to come falling from the sky. Then Jimmy and I share a glance and suddenly giggle.

'That'll be him, then,' Dad says to me. 'You'd best bring him in.'

By the time I get there, Ruari is standing nervously at the door, and I notice his hands have been scrubbed shiny. If he had a hat, he would be scrunching it between them. I cast him a reassuring smile. 'We're not going to eat you. Come on in. The family's waiting in the kitchen.'

Ruari seems to fill the doorway as he enters, bowing his head under the low lintel. Dad manages to provide a weak handshake. Jimmy greets him with a barely discernible wink. Micheal just nods, and Mam wipes her hands on her apron before nervously reaching for a handshake as though Ruari were the devil himself.

'Sit ye down,' she says and turns her back to fetch the pot from the range. She plonks it on the table and serves it into bowls with her big ladle. The dishes are passed around the table. She wields the big bread knife to cut slabs of fresh bread which are equally distributed, before sitting down herself.

You could cut the air, I'm thinking, when Jimmy asks Ruari with false indignity, 'So, why does Ginny get a Land Rover? Got any more going begging?'

Dad snorts, and the tension is relieved slightly.

'Ginny was struggling over potholes in a town car,' Ruari says. 'She smashed the sump on a rock, and from the state of it, that wasn't the first time it had bottomed out. I just thought...' He shrugs, embarrassed.

'And we're very grateful to you,' Mam says unexpectedly. 'We do worry about her, going up those mountains. I expect you want to see Molly's picture?'

'Molly's picture?' He glances at me in surprise.

'In Davan's sketchbook,' Mam says. 'He made a picture of her. She was beautiful if the picture is anything to go by.'

'Ginny didn't mention that. I've never seen a picture of her.'

'So, eat away,' Mam says, 'then Ginny can take you into the best room to look at the drawings.'

I raise a brow to her, and she colours slightly. 'I have the laundry draped in the other room.'

. . .

The best room smells of mould and furniture polish. The chairs by the small gateleg table under the window are fine walnut. Mam has an idea they might have come from the abandoned Roone Manor, because they are certainly not country-made. I lay the home-made parchment-book down and open it carefully. 'I want you to see the other drawings first, to get an idea of his talent. Then when you see Molly's portrait, you'll understand.'

Ruari sits gingerly in one of the chairs, which seems too fine for his bulk, and peruses the images with intense, silent contemplation. When he finally turns to Molly's image, I have to bite my tongue to stop myself from asking what he thinks. When he finally looks up with a sigh, he doesn't comment on Molly's beauty at all.

'They are exquisite,' he says softly. 'What talent. I wonder if he was able to use his skill, wherever he ended up. What a strange world it is that someone with that kind of ability should be destined to milk cows for a living.'

'That's exactly what I thought. But she's beautiful, isn't she? Molly?'

'She was,' he amends. 'If she's still alive, she'll be in her late sixties or early seventies by now,' he says, reaching out to almost touch the parchment, then hovering, before bringing his hand back. 'I'm no expert, but shouldn't this be protected in some way? It almost belongs in a museum.'

'It should, but I didn't know of its existence until recently, and I'm feeling a bit possessive about it.' I muse for a moment. 'You know, I never thought of the possibility of her and Davan still being alive somewhere on this earth. In my family, the thought is they must have died, because Davan wouldn't have left his mother wondering. Wouldn't it be grand to bring them back to their home, though, and let them know the bother between the families is finally over?'

He sits back and stares at me. I hear the fragile walnut chair creak ominously. 'Is it?'

'You broke bread with my family. That's a start.'

'But,' he says, 'are you prepared to break bread with mine?'

The reality hits me, and I'm sure he sees me wince. 'Maybe sometime.'

'Maybe never. What is it you're not telling me, Ginny?'

I feel the red dots of panic rise behind my eyes. His hand rises again, almost as though he wants to reach out to me, then recalls what happened down at the quay. I force myself to breathe. 'It's too soon, Ruari.'

'Okay, but the invitation is an open one. I told my family what you said about your relationship with Ben. They were moved. They had no idea why you were with him. There was a suggestion that you were brazen, leading him on.'

'I was a teenager. I didn't have a clue what I was doing.'

He smiles softly. 'And my family don't have much of a clue about young women. We seem to breed boys.'

'And you breed them big,' I say, half-laughing.

'You see, that's why Molly was so precious to her father. She was the first girl in two generations, and we've had none since. None that lived, anyway.'

That thought hadn't occurred to me. 'That's why she was protected to the point of being hemmed in,' I say softly. 'And William wanted to put her on a pedestal. It's a shame he couldn't see that Davan was sensitive, unique. He would have been her ideal mate, protected her totally.'

'Maybe. I don't know. My grandfather didn't talk about the past at all, and if anyone mentioned Molly, he got mad and started saying the rosary, over and over. It was weird. We were careful not to mention her in the house.'

'Are any of Molly's other brothers still alive?'

He shakes his head. 'My family die young. Heart attacks, strokes, whatever. One of the great-aunts is still alive, though. Winnie would be William's sister-in-law. She inherited a farm over on the Mizen Peninsula and was married to one of

William's brothers. I can't say I've had much to do with her, but maybe she'll talk to us. The other brother and his wife went to America. That's a bit of a trek for a chat. Noel O'Donovan was just a boy when all this was going on, but he has a good memory on him. He might be able to add something.' He gives me a sly grin. 'There's a rath up behind the manor, too, so you have a good excuse to go calling.'

'I already did. It was him who told me what really happened to Ben. Mam told me he'd been born unpredictable and angry, like William. Why did your mam keep that a secret?'

'Not a secret exactly. Mam just didn't see that it was anyone else's business.'

Today has been somewhat traumatic, and all of us collapse like empty sacks when Ruari makes his excuses and leaves. We might have crossed a hurdle, but there are quite a few more to go.

I find myself lying in bed staring up at the painted white boards of the ceiling, thinking about Molly being sent off to the nuns. I expect she was probably hoping Davan would go and rescue her; it's possible she didn't even know he had been put in prison at that time.

And again I wonder what happened to her baby.

20

MOLLY, 1921

Molly didn't actually know where she was taken. At some stage on the journey, she had fallen asleep and awoken to the sound of the angelus bell. She was hustled into the church, catching no more than a glimpse of a long grey building with rows of tiny, barred windows. It wasn't built for the glory of God, it seemed, but simply to house those who spent their days worshipping Him. To Molly, it looked like a prison, and once she stepped through the forbidding oak doors, it became one.

When mass was over, she was taken to a cell containing nothing but a cot and a bedside table bearing a bible. She was not to leave the room except for meals or mass, despite the door being open during the day. The temperature in the whole building couldn't have been much over freezing, the gloomy rooms having a cave-like atmosphere in which she could see her breath more often than not.

She learned to quickly slip to her knees and clasp her hands in prayer if she heard a nun walking down the corridor. That would have been the end result, anyway, preceded by a lecture or even a switch across her hands. She was wicked, apparently, and the more she prayed, the more were her chances of eventual salvation.

She was escorted to the church three times daily to further wreck her knees on the flagstones – no cushions were provided for the wicked, as if pain was part of the penance required for sins she had not even thought of let alone committed.

Molly waited and hoped and prayed that Davan would arrive and take her away from this grim mausoleum, but as time passed, she realised he wasn't coming. *Of course*, she thought. *He doesn't know where I am, and my family won't tell him.* But when she got out of this place, she was going to take her baby to Davan and do what he had begged her to do: run away with him, start a new life somewhere else.

She didn't mind being in the church because it was a tall space, as churches tended to be, the builders raising the ceiling as near to God as the structure permitted; unlike the cell, the ceiling of which seemed to close down during the short night while she shivered under the thin blanket. The church was equally as cold as her cell but relieved by tapestries of religious scenes devotedly stitched by past nuns, and ornate accoutrements brought out of locked cupboards for the services provided by visiting priests. These items shone like jewels in the shadowed space: the polished ciborium and plate used to hold the body and blood of Christ, the pair of heavy gold candlesticks, the brass thurible on exquisitely thin chains, whose diamond-shaped holes allowed the sweet and fragrant incense to drift up to Heaven with their prayers.

Molly turned fifteen and had never had such a bleak and unremarkable birthday. Her mother had not once visited, nor her brothers. Maybe they were not allowed or hadn't found the time from the farm. Maybe they didn't know where she was, either. Everything she had once believed now became challenged by her churning thoughts – after all, her mind was free to wander, even if her body was confined. She had never questioned her religion before. She had felt safe within the comforting arms of Christ and her community, but now she wondered how God could have given her something so wonderful as her love for Davan and all that came of him, yet His servants treated her as a fallen woman, as they had Mary Magdalene.

A disconnect was beginning to open cracks in her childish acceptance. The nuns could mutter all the prayers they liked, but it took a man to conduct the services. Her mother had to bow to the dictates of her father even in his drunken rages. Women, it seemed, in all parts of society were of less value than men despite the fact that men came out of women's bodies. Was that because God was a man? Up to now, she had offered great respect to the women who chose to give their lives to God, but now, subject to their often vicious piety, she wondered quite why God would ask this barren existence of anyone. And if fornication truly was a sin, as the last priest had declared, bathing himself and the nuns in sanctimonious self-righteousness, it occurred to her that their own parents had all committed sin to bring them into the world.

She closed her eyes and thought of Davan. Her thoughts and memories brought him to her as she recalled their time together. If it was, indeed, sinful to love a man, then she was unrepentant. She would endure this sentence, imposed by her own heartless parents, because she would one day be reunited with Davan. This she knew without doubt. This secret knowledge kept her dauntless in the face of the inhuman conditions: the cold, the hunger, the endless prayers, the lack of conversation, the lack of sunlight, and the disdain with which she was treated. There were no comforts for the fallen. No conversation other than to God. No singing and certainly no laughing, as if she had anything to laugh about.

She passed other whey-faced girls in the corridors, saw them kneeling in the church, pain written clearly on their faces.

Their eyes would glide past each other, not betraying sympathy in their shared predicament, for fear the nuns would see and impose additional penance. They came, swelled and one day disappeared. Molly had known of another girl in Roone Bay who had 'taken sick' and been sent away, to come home thin and pale. She now understood what had happened. What she didn't know was what had happened to the girl's baby. She hugged herself and rocked on her wooden cot, frightened by the unknown.

As the months dragged by, she lost the bloom of good living; her rounded arms and legs lost their fat, the pale skin sagging on the bones. Beneath her budding breasts, her ribs were visible. Below them, the tight bump of her belly grew harder and bigger, and the baby moved within her. She must be near her time. No one gave her advice or told her what to expect, but she counted herself lucky to have lived on a farm. She had watched the lambs being born, the dams pushing them out in quiet determination before turning to nuzzle them, and assumed it would be something similar.

What she hadn't expected was the sudden rush of water between her legs when she tried to stand up in the church. There was a frantic screeching of nuns as they grabbed her arms and almost dragged her bodily from the holy space she was desecrating. She was taken back to her cell, and then the pains began in earnest. She was left alone with no words of comfort, nor advice or instruction. She whimpered through the pains and bit the blanket to stop herself crying out. The nuns had told her the pains were the price of sin, and they didn't need to hear her complaining, thank you very much. They came and checked on her now and again, but didn't bring food or water, even when she begged; they were not her servants. Molly was delirious and exhausted, barely aware, when, with a searing pain, the baby finally tore its way into the world.

Struggling onto one elbow, Molly saw the healthy girl baby

lying in a pool of liquid between her legs. The baby gave a hearty yell, and Molly slumped back and closed her eyes with exhaustion. Davan's child was born. When she next awoke, she was on her own, and the baby was nowhere in sight. She screamed, and a nun came running in. 'My baby,' she said frantically. 'Where is my baby?'

'It was born dead,' the nun said.

'I had a girl,' Molly argued tearfully. 'I saw her. I heard her!'

'The baby is gone,' the nun insisted. 'Now you will go back to your father and it will never be mentioned. Do you understand? Never! That is the price of your sin. Now, pray for the baby's soul, because it is unshriven and destined for everlasting perdition.'

'No, she was alive! The priest must bless her. Please, I need the priest!'

Molly tried to rise from the bed but was too weak and collapsed to the floor.

The nun scowled. 'If you're going to be difficult, you can just stay here until you have repented.'

As Molly clawed her way onto the hard, wooden bed, she heard the door close and the key turn in the lock.

A week later, she was bundled into a cart and taken back to Roone Bay, arriving there exhausted, losing blood and only half coherent.

'Where is Davan?' she begged over and over. 'Why doesn't Davan come to me?'

She had not recovered well from the birth and her condition was critical. Her mother fed her and nursed her, but no one would tell her what had happened to her child or Davan. She discovered that no amount of cajoling or begging produced any kind of answer to her questions. It was as if it had never happened. Her baby gone, Davan gone, she was totally bereft.

There were times she prayed for Davan to return and other times she prayed to die, but God didn't see fit to end her suffering.

One of her brothers finally took pity on her and whispered that Davan was in jail. In some respects that helped, because at last she knew why he hadn't come to her, why he had left her to suffer in that awful place that had been her own prison. She became determined to live, for Davan, for when he came home. Over the months, her health improved and she started to do small chores around the house.

One day, William came in from the fields and informed her that she was to be wed. Her eyes lit up. 'You found him! You found Davan?'

Her father sneered. 'Davan is dead, girl. If you had been dutiful, none of this would have happened. It's all your own fault. Just remember that when you're saying your prayers.'

'Davan is dead?' she said blankly. Her vital, beautiful Davan was dead? 'How can he be dead?'

Molly was too stunned to cry.

William told her harshly, 'Forget about him, and for God's sake, girl, stop whining and put some weight on your bones. Jacky Marsh doesn't want a wife who's fainting all the time.'

'Jacky Marsh?' It wasn't so much a query as disbelief. 'But he's an old man.'

'You're not in a position to be choosy,' her father said. 'I had to pay him to take you, God help me. And he will provide me the money back when you produce a living boy child. He knows our family produces boys, and he wants an heir for the farm.'

'I will not marry him,' Molly said slowly.

William swung on his heel. 'You what?' he said in furious disbelief.

She lifted her head resolutely and looked him in the eye. 'I won't marry him.'

'You'll do as you're told,' William roared, 'if I have to drag you to church myself!'

'You can drag me to the church,' she said. 'But I will not say yes. I would die first. If I can't have Davan, I'll have no one.'

Furiously, he pulled his arm back and raised his riding crop.

Molly smiled. 'Go on. Do it. Let the world see how you abuse me. Let everyone see the marks on my body. Do what you will. If I can't have Davan, I will marry no one.'

William turned on his heel, red in the face with fury, and for the first time in her life, Molly realised that she had free will and knew what she would do with it.

21

GINNY

Ruari's invitation to visit at his home spooks me, but it's my choice whether I accept the invitation or not, isn't it? Micheal told me it was our own parents who stopped the rift from healing, not the Savages, and that hit me hard. I thought all the anger was on their side. I tend to forget that Mam is a force to be reckoned with when it comes to protecting her brood, especially one who was betrayed and hurt as badly as I was.

That knowledge challenges the self-pity I've wrapped myself in for years. I'm not the only one hurting, it seems. I've never admitted to anyone, not even my family, that my decision to traipse the landscape is partially derived from a feeling that being alone is safer than being with people. I don't have to worry about them, what they're thinking, what their intentions are. Being alone is a bubble of self-protection I've cultivated for years, and it will be difficult to step out of it.

If Micheal is right, that I'm the one keeping the generations-long antagonism going, that doesn't put me in a very good light. Maybe everyone knew that except me. Maybe it is my job to heal the rift now, because Mam will continue to protect me, for as long as I need her to.

I need to act. But what if I crack out of my protective shell and find I can't cope? Meantime, I plough my energies into my job, exhausting myself into almost catatonic sleep every night. As the weeks pass, I face the realisation that I'm procrastinating. I'm afraid to face my own demons. Perhaps that's why a kind of silence sits over us at the dinner table, with Dad paying particular attention to his meal, Micheal grunting and leaving the table sooner than sit with us, and Mam emitting sighs she has no idea we can hear.

Early one morning, after Dad and Micheal have left the table to head out to the fields, the phone rings. Mam calls me over. 'It's Sarah, for you,' she says, handing the receiver to me. We share a worried glance, because it's out of the ordinary for Sarah to phone when she'd be getting the children ready for the school run. Or are they on the long holiday now? I'm out of touch.

'Hi, sis,' I say, my voice rising in query.

'I'm coming over to see you. I need you to be there.'

Something in her voice makes me wary. 'Isn't it a school day?' I ask.

'It's just me and Ivy.'

Her words fall into a dark pit. My mind, already heavy with the past, blanks off with panic. I know without her saying it that the past is coming back to bite me, with a vengeance. The status quo, which has been hanging in precarious balance for a long time, is broken. I want to do exactly what Sarah's telling me not to do. I want to run. Back to Cork – or further, to Dublin or America or the moon. Mam has overheard the conversation. We share a quick glance. She compresses her lips and nods. She knows, too.

I sit in the old deckchair in the backyard and wait, distantly watching the blackbirds and thrushes go about the business of raising their young. They seem to instinctively know what to do, and I wonder why we humans often get it so wrong. The summer has arrived in the way it rarely does in Ireland. The sky is wall to wall blue interrupted by fluffs of little clouds that drift serenely by. The sun beams relentlessly onto the land, making the exposed rocks' tops gleam like polished teeth and creating jewels out of the yellow gorse. Drooping bluebells have emerged as the primroses and daffodils fade. The blossom on the whitethorn bushes that line the hedgerows is turning brown, exposing tiny fruits that will slowly swell towards autumn into red berries for the birds. Dotted more thinly between them, the blackthorn is secretly nursing its bitter sloes.

I sit among all this beauty and it means nothing.

When Sarah rang, she sounded brittle, upset. Life is rolling towards me like an avalanche, and all I can do is stand and watch until it engulfs me, because running isn't an option.

Eventually I hear the car struggling up the potholed drive. I don't feel old enough or strong enough to have this conversation, but it's been taken out of my hands. I rise out of the chair, shaking, and walk slowly into the house, through the kitchen, and open the front door.

I feel the pounding of my heart as a physical rhythm driving up through my head, like a migraine in overdrive. This is the moment I've feared and dreaded and longed for all in the same breath. I fear it's not going to go well and struggle to retain a little smidgen of hope. I am waiting at the door as the car swings into view, pulls in and stops.

Sarah climbs out with the tiredness of an old woman. Her face is swollen and splodgy with crying. Even as she turns red-rimmed eyes to me, she swipes a hand over her brow. Then Ivy slips out of the passenger side looking equally distraught. She stands and assesses me for a moment, as if I'm some kind of alien. I hear her voice in my mind. *I hate you. I hate you. I hate you. I'll hate you forever. I never want to see you again...*

She rushes over and hugs me, and we're both crying.

I love this daughter of mine so much it hurts.

In the kitchen, Mam is making the tea, the Irish cure-all. She bustles and fusses, and then we're sitting around the big pine table as we have many times: Mam, her two daughters and her granddaughter. It looks as if nothing has changed.

But everything has changed.

'Did Mam tell you?' I ask Ivy.

I glance at Sarah over the top of her head, knowing she wouldn't have, not without me present. But I want to hear it from Ivy. She's eleven, and at that age, they're seeing the big wide world from within the encapsulated boundaries of family and school. But for her, the outside world has plunged in, with all its crazy values. How do we explain something this big?

I can't take my eyes off her. She can't take her eyes off me, because she's seeing me in a totally different way.

She says, 'We're doing family values in school.'

I wince visibly as she carries on.

'The teacher was talking about how God made marriage sacred, and how we all come into the world blessed. She told us about how her parents met, and how they went to church and got married so that God would give them children. She showed us her birth certificate and asked if we had seen ours.'

'The nosy cow,' Sarah mutters.

'Sarah,' Mam warns.

Ivy flashes a shaky grin, but Sarah takes the reins. 'Well, she's fishing for gossip, so she is. She told the children to bring-and-show, and sent the whole class home to look out their birth certificates. Ivy knows where Thomas keeps all our family documents and the like. She's not supposed to look in his desk. She knows that.'

She glares at Ivy, who grimaces, and I give her a secret smile. What child ever did what she was told? I certainly didn't. Most parents would die a thousand deaths if they ever learned what their children really got up to when they were supposed to be at school or at playdates or sleepovers. Maybe parents know, really, but you can't keep a child locked up, overprotected, as the Savages did to poor Molly. There are consequences. There's nothing easy about growing up. It's hard all the way, and no one learns from the mistakes of the past; everyone learns afresh from their own mistakes. I know that all too well.

Sarah carries on, 'Anyway, she came into the kitchen holding the certificate. And, well, that was that, really. We had a little talk. Tom took the day off to look after Ellen, and I came over here.'

She looks at me as if to say, *Well, now it's up to you.*

'It's a lovely day,' I comment. 'Ivy, perhaps you'd like to walk up to the high rock with me? Maybe we'll see the buzzards.'

She knows it's an excuse to extract us from the family.

It's a hard slog uphill, but being outside, expending physical energy is a good way to dissipate tension. I let Ivy lead the way, and she scrambles like a monkey up the steep bits, using hands as often as feet. She's nimbler than me, though I lead a fairly active life, and knows to avoid the small patches of virulent green moss that innocently disguise depressions filled with water. Bogs, some would say, though that's not entirely true.

Half an hour later, we haul ourselves onto the flat rock, gasping for breath. We're a little too far inland to see the sea, but the high rock, so labelled by the family, being the highest point on our land, exposes a wide vista of land too rugged, marginal and harsh to farm.

We're close but not touching, separated by nearly twelve years of lies. I wasn't sure how we were going to get through this moment, but I feel lighter and freer than I have for years, now that the time is upon me. I'm glad she learned while she's still young enough to adapt. Sarah and I had discussed how and when to tell her, because it was always the intention to tell her before she found out by herself. But good intentions became procrastinations, for so many reasons.

'I should have brought a picnic,' I say, somewhat inanely, remembering past excursions, as we scan the still and hazy expanse of scenery. Below, the land is fertile and green, but the ice-scoured peaks wear grey and yellow toupees of rock and rush. From here, the farmhouse is like a toy, nestled on the side of the hill. From here, I can also see the rath on the Savages' land, with all its memories and heartache. I have been procrastinating about that, too. I need to visit it, but the memories are wounds stitched with barbed wire.

'There's Grandpa.' Ivy points out Dad's tractor making its way down the boreen pulling a tall-sided trailer full of fresh grass destined for silage, to feed the cattle during the winter. 'He's still my grandpa, isn't he?' she says, working through things.

'He is. And Jimmy and Micheal are still your uncles.'

'But you're my mam and my mam is really my aunt, but I'm still to live there and she'll still be my mam?'

'You're happy with Sarah being your mam, aren't you?' I ask anxiously, 'And having Patrick be your big brother and Ellen your baby sister?'

She nods. 'Mam explained it to me this morning, how you were too young to look after a baby and Mam had been wanting another baby and it didn't come, so you let her have me.'

That's as good an explanation as I could have come up with. I wonder how many years Sarah has had that little lie stored in her mind. It makes me out to be a saint, though, and I sure don't feel like one. 'But you know I still love you, lots,' I stress. 'Sometimes, when girls have a baby and can't look after it, it's adopted by a different family altogether, and sometimes they never find each other even if they want to. But because you're with my sister, I haven't really lost you at all.'

'Mam said Gran and Grandpa would have brought me

up, but they're too old, and you were still at school, but my mam had a house already and a little boy already, so it made sense.'

'That's right.' It made sense, but making the sensible decision tore rents in my emotions. I shuffle closer and put my arm around her. I can't imagine the confusion that's going through her mind, but what I hadn't expected at all was her acceptance of the situation, her lack of blame, her almost uncanny, grown-up understanding of the situation.

'Auntie Ginny...' she starts, then thinks about it. 'I can't call you mam, can I?'

'Auntie Ginny is probably best,' I say, 'otherwise it would be confusing about which mam you're talking about.'

She grins. 'Yes, it would. But if Mam isn't my real mam, then Dad isn't my real dad, either, is he?'

'No,' I say slowly, knowing where this is going.

'So, who is my real dad? Can I see him?'

I sigh. 'Ivy, love, your real dad died several years ago.'

'Is that why you couldn't marry him?'

'Sort of.'

'Did you love him?'

'I sort of did,' I say. It's not altogether a lie. 'Can I tell you about him another day? Because it hurts to remember, and really, Thomas is your dad in every way that matters. He's looked after you, the same as Sarah has, since you were born. He loves you very much. And now that you've discovered all the secrets, he must be very worried that you won't love him any more. Perhaps later we could nip into town and buy him something special, just for being a good dad?'

She nods seriously. 'And something for Mam, too?'

'Something very special for your mam.'

We scan the sky for a while, but there are no buzzards to be seen. They flew over to Ireland from Scotland back in the late thirties and have been working their way south ever since. Last year, I saw a pair courting by the scrubby trees below. I'm hoping they managed to rear some chicks.

'Will we go back down, now?' I ask. 'I expect your mam is worrying, and Grandma will have lunch on the table.'

'I hope she's made scones,' Ivy says, jumping up.

I laugh. 'She makes the best scones in Ireland!'

'With lashings of butter and jam!'

'Absolutely.'

'Will we stay overnight, so I don't have to go to school in the morning?'

'That's up to your mam.'

She grins. 'You're my mam.'

Oh, Lord, this is going to be difficult. She's known this for just a few hours, and already she's working out how to play us off, one against the other! But this, I think, is the lull before the storm. Despite her seeming acceptance of the situation, something this big is going to generate a rollercoaster of emotions, one day to the next, and poor Sarah is going to bear the brunt.

But Sarah has a different view.

After lunch, Dad takes Ivy out to feed the geese and the two goats, leaving me and Sarah and Mam sitting with our hands wrapped around what seems like our fiftieth cup of tea.

'I can't send her back to school straight away,' Sarah says. 'She has to learn not to blurt it out to everyone. That blasted sanctimonious teacher of hers will call her out on it and next thing the children will be calling her a bastard.'

'That would be harsh,' Mam agrees.

Sarah looks at me with a determined glint in the eye. 'It's nearly the summer holidays. How about I call her in sick, let her stay here for a few weeks?' She looks me straight in the eyes. 'Give you two time to come to terms with the situation. Ivy and I can go home and pack some things, and come straight back here again in the morning. By the time she goes back to school, we can all have our stories straight.'

'But—'

'No,' Sarah says mulishly. 'No buts. You can call in sick, too. She's your child. Don't tell her you love her – prove it.'

I stare at her, stunned, with no ready answer, because actually, she's right. She's been caring for my daughter all this time, and now she's telling me to do my damn job.

'And we've told her lying is a sin,' Mam sighs.

I'd already experienced the way religious dogma provides fuel for the self-righteous. I love the way religion binds our fragile community together, but I learned early to question its antiquated doctrines.

'It's the school that's the problem,' Sarah says. I don't think she believes in God, either, though we were brought up in the faith. 'They still bring the priest in to do religious assemblies once a week, and the children are encouraged to go to confession.'

'I'd knock that on the head sharpish!' I say sourly.

'It's easy to say what you would and wouldn't do when you're not her mother!' Sarah snaps.

'Girls,' Mam reproaches gently. 'It is what it is. And it could be worse. The girl is well-balanced altogether.'

I put my hand over Sarah's in apology. 'She is. We just need to undo all that and teach her how to lie.'

22

GINNY

Ivy has been with us for a week, now, but my ten weeks has been extended to cover my fictitious illness, which is a relief. It's been hard for both Ivy and me, but it's been fun, too. We've talked so much my throat is sore. All the reasons why she must not tell anyone she's my child have been picked apart in discussion. For me, it's heartbreaking all over again, not so much to know that she will go back to Sarah, when we are just starting to create a bond, but that she has to learn the folly of the world so early. But I can do nothing else. When she's left school behind, she can tell whoever she wants, but right now I don't want her future blighted by mean-minded prejudice.

Don't give people information that makes them feel superior, I said. *Don't hand other children a reason to bully you, because they'll grasp the opportunity with glee.* She's seen a clique of girls in her class be horrible to a little girl whose crime is vested in the ugly National Health glasses she wears like a badge of dishonour because her mam can't afford better ones. They run behind her in the playground, chanting, *Goggle-eyes, four-eyes.* Ivy says it's horrid and makes the girl cry. She doesn't understand why the teacher stands and glares from the doorway but doesn't interfere and put a stop to it. But she does understand that she doesn't want to be like that picked-on girl.

Ivy is enjoying her illicit time off school as much as being with me and the family. She likes being outdoors, helping on the farm, but wants to come and help me with my work, to measure and record the old monuments. That's a relief, actually. She's enchanted by the Land Rover. She's never been in one before and loves the way the door creaks ominously when she forces it open, and laughs through the struggle to climb up into the cab. She enjoys undoing the little sliding windows in the door with their old-fashioned catches and the overwhelming noise of the engine as we rattle along the main road, so loud we can hardly talk. She shrieks with delight, holding on to the ledge at the front – too basic to be called a dashboard – as we go bouncing up rutted boreens or farm tracks. She deliberately directs me towards potholes I would previously have tried to avoid, like an obstacle course where you don't go around the challenges, you simply drive over or through them.

She's on a high at the moment, because we're making her feel special, and she's bunking off school, but when she goes back home, I suspect the bubble will burst. Then we'll see the true results of our subterfuge. Sarah is, meanwhile, explaining things to Patrick, so that there don't have to be lies within the family. Ivy knows that a secret told is a secret no longer. But I do hope it can be contained, for a while, at least.

Sarah has often moaned about the whole heavy business of children; the never-ending chore of bathing, washing, feeding and deadlines such as school runs – now with baby Ellen in tow, as well. She only ever wanted two children, and Ellen's unexpected late arrival (despite illegal contraceptives, she whispered) was as much a shock as a pleasure.

I used to think being a mam was a part-time job, leaving plenty of time for shopping and hairdressers. I was too young and too wrapped up in my own problems to realise what a huge thing it had been for her and Thomas to take on my baby.

What I had never experienced before was the sheer terror of being responsible for my own child. What if she slipped from a rock and broke her leg? What if she opened the door of the Land Rover and got knocked down? What if she slipped off the quay into the water? She can swim, but what if a motorboat was coming in at that exact moment... My imagination comes up with a zillion scenarios in an instant. I've been looking after her for just one week, and I'm exhausted, while Sarah has had this responsibility for eleven years. I feel chastened and guilty for my previous lack of understanding. I also want to stand on the mountain and scream my frustration, because she's my daughter and I can't have her.

23

GINNY

One morning, after breakfast, the phone rings. Mam hands the phone to me with her brows raised. 'It's Ruari *Savage*.' She hisses the last name in warning, but I don't know any other Ruari who might be calling. I have been living in fear and dread of this call, and suspect he's been waiting, hoping that I would make the first move. He has no idea of the trauma I've been coping with in the meantime.

'Hi,' I say brightly.

'Ginny,' he says, sounding relieved at my tone. 'How's the Land Rover going for you?'

His deep voice, so like Ben's, sends a trickle of excitement through me, as would happen when I found Ben waiting for me by the lane after school to show me some wonder of nature he'd discovered, like the coal tit's eggs in a tiny hollow in a stone wall or the magic ring of translucent toadstools in the rath, which were beautiful one day, their little caps bouncing on slender stems, and the next day were melted to slime. *The most poisonous toadstool in Europe,* he had whispered. *Death angels. Eat just one and you'll die, not immediately, but a few days later because it destroys the internal organs.*

'The Land Rover is great,' I tell Ruari, which isn't at all a lie. 'We've been having fun in it, actually. I'm truly grateful. I'll pay you back one of these days.'

'We?'

'My niece – my sister's daughter – is here for a couple of weeks. Ivy has been helping me with my job.' I turn and smile at her, where she's sitting in the kitchen, drawing on a sheet of paper, all ears tuned to the conversation, though she's pretending otherwise. I see a faint smile emerge. She'll task me with the lie later.

'Look, I've talked to Anne Doheny about you visiting my great-aunt Winnie. Anne is her carer.'

So much has happened in the meantime, it takes me a moment to recall that the old lady had married Cillian Savage, one of William Savage's brothers. She must be ancient. The last of that generation, I think Ruari said. 'Oh,' I say, perking up. 'That's great.'

'Anne said we can visit pretty much any time, but I'll take you there, if you don't mind. I'd like to hear what she has to say about it all, and as she knows me, I might be able to get her to open up a bit. But be warned, she can get confused, sometimes.'

'Sure, that's fine. When were you thinking?'

'How about this morning? If you can, I mean. I have a couple of commitments tomorrow and the next day that I can't get out of.'

'I was just about to make some calls and plan my day, but this works for me, if you're sure it's not inconvenient.'

'No, it's fine. I have a couple of lads working with me here; they can manage to keep the shop going for a morning – can't you, lads?' he adds in a shout. There's some muffled laughter in the background. He must have a good working relationship with his 'lads'.

'So, we'll drive down to Roone Bay?'

'Any time. I'll be here, at the garage.'

And that's our day sorted.

I think the weather is going to turn soon, because as we drive down the hill, to the west I see tall clouds gathering. *Don't fall on us today*, I beg silently. I've got so used to the good weather I forgot my own rule – to always have wet weather gear in the car. But they aren't the ominous grey clouds that darken the landscape, or the doom-laden anvil clouds of thunderstorms. They're the thick white clouds that Ben's imagination used to turn into bears and whales and crocodiles as they rolled and churned before the wind.

Ruari must have heard us coming as he steps from the office as I pull up. 'Climb over the back, love,' I tell Ivy, and she does so without quibbling, which is quite a milestone. Perhaps because the man I'm picking up seems large and daunting.

He peers in and grins at her before climbing in and presenting his back. 'Hi, I'm Ruari. Who are you?'

I hold my breath.

'I'm Ivy. Auntie Ginny's sister is my mam.'

I let my breath out in silent relief.

'So, do you mind if I sit in front? You see, my legs are a bit long for the back seat. They'd be up around my ears.'

She giggles. 'No, I don't mind. I've been sitting in the front all week, so you can have a turn.'

'Thank you,' he says, climbing in. 'You can call me Ruari. I'm not old enough to be Mr Savage.'

'Have you got any children?'

He shakes his head. 'Not yet. Though I would like to one day. My big brother has, though. He's got two boys, Andrew and Mark. They're about your age. They live in America. Are you staying here for the summer? They'll be visiting. Maybe you'd like to meet them?'

'No thank you,' she says politely. Boys are definitely not

playdate material for little girls who are practising being women.

'Okay, so,' he says and settles, looking at me. 'You know the way. I'll direct you when we get close. We could stop at the Altar Tomb on the way, if you like.'

The wedge tomb at Altar is a mystical landmark – one of the best in Ireland, to my mind – created around five thousand years ago, pointing south west, directly at the Mizen rock. I wonder at the significance of the orientation. The prehistoric monuments can usually be identified as aligning to celestial targets, sometimes even specific events such as equinoxes, but the significance is unknown. What rituals led to the huge effort of creating them, and what gods were worshipped, no one knows.

'I know you'll have that on the map already,' Ruari is saying, 'but perhaps Ivy won't have seen it? It's one of those things you can tell people about, but to truly get the feel for it, you have to stand where the ancients once stood, don't you?'

Though I'm driving, my eyes glued to the road, I sense his gaze drift over me. He's not expecting an answer; he knows it already. He's surprised me, though I shouldn't be surprised. His big brother had been passionate about ancient Ireland, and to some extent had passed this interest on to me. Maybe it's in his whole family. Historically, owning land in Ireland can breed a love of the landscape into a person, as it has me. But not always. Some who inherit just see the land as a resource to sell or generate an income, missing the whole beautiful, somewhat ephemeral sense of past, present and future all being part of the same moment.

'You're smiling,' he says to me. 'You should do that more often.'

Now I do glance at him, briefly. I realise I was thinking of Ben as he had been in those magical moments, before everything went wrong, when we were somehow bound by a deeper love of nature, when we could almost say the same thing at the same time. If Ivy hadn't been present, I might have told Ruari this. I might even have admitted to myself that I feel the same attraction towards Ben's younger brother, a huge presence in the vehicle beside me, and I'm not talking about his physical size. But I'm not daft enough to repeat a past mistake.

We stop at the Altar Tomb car park and walk over to where the massive rocks seem to grow out of the long grass. Ivy, of course, wants to clamber up onto the capstone for the view. I can't see the problem, as it's been there for thousands of years and seems as immoveable as the very land we're walking on. The scenery here is stunning, the bay before us, the sea gently twinkling under the sun, the hills rising into the distance, the low, rocky cliffs of the bay's opposite shore. Ruari crouches beside Ivy and puts his arm around her, pointing with the other hand, directing her gaze. I have a brief moment of panic, but his contact is so innocent I bite my tongue.

'See those little seagulls up there? They're kittiwakes,' he's saying. 'See the ends of the wings? They look as if they've been dipped in ink, don't they? And that pair standing on the edge of the cliff? You're lucky to see that. They're guillemots. They must be breeding, because they spend all their lives at sea, and just come to land to lay eggs and rear their young.'

Yes, he's so like Ben it's weird. His interest in the birds and the landscape is dimmed in comparison, less consuming, less passionate. Passion was Ben's best and worst feature. He could be so gentle but could fall into a rage in an instant, like the time he discovered that a bird's nest he'd been watching had been vandalised, the eggs destroyed. He had actually cried great gulping sobs as he gathered the pieces as if he wanted to glue them back together. I'd never seen a grown man cry before and it had scared me, before he wiped his eyes and became my gentle Ben again, so suddenly it was as if a switch had been pressed. Perhaps I should have understood,

then, that his swings of mood were unnatural and uncontrollable

We carry on, rounding the bay before heading west again. Ruari
directs me up some tiny, winding roads, to a newly built
bungalow beside an old, almost derelict farmhouse.

Anne Doheny bustles out of the new bungalow and leads us
into the kitchen of the old house, which has surely been
forgotten by time. There's just one sash window, propped up by
a length of wood as the sash is long gone. An ancient fireplace
dominates one end, with an oven on one side, a hotplate on the
other and a tall grate between made of horizontal bars. There's
an iron crane in the wide chimney opening, supporting a black
cast-iron kettle that has been swung over the open fire, and is
steaming gently to itself.

There's a rocking chair to one side of the fireplace in which
an old lady is seated, her sunken eyes closed. She's wearing
black clothes down to her ankles, a grubby white apron and a
white cotton cap with a frill around the brim, tied under her
chin. She could be mummified, save for her foot, which presses
with relentless monotony on the flagstone.

'Gran!' Anne yells. 'Here's Ruari to see you, and he's
brought young Ginny Kingston.'

Anne spoons tea into a crockery teapot, grabs the tail of a
lazy boy with a cloth and tips boiling water into the pot. She
places the teapot on a solid table made from rough-hewn planks.
She grabs milk from an antique fridge, pulls mugs from hooks
on a dresser. 'There's sugar in the bowl, and a teaspoon already,'
she says with satisfaction. 'Just let that brew for a while, Ruari,
love, and would ye mind pouring? I'll leave ye to it.' At the door,
she glances back over her shoulder with a broad smile. 'Good
luck, altogether!'

Ivy hovers by the door, in awe. I don't think she's ever seen anyone so old. I don't think I have, come to that. She must be getting towards a hundred years, a whole century. And what changes she must have seen in that time!

'Auntie,' Ruari says loudly, 'I've brought Ginny to see you. She's Sally O'Brien's granddaughter. You remember Sally? Davan O'Brien's sister?'

'Will she remember?' I ask quietly.

'Maybe,' he says quietly. 'Her mind tends to wander these days. I don't think she's long for this world. Her family gone, William's brothers all gone. When Auntie Winnie passes, there will be none left who remember Molly at all, just the story in the telling. Everyone gets lost in the end. I guess that's how it's meant to be.'

He shouts again, 'Auntie, tell Ginny the story of Molly and Davan.'

The old lady's wrinkled eyelids crack to betray faded grey eyes. Her tongue wets dry lips. 'Ah now,' she says. 'A right sad do, that was, with William losing his nob altogether when he found out that his daughter was sweet on Davan O'Brien and her only fifteen years old at the time. Sad it was. She was such a lovely thing, but, sure, didn't she have bad blood? Didn't listen to the Word but ran off, giving herself to the first lad who came along.'

I feel an instant antipathy towards the old woman.

Ruari begins to fill the mugs and takes one over to his great-aunt. He wraps her hands around the mug on her lap.

'William sent her off to the nuns. He said it was for her health, but we all knew what she'd done, didn't we?' she continued, casting a sly glance. 'She came back thin as a reed, of course, and William was trying to get her married off as if she was untouched.' She cackled.

'Where was she sent?' I ask.

The old lady considers, then shrugs. 'William never said.'

'What happened to the baby?' I ask.

'It died. There was never a word said, after.'

Not openly, maybe, given William's temper. But no doubt the secret was whispered all over the townland. God forbid a family should have to admit to having a bastard in the house, I think sourly. But I grew up with the story and feel sad for Molly, the child-woman who had her baby taken away from her even though Davan would have married her.

Winnie falls silent for a moment, lost in the past, but she perks up again. 'Of course, William got the law onto young Davan, just so. He said if he was seen around again, he'd kill the spalpeen with his own bare hands. When Davan came back from prison a year later, William was like a man possessed. He said Davan should surely be dead – hadn't he arranged it himself? But didn't the boy turn up and start asking about Molly? But sure, wasn't he too late?'

Ruari and I exchange a shocked glance. Had William arranged for Davan to be murdered in prison?

'What do you mean, too late?' Ruari asks, picking up on her next statement.

Maybe they'd forced her to marry another man.

Winnie puts her mug to her lips and slurps noisily, but I see her eyes flick slyly to Ruari, then wander guiltily around the room as if having been caught out saying too much.

Her wandering eyes catch sight of Ivy. She gives a cry and drops her mug on the firestone, where it explodes in a cascade of hot tea. She puts shaking hands on the arms of her chair and half-rises to her feet, shaking and gasping, before she finds her tongue again.

'The devil's brought her back to haunt me,' she screams, pointing, spittle lining her thin lips. 'Get that whore out of my house, do you hear me? Anne, Anne, the divil is on me! I'm cursed. William made me swear, and I prayed, didn't I pray? Get me the priest. Anne, Anne...'

Her screeches warble higher, and I run to Ivy, who has

burst into shocked tears. I turn her around and march her swiftly out through the open door, hugging her close as Ruari tries to calm the old woman down, making inadequate shushing noises, stopping her from falling onto the fire.

Anne bustles past us, through the door, and takes charge. 'Gran, Gran, there's no one here at all. You must have been dreaming. Gran, calm down. Sit down. I'll get you some fresh tea. See, there's no one here.'

Behind her back, she indicates for Ruari to leave, and he does so, hastily. He closes the door firmly behind himself, but not before I hear the querulous voice say, 'It was Molly. Molly, come back to haunt me! Anne, my soul is going to the divil. William did a wicked thing, and all these years I've been confessing my sins and keeping the faith, but now her ghost is come to haunt me, ah Virgin Mary, blessed mother of God, save me!'

I stand by the Land Rover, holding Ivy close, rocking her like a baby until her panicked breathing has slowed. I kiss her head. 'It's all right, Ivy, love. She didn't mean you. She thought you were someone else.'

'I didn't like her at all,' Ivy hiccups. 'She was like an old witch.'

She was that, all right. 'I know, love. Don't worry – you never have to come here again. We'll go back to Roone Bay, see if we can get an ice cream on the quay.'

She wipes her eyes with the backs of her hands. 'But who is Molly, anyway?'

'Well, it's a sad story, one that my grandpa told me a long time ago. You have to feel sorry for the poor old woman, because she's confused and doesn't know who's who any longer. It happens sometimes when people's brains get old and tired.'

'I know. Mam told me that happens. I do feel sorry for the old woman, really,' she says, wiping her eyes.

Which is more than I do.

Whatever she knew about William has been locked in her head and in the priest's confession box for fifty years. If William had committed the kind of sin she believed would bring the devil to her deathbed, perhaps he did kill Molly, after all, and maybe Davan, too.

Ruari's shock is written clearly on his face. He's also realised that his great-aunt has been hiding a secret all these years. We don't know what, but I have the strongest suspicion that Molly and Davan didn't elope, after all, that something dreadful happened to them right here in Roone Bay, and if Winnie dies without speaking, whatever happened is going to remain forever undiscovered.

24

GINNY

Ruari apologises profusely as we drive, and when we get back to the garage to drop him off, he stands at the open door and speaks directly to Ivy as she climbs back over into the front seat. 'I'm so sorry you had to experience that. I knew my great-aunt was going a bit doolally' – he makes a weird expression while making a circling motion with his finger around his ear, making her laugh – 'but I had no idea she'd gone that far downhill. She's surely deranged. I'd really hate it if this stopped me from seeing your Auntie Ginny again.'

Ivy glances at me, surprised, and I can see that she's added two and two to make five. I laugh self-consciously. 'We're just friends, that's all.'

The half-smile Ruari shoots towards me doesn't suggest that at all, and makes me feel a bit warm and fuzzy, which is strange in the circumstances. After his aggressive attitude when I arrived back home, I never would have guessed that I'd one day feel comfortable in his presence and even enjoy his company, but so it is.

'Did you know Winnie, when she was younger and presum-

ably *compos mentis?*' I ask curiously. 'Did she ever speak of
William and Molly?'

He shakes his head. 'I admit, Winnie was never my
favourite great-aunt, but really, I never had much to do with her.
Just family gatherings, you know. Just as well, I guess. She could
turn milk sour,' he adds with a laugh. He slams the door and
asks through the open window, 'Has this put you off coming to
dinner with my family?'

I flush slightly. 'I never agreed to.'

'No, you didn't,' he says. 'Ivy, what do you think? Would
you like to come up and meet my mam and dad and my brothers? They're all a bit like me, big and scary.'

She giggles. 'You're not scary.'

'And we've got donkeys,' he adds. 'And horses. You can ride
one, if you like.'

Ivy turns to me, her eyes shining with hope. I glare at Ruari,
who smiles back innocently and says, 'That's settled, then. I'll
talk to Mam, and we can arrange a day.'

At home, Ivy gives Mam a rundown of the day, and Mam looks
at me worriedly. 'The auld one scared her, so?'

'She scared me, too, but there's no real harm in it.'

'Are you going to be all right going up *there*? Ruari seemed
nice enough, but so did Ben until he wasn't.'

'Ben was different,' I say after a moment's thought. 'We
know that now. I think it would be a good thing to go and visit,
don't you? And if it gets stressful, I can always come home.
Mam, I'm twenty-seven, not a schoolgirl any longer.'

'Well, if you're sure. It just seems a bit strange, is all.'

I kind of forgot that Ivy was watching, her eyes batting
backward and forward between us, taking it all in. 'What
happened? Who's Ben? Why wasn't he nice?'

I sigh. 'Ben was Ruari's big brother. He had an accident on

his tractor and died, a long time ago. He could sometimes seem a bit angry, but I don't think it was his fault. He had something wrong with his head.'

'Oh,' she says, accepting this.

'And if you want to go on a horse I don't mind, if someone is looking out for you and holding the reins.'

I'm thinking I should make a few more visits to monuments when there's a long roll of thunder overhead, so loud it rattles the crockery and the lights flicker. 'Darn,' Mam says. 'There goes my washing. Help me bring it in, quick, now.'

We rush out and unpeg the washing as the first huge drops of rain splash onto the dusty earth, and a flash of lightning cuts across the lowered sky. We barely get back in through the door when the heavens open, rain falling as thick and heavy as I've ever seen it. A half hour later, Dad and Micheal come in, drenched, having brought the cows back down to the barn. The marginal fields can get waterlogged very quickly, and cows tend to spook in bad storms.

Just as they're shaking their coats out to hang in the hallway, the lights flash again then go out altogether. Mam shakes her head in the gloom. 'This backward auld country,' she sighs. 'Well, we have wood for the fire. Get it lit in the living room, won't you, Micheal? Have we candles handy? Sure, it could be night already. Let's hope the power-out doesn't last for two weeks, like it did that Christmas. And there was me trying to cook a turkey in a pot on the fire, like they did back in the day!'

'I don't think they'd have had turkeys back in the day, Mam. A chicken, maybe.'

'And spuds,' Dad jokes. 'Don't forget the spuds!'

It's kind of atmospheric in the old house with just the fire going and candles around the room and us sitting around the little table playing cards as we had when we were children.

'It's just like the old days,' Mam says, 'without electric.'

'Not quite,' Dad disagrees, having been brought up in the

house. 'We wouldn't be playing cards, that's for sure. We would be making and mending, ruining our eyes doing the work all the same. But thank the Lord we got the silage in last week.'

How we've come to rely on electricity in just one generation, I think. But in a funny sort of way, it's kind of exciting. Sitting by candlelight somehow brings us closer together as a family.

Mam is on a roll about what it was like when she was growing up. There's nothing like a power outage to start the reminiscing. But because we aren't so far off the beaten track Dad got electricity brought to the farm in 1948, a few years before I was born. Not all farms were so lucky. But the worry now is that everything, including the milking parlour, is run on electricity. Gone are the old hand-milking days. Sure, I've helped milk an ailing cow by hand, but we would be there forever trying to get through the whole herd tomorrow.

The storm drives through and is gone the next day, but Dad's seriously worried about the cows, which have already missed a milking. They're in discomfort, and being left too long invites mastitis and worse. He's wondering about trying to get the loan of a generator, but when he picks up the receiver, the phone is dead, too. He's talking of driving down to Roone Bay to see if the phone lines are open there when Ruari appears in the pick-up truck.

'I just wanted to make sure you weren't cut off,' he says, standing dripping, just inside the door. 'There was a tree down on the main road. I just helped to pull it free, but it's taken out the phone line.'

Dad rattles the dead phone. 'Found that out. I was just going to phone around for a generator.'

'When the brothers have finished the milking, I'll bring ours down,' Ruari offers. 'I just need to go and check on the Misses

Breams up the road, them living on their own. I'll be back in a bit.'

'That's kind,' Mam says, watching him scoot back to his truck.

'Why now, after all these years?' Dad says in wonder, after Ruari has gone. 'Last time Connie Savage spoke to me, he asked to buy the farm. He made it sound like he was doing me a favour. I maybe said things I shouldn't have.'

'Perhaps he really was trying to help,' I say.

The Savages have a strong farm with many acres and two hundred cows, unlike our little patch of land that once just supported a family with eight cows and now has to run sixty to just break even. Dad couldn't afford a generator. Small farms are going under all the time, and ours is hanging on with difficulty.

Ruari calls in again on his way back down, and we wave him on with thumbs up as the power pops back on. I think about his father wanting to buy Dad out. I hadn't known that. It must have hurt Dad's feelings, though he's hinted that the farm might not survive another generation if the government doesn't step in to help. And what about Micheal if the farm isn't really viable? All he knows is working the land.

The phones are out for another day, but as soon as we're reconnected, I phone Sarah to let her know all is well.

'Why would I be worried?' she asks, much to my amusement. They hadn't experienced a power cut in Clonakilty, so it never occurred to her to check on us. She has a good chat with Ivy, asks her how her holiday is going, meaning how is she getting on with me, given the new dynamics between us. Ivy says *fine* and tells her about helping me with my job, and about taking Ruari up to visit an old witch on the hill, and how he came over to offer Dad the generator. More is said, at which point Ivy shrugs and passes the handset to me.

'Ruari Savage,' I say in answer to her question.

There's a silence. Then, 'Is he safe?'

I find myself smiling. 'Sis, he's nice. I kind of like him. He's invited me and Ivy over to his place for dinner, to meet his family.'

As soon as it's said, I realise that she'll read more into it than she should.

'Is that wise?'

'I don't think there's any danger in it,' I say dryly, 'but it will be a bit daunting as the whole family will be there. But Ruari is good with Ivy. He's kind and funny.'

'Do they know?'

'No. And I'm not going to tell them.'

She's silent again, and I can almost hear her thoughts churning, then her breath whooshes out audibly. 'Well, I guess you're old enough to know what you're doing.'

I'm not so sure about that myself, but the tide carrying me is too strong to fight. It's time to face the past. Trying to close the door now it's cracked open is counter-intuitive. But that thought leads me back to the past. 'Did you know that Mam and Dad have Davan's sketchbook?'

'Sure. Grandpa still had it when I was at home. I never saw it, though. Was he good?'

'Superb. Amazingly so. I might take it up with me. I think Ruari's family would be interested. There's a beautiful sketch of Molly. He really brought her alive.'

'Good Lord! I'd like to see that.'

Of course, she recalls Grandpa's stories well enough, too. It's a shame no one has a picture of Davan. He worked on the farm but must have had a sensitive side, to be able to draw the way he did. I wonder again where that gift came from. No one else in our family has ever shown a smidgen of artistic ability, least of all me.

Ruari calls to ask us to go up the following afternoon. I must have swallowed loudly, as he laughs down the line. 'Tell you what, I'll come and fetch you both, which will make it easier for you. If I bring you up early, we can take a tour around the farm. I think the water in the stream will have subsided a bit, so we can maybe visit the rath, too. I'd like you to tell me about your work. I'm curious. And while we're there, Teddy can teach Ivy a bit about the horses, and let her ride one. He's good with kids, I promise. He won't let her fall off.'

'Okay,' I say dubiously and belatedly remember to add, 'Thanks.'

Ruari's laugh echoes in my mind as I put the phone down. It's so like Ben's a shudder of unease ripples down my spine. I feel an attraction towards Ruari – and I'm sure he feels the same towards me. Is that almost sinister echo from the past real? Is this strange attraction the same as the one that makes some women fall for men who are in prison for appalling crimes? Some kind of inbuilt need to self-harm, perhaps?

I don't mention any of this to Mam, but I'm filled with a need to take to my heels before it's too late. If I didn't have Ivy here, maybe I would, but Sarah – bless her! – has decided it's time I took some responsibility for my own child. It's strange how burdened I feel, not to be free to simply go where I want without thinking about Ivy's well-being. Her parting shot – *Maybe it's time you grew up!* – is not so far from the mark.

I don't exactly dress up for dinner at the Savages', but out of respect for Ruari's parents, who I've never met, I do heave a clean pair of jeans out of the wash basket. Being an archaeologist, always out and about, I don't have much in the way of decent clothing and certainly didn't bring anything clever with me. I haven't yet achieved the status in the academic community that requires cocktail dresses for those upmarket functions I hear about. I smile to myself. Maybe one day!

When Ruari arrives in the rescue pick-up, I plaster a smile of welcome onto my face and let Ivy climb up first to squeeze between myself and Ruari on the bench seat. 'Have you got wellies?' he asks. 'I went up the fields this morning. It's pretty wet, still.'

'We have.' I nod towards the carrier bag at my feet, then ask, 'Don't you have an ordinary car?'

'Sure, I can borrow a car any time I need. Mam has one. So have Dad and Noah and Ted. But the pick-up's got four-wheel drive, and there are still a few trees down after the storm. I keep the chainsaw in here, too, just in case anyone needs a bit of a hand.'

I have no answer to that. Perhaps he sees it as work, but maybe he just likes to help people simply because he has the wherewithal. I lean into the corner by the door and watch him as he drives. His jeans and checked shirt are as used and worn as mine, and the tough work boots are worn down to the shiny steel toecaps in places. He has the faint whiff of soap and after-shave with a hint of car oil. Despite coming from a fairly affluent family and owning his own business, I gather he's not bothered about shopping for new until the old things simply don't do their job any longer.

Of course, he's attractive, too, in a very macho kind of way, and I suspect he knows it. His wide shoulders have an inherent strength, and his thick forearms, bare to the rolled-up shirt sleeves at the elbow, are dark from exposure. His thighs flex against the worn fabric of his jeans as he works the clutch and brake, and I feel myself grow a little hot under the collar as I realise quite what I'm assessing. I turn my head away rapidly and stare out of the front window, hoping I wasn't caught looking.

What is it about a man's physique that makes a girl go all

gooey? I remember looking at Ben that way, with the fascination of a young girl who had never seen a man's naked body – though that part remained just imagination! I'm not naïve any more, of course.

We turn the final corner to see three houses. The old farm-house, similar to ours, is in the middle. There's a bungalow on the right and a big two-storey house on the left, which we stop outside.

'Granddad had the old house until he died,' Ruari says. 'It's empty at the moment. I've been doing it up. See, the new slates on the roof, and new windows? Noah has the bungalow. He's recently married. You'll meet Anita later. They'll be having a baby in a couple of months, which, of course, Mam is really excited about,' he adds with a grin. 'That will be her first grand-child in Ireland, and the poor mite is going to be horribly spoiled. Us Savages seem to be late starters. Too busy working to go romancing.'

Ruari casts me an assessing glance. He knows Ben got me pregnant and believes the baby to have been aborted. With a jolt, I realise that Ivy is actually his mam's first grandchild in Ireland and imagine how hurt she would be if she knew I'd been keeping this from her for eleven years.

His mam, Jenny, opens the door, and stands there waiting. She has a smile of welcome on her face and no trace of the accusatory glare I'd been envisaging if I ever bumped into her by accident. Unlike me, she's tall and well dressed; her hair, black going silver, is caught up in some kind of clip at the back; and she's wearing dangly earrings. As I walk forward and take the hand she's holding out, she pulls me into a familiar one-armed hug and brushes my cheek with her lips, which I wasn't expecting at all.

'Ginny,' she says. 'Ruari's told me a lot about you. Welcome to the Savages'. I'm sorry I didn't make it to your talk, but I had another commitment.' She makes a wry grimace. 'For my sins,

I'm on various committees. I'm looking forward to hearing a bit about your work, over dinner. And who's this pretty young lady?'

Ivy preens, and I find myself holding my breath.

'I'm Ivy. Auntie Ginny is Mam's sister. I'm staying with Auntie Ginny and Gran and Grandpa for a holiday.'

She frowns slightly. 'Has school finished for the summer? It's early, isn't it?'

'Mam said I could come over because Auntie Ginny wants to spend some time with me and I had a sore throat, but it's better now, and there's no point going back to school for just a couple of days.'

She casts me a self-satisfied look. I'm shocked at how fluently the lies slip out. Sarah is going to have her work cut out!

Jenny backs inside and holds the door open. 'Come on in – make yourselves at home. The boys will be in from the fields any minute. Apparently, Ted's going to take Ivy riding?'

'It was discussed,' I say, 'but I'm not sure...'

'He'll be careful, don't you worry. They can just walk around the track; see how she gets on. The horses are getting old, now, so you don't have to worry about them being skittish or bolting.'

'Noel said you used to ride,' I say.

'Noel O'Donovan?'

I nod.

She laughs. 'The old gossip! But I did, and I like to think I was pretty good at it. It's been my passion, since I was a child. I used to hunt when I was younger, but times are changing. Hunting is a bit passé these days, and age is catching up on me, too. Brittle bones, arthritis, the works... Well, there it is.'

I suspect she came from a fairly affluent background, in a household where horses were for pleasure, not work. 'You're not Irish, though?'

'Absolutely not! I was brought up in Kent, England. I came

over here to bring a young colt to race, met Connie, and that was that. Just one sight of him had me quivering in my riding boots. I never thought I'd end up as an Irish farmer's wife!' She gives a belly laugh, and I find myself laughing with her. 'My only regret is that there are no grandchildren here. My boys are taking far too long to get hitched! Martin is gone away to America and got married over there, and I do wonder if I'll ever get to see his children, and Noah, Teddy and Ruari have been busy building careers. When I was young, girls were married with a bump on the belly before they were twenty. Noah's wife – that's Anita – is pregnant, now, and I'm really hoping to have a granddaughter to pamper, but Ted tells me not to count my chickens. The Savage men seem to be good at making boys!'

And just like that, all the bad feeling I had imagined Ben's mother would be projecting is gone. Ruari said he took it hard when his big brother died, and blamed me in some way, but maybe his parents never did.

We're seated at a modern dining table, our hands wrapped around mugs, when the door opens and the room seems to shrink as Ruari's father and two brothers come in. I stand up and Ruari introduces them. 'Noah, Edward, but we call him Teddy, and my dad, Connie.'

In turn, they give me the kind of hug Ruari's mother had given me. I try not to wince at the overwhelming male physicality as I'm dwarfed by the size of these men. I surreptitiously assess them, wondering if there's any noticeable resemblance to Ivy. At her age, it would be hard to know, but nothing stares me in the face, which is a bit of a relief.

'So,' Jenny says, when things have calmed down, 'finish your tea and get out of my kitchen, lads; haven't you got work to be doing? Ivy, Teddy here is going to take you out to the horses; Ruari, you're going to take Ginny up to the rath; and you two, well, get on with whatever you were doing! Dinner will be about an hour.'

'Yes, ma'am,' the latter two say, grinning, and kiss her cheek before departing.

'You can tell who rules the roost here,' Ruari says to Ivy in a loud whisper.

Ivy snags a grin with Jenny, then Teddy indicates shyly for her to follow him out. Any nervousness I felt about leaving her with Ben's brother has somehow evaporated. These are nice, wholesome people, after all.

I slip into my wellington boots at the front door, and Ruari does the same. 'I'll show you around first, then we can head off up the hill.' He indicates the hill rising behind us, the darker ring of the rath clearly visible, my own family farm nestling over the hill, just out of sight.

This farm is as unlike ours as anything I can imagine. Dad and Micheal are always making do, replacing fence posts as they rot away, inserting new bits of corrugated iron on the shed roofs rather than fork out for whole sheets, but here the fence posts are all upright and pristine, marching around the farm as though they wouldn't dare so much as lean. At the front of the house is a large, well-maintained field, more like a lawn, with a few horse jumps dotted around the place.

'That's Mam's,' Ruari tells me, indicating with a wave. 'Dad wanted to put the cows in here one time, after she couldn't ride so much, and she went spare, told him he could do that when she was dead. She still rides sometimes with Teddy but doesn't jump. She had a bad accident many years back and didn't heal so quickly.'

'That's sad,' I say, not revealing that I know exactly how bad his mam was hurt. I wonder how I would feel if I couldn't walk up the hills any longer. No doubt I'll find out one day.

'Well, Mam's not one to let herself get down about things, like when Ben died. She was grief-stricken for a few months, because he was her first son, of course, but she made a decision to move on. She said she had four more sons and wasn't going to let her grief impact on our lives.'

'She sounds amazingly strong-willed.'

'She is. As kids we were far more scared of her than Dad.'

We're walking as we talk, and he shows me a huge barn where farm equipment is kept and another where the cows are brought in for calving. The milking parlour is twice the size of ours, fifteen a side, and so clean you could eat dinner off the floor, mam would say. Not that you'd want to.

Maybe Ruari knows I'm wondering how they came by the finance to do all this because he explains without being asked. 'Dad took over the farm when Granddad got too old, and a few years later, he bought out the farm on the other side, because McCarthy's boys just wanted out. Dad's pretty canny, but he was also lucky. Mam inherited from her parents in England, which is why the farm is in good shape. Come on around this way.'

Behind the barn there's a stone-built stable with a red-tiled roof, which could have been uplifted from an English country estate.

'Mam had this built. Brought two horses with her. Thoroughbreds, of course. Roone Bay had never seen anything like it.' He grins. 'She got a name for being the mad Englishwoman who got dressed up to go riding. But she also got known for being kind and not minding getting her hands dirty.'

We glance inside, where Teddy is showing Ivy how to hold a sugar lump out and let the horse take it gently from the palm of her hand. They glance at us and smile, but are too engrossed to engage. I suppose Teddy inherited his love of horses from his mam, as Ben had.

'So, shall we go up through the fields?' Ruari says.

I nod, and he opens a gate for me to walk through. There's a kind of stony path up through three fields, then we're out onto the boggy fields scattered with bright green rushes that fringe the rock line. 'We only use these fields in summer, when the weather's kind,' Ruari says. 'They're no good for hay. The cows crop the grass between the stones, but the rushes cut their mouths. It's not good land at all.'

I stumble on a rut and immediately Ruari's hand is on my arm, steadying me. I flinch. He recalls that I don't like being touched and lets go instantly, as if burned. So why did I flinch when he touched me, yet I managed to hide it when his parents and his brothers did?

'Sorry,' he says. 'I didn't understand, before.'

I flush brightly, and he stops short.

'Was it Ben? Did he hurt you?'

'I don't want to talk about it,' I say and walk on.

I feel his eyes on my back and realise he's churning new thoughts around in his mind. Eventually, he says, 'Look, Ginny. We all knew Ben was off the wall. He was kind and loving and gentle before the accident, but after he had violent mood swings. He could sometimes flip for the slightest thing and go off into a rage. Mam had no idea he was seeing you at the time. She said, if she'd known that, she would have warned your mam. When your mam and dad sent you away, Ben told the family he was going to find you and bring you back and marry you. Mam said you were too young, and when your family wouldn't tell him where you'd gone, he went mad. He calmed down after a while, went a bit quiet and strange, but then he went and had the accident.' Ruari takes a deep breath. 'I was just a lad myself and didn't understand. I loved Ben, and when he died, I needed to blame someone so decided it was your fault. Mam told me not to be stupid – you were too young to know what men were all about.'

I stop and look back at him. 'She said that?'

'She did. But Ben did love you, you know. In his own way.'

'I know. I'm sorry he died, Ruari, but he scared me.'

'I can see that he would. But I'm not him, Ginny. I like you, and I don't want you mixing us up in your mind.'

'I'm not,' I say but wonder whether I am. Why did the Savages' youngest child have to look and sound so much like the older one? Or is it just my memory playing tricks?

When we reach the rath, although it's slightly larger than the average thirty metres across, built up at the front with a metre-high stone wall, it seems smaller than my childhood memory allowed for. With all its early magic and the later trauma, I had built it up in my mind to something far greater.

Ruari puts his hands on the wall and kind of frog-leaps up, then he turns and reaches his hand down to me. I stare at it for a moment, then reach up to grasp it. He lifts as if I weigh nothing at all, and there I am standing on the bank above, finding my feet, being steadied by him. 'Okay?' he asks.

I nod. A hurdle crossed, maybe.

He smiles and turns to the gorse. 'I should have brought a billhook. I think we can squeeze through, though. Mind yourself on the spines.'

He pushes through using his shoulders, and I follow closely, laughing at his occasional blasphemy as a sharp thorn digs in. He looks back over his shoulder. 'Good job Mam's not here!'

'I've heard worse,' I say.

'We should have cut around by the stream. It's easier from the other side. But there's a clearing in the middle, past the trees. Well, there was when I was younger... Ah, right. Here it is.'

I push through after him, emerging into a small area with a large rock on one side, where bluebells are fighting to get their heads above the rampant grass. 'There are toadstools here, sometimes. I wouldn't advise eating them, though. I looked them up once, they're so beautiful. They're called amanita toadstools.'

'Ben showed them to me, but I don't think it was that name.'

'He might have called them death angels. They're the dead-liest of all. Just one cap can kill a person, and the ironic thing is, they taste nice. Apparently.' He grins. 'Not that I've tried, or I wouldn't be here. It can take days to die, because even if a person gets over the initial sickness, and looks as if they're recovering, they'll die, anyway.'

'That's fairly scary. Shouldn't you get rid of them? What if a child tried one?'

'I'd tell any child of mine never to eat any toadstool unless it came from a shop.'

'Me, too. I wouldn't even eat a mushroom from the wild, just in case, even though a lot of people do. I'm not that good at identifying them. You can apparently eat some of the red ones with white spots, but another one that looks similar is deadly. You'd think no one would be so daft as to eat a red toadstool. I mean, they even look poisonous!'

'Fly agaric,' he says. 'They grow here, too, in the autumn.' He glances up. 'They like growing under birch trees. The slugs seem to like them well enough, which is strange.'

'You seem to know a lot about them.'

He shrugs self-consciously. 'Ben told me a lot, too. I was interested. After he died, I didn't go out in the fields so often, though. Or up here. This was his special place.'

'I know.'

He's silent, remembering. 'Sorry, I forgot. Right. So, let's go out the easy way. Well, as long as the stream has subsided a bit.'

He leads the way towards my farm, the way I used to come in with Ben. The back of the rath, as it's seen from our farm, is built into the hillside, which is why I've never seen the wall at the front.

'Careful, the ground seems to have collapsed here,' Ruari says, and just as he takes another step, he slides forward into a depression and ends up on his backside on loose soil, and his feet in a hole.

'Oh,' I whisper in excitement. 'Ruari, you've found a souterrain!'

'Well, well. I had no idea there was one here. Is that significant?'

Ruari heaves himself up, shuffles around and crouches to try to look in the hole that's appeared to one side.

I suggest, 'I don't think we should try to look in, not with the ground so wet. It might collapse. Besides, no one's ever found anything much in a souterrain. I expect they were all raided and searched many times after being abandoned.'

'So, they weren't used for burying people?'

'No, they're thought to have been created to store food in, to keep it away from animals, and maybe as safe places for women and children to hide in if the family was attacked. They usually have two or three larger chambers joined by low tunnels. Easier to bash someone on the head if they have to crawl in.'

'Nice,' Ruari says, rising and brushing the dirt from his jeans.

As he steps back onto firm land, he brushes a white stone with his foot, which shifts, betraying a pair of empty eye sockets. I give a little scream of shock and point. Ruari shunts it with his foot. 'I thought you said they weren't used for burials.'

'They weren't. And no ancient skulls have been found in West Cork. The land is too wet, too acidic. Everything is eaten away. That's not so old.'

I bend down and look, careful not to touch. 'Not so recent, either. Maybe from the famine?'

'Whatever it is, we're going to have to call in the guards and probably archaeologists, too.'

I nod. 'Sorry. It's going to be a mess. Archaeologists would be careful, but I wouldn't put it past the guards to want to bring in a digger.'

'Shall I bring that down?' Ruari points to the skull.

I shake my head. 'Leave it there. There's probably the rest of him under there. Whoever excavates will want to see him in situ.'

'Him?'

'Figure of speech. Could be a her. We wouldn't know without the rest of the bones.'

'Could it be our Molly?' Ruari says ruminatively.

'Or Davan? I don't know. Maybe the rumours are true, that William killed her and buried her body on the farm.'

'Mam's going to love me,' Ruari says, 'now she's made a dinner and all.'

'We could tell her after dinner. After all, it's been here for years – there's nothing to be rushing for.'

25

GINNY

Dinner is quite strange as the family, unaware of our grisly discovery, enjoy the roast beef that Jenny has expertly prepared, along with the traditional Yorkshire pudding, cabbage, roast potatoes and lashings of gravy. Anita turns out to be a small, bubbly Irish girl from Roone Bay, who laughs at everything, and is totally unfazed about being in late pregnancy. I wish I had her confidence. But then, she is in a safe place, with a close-knit family around her and probably another just down the road.

Ivy talks volubly about her riding experience and tells us that Teddy led her around the field at the front several times, tutoring her, and at one stage Jenny came out and gave her a thumbs up. She is veritably glowing with the experience and the praise.

The family go on to talk about farming policies and local news, and although it's sometimes controversial, it doesn't descend into argument. It's strange to think that if it weren't for Ruari, I might never have arrived at this point in time, at dinner with these people who, for years, I was vaguely afraid of, and who I had assumed blamed me for Ben's death.

Ivy's eyes and ears are all over as the conversation shunts and shifts, and what I thought was an enormous quantity of food is demolished down to the last potato. Ben's name is mentioned at one stage, and she chips in with, 'Is that Ruari's big brother who had an accident?'

'It is,' Jenny says, glancing at me.

I'm not sure quite how much she knows or guesses, but we move on quickly.

Eventually, Ruari breaks our news, which is greeted by a stunned silence, before Connie asks, 'A skeleton? Are you sure?'

'Positive,' Ruari says. 'I need to call the guards, but I'll do it in the morning. As Ginny pointed out, it's been there a while, so there's no point in ruining our evening. It's going to get manic once the news is out.'

'All this time, and I never knew?' Connie shakes his head in disbelief. 'Could it be Molly?'

'Who knows? We wondered if it might be Davan. It might be neither. We might never know, but the coroner should at least be able to tell if it's a man or a woman.'

Davan's name being mentioned has me leaping my chair back and jumping up, surprising everyone. 'Oh, I forgot! I brought Davan's sketchbook with me.'

'I didn't know there was one,' Connie remarked, looking interested.

'Nor did I until recently. Apparently, Dad ended up with it a few years back, when Grandpa died. But the thing is, there's a drawing of Molly. Would you like to see it?'

'Well, of course we would!' Jenny answers for him eagerly. 'We don't have any photos from that far back, not in this family, anyway.'

'Maybe the table could be cleared first?' I ask diffidently. 'It's survived this long, and it would be sad if it got plastered in gravy now!'

The boys laugh, and Noah and Ted jump up to gather dishes, crashing them loudly into the sink, making Jenny wince dramatically.

I go and fetch the sketchbook from my bag. On the table, I carefully unwind it from the rags it came wrapped in, and the family surrounds me, looking over my shoulders, exclaiming with wonder at these drawings that have materialised unexpectedly out of the past.

'They're so clever,' Jenny says in wonder. 'Where did that talent come from?'

'I wondered that myself,' I admit. 'I think pure talent like this is something a person is born with. It can be honed or practised, but it has to be there in the first place. Maybe whole generations of people inherently had this talent, but time and circumstance didn't allow them to even discover it.'

'My aunt said Davan was a dreamer,' Connie remarks. 'Always skiving off to hide away from getting his hands dirty.'

'He was probably just drawing,' I say. 'That's exactly what I mean – that people who are busy simply trying to survive don't even understand what having an artistic bent means. I mean, he didn't even have a proper sketchbook – or paints. Just a pencil.'

'Noah does a bit of drawing,' Jenny remarks.

'Not like that.' Noah shakes his head. 'Look at the clarity of those leaves. I can almost see them rippling in the wind, they're so lifelike. I couldn't do anything like that.'

'No, you couldn't,' Ruari agrees, making everyone smile. He carefully turns the pad to the last page once more, to the portrait that has us all speechless for another long moment. He says, in a kind of wonder, 'But look at Molly. What a scorcher she was! No wonder Davan became obsessed.'

'She was just a name in a story when I was growing up,' Connie says with a sigh. 'And now I see her, I get what all the bother was about.'

'I can see why William was so protective,' Noah comments.

'Overprotective,' I correct. 'They treated her like a porcelain doll, from what I gather, and behind all that she was a girl wanting adventure and freedom. If she'd been ugly as sin, I doubt she would have been treated the same. She might still have been a lovely person inside, and Davan might well have still fallen for her. It must have been a real burden, being born so beautiful.'

The book is left open on Molly's image.

Her portrait had been drawn with a clarity that shouted of familiarity, of Davan's love. Again, I'm thrown by the exquisite attention to detail and in some ways feel that I've seen this girl myself. 'Would you like the picture?' I ask Connie. 'I could have it framed for you.'

'That would be really generous, thank you,' Connie says, surprised. 'But I wonder, would you be wanting to keep it?'

Noah glances up from his probably jealous appraisal of Davan's talent. 'But isn't it strange? Don't you think she's the spitting image of Ivy? If she had hair like that, I mean?'

As one, our faces all turn to Ivy, who colours under the open perusal.

'But I don't see how,' he adds, perplexed. 'Seeing as she's not related in any way.'

They are so busy comparing Ivy to Molly's image that they don't notice the betraying hint of warmth that's creeping up my own neck.

Dinner is over early, which is the way for folk who work the land and still have chores to complete. *Up with the sun, down with the sun,* the saying goes.

Ruari gives us a lift back home. Ivy jumps out of the pick-up to run in and tell her grandparents everything, and he stops me from following by touching my shoulder in query. I turn to him, to find his face softened. I surprise myself by reaching up and putting my hands on his shoulders. He leans his head down, and as his lips touch mine, my eyes close automatically. He kisses me softly, then, after my hesitant response, puts his arms around me, pulls me close and rests his chin on my shoulders. I breathe in the scent of him, the ever-present engine oil, the hint of roast on his breath, a natural underlying dose of the day's body odour that isn't at all unpleasant. His stubbled chin scratches at my neck. He nuzzles my hair and breathes in deeply, pressing himself against me. It's been a while since I had such close proximity to a man, and I'm left in no doubt of his desire. What I hadn't expected is the hot burst of yearning that rushes through me, too.

'Do we stand a chance, Ginny?' he whispers.

He can't see my smile but maybe senses it as I melt in towards him. 'Maybe,' I whisper back.

We stand like that for a moment, then he releases me and takes a step back. 'Right! See you tomorrow, then.'

'Tomorrow,' I echo.

He leaps into the cab with an almost childish vigour and gives a brief wave as he drives away. I watch the vehicle until it's out of sight, the twin halos of its headlights fading softly into the dusk.

When I'd first seen him at the back of the hall all those weeks ago, I'd felt a thrill of fear, and his later words had been designed to scare me, but it was as if I'd known, even then, that the words of aggression hadn't come naturally to him, as if he'd practised them, trying them out for size. Inherently, I'd known that despite his daunting presence, the pretend anger somehow hadn't fitted his character. He'd left me, back then, with a fear that was more of the unknown than fear of harm. And now I know why. Maybe even then, I'd suspected that this moment would one day arrive.

As a child, I'd been fascinated by Ben, but it had been for

his vibrant interest in the landscape. There might have been a little titillation, too, from the illicit friendship, because I knew I wasn't supposed to be with him. But I'd been brought up safe and sheltered, and thought Mam and Dad's wariness was over-the-top silly. Wasn't Ben our neighbour? I'd been too young to recognise the signs of his hunger, and he'd been too immersed in his own needs to take my immaturity into account. I learned, too late, that my parents had been right, that Ben was danger-ously unstable.

But Ruari is not Ben, and I'm no longer a callow schoolgirl. My fascination with Ruari is that of a grown woman, with all the desire that nature has instilled in me, added to an under-lying knowledge that we have so much more in common than physical attraction.

Yes, I think. *We have a chance.*

But only if I can somehow make things right.

The following day, I drive up to the Savages' farm, only to be stopped at the gate by a local guard, who lets me through when I tell him I'm the archaeologist who discovered the remains. Ruari has obviously phoned the discovery in, and the law-enforcement machine has jumped into action. The guard tells me he went up, his very self, this morning and it is, indeed, a skull; as if there might have been some doubt. He had person-ally phoned the guards in Cork, and was told to keep the site clear of news reporters, chancers and treasure-seekers until a detective arrived to take over. Gold has never been discovered in a souterrain, but there might be a first time, and it wouldn't surprise me, too, if news of a find has already flown down the grapevine.

Jenny welcomes me in like a member of the family. Perhaps she knows or suspects that Ruari's interest in me is more than a wish to carve a new relationship between our two families. We chat about archaeology, and I get the sense she's trying to engage with me, so I try not to bore her with my passion for the subject. In return, she tells me a little about her heyday, riding horses in major tournaments, before marrying an Irish farmer. She always laughs when she calls him that, knowing that the very phrase lends an image of someone uneducated and rough and Connie is anything but.

After a few hours, a cavalcade of cars arrive, ejecting a phalanx of excited professional archaeologists who, despite their high degree of self-importance, are refused entrance to the farm until the detective from Cork arrives with his own team of experts.

Ruari and I eventually lead them up to the site as the detective and the professor of archaeology discuss the process of exhuming the remains. The archaeologists want to excavate the site according to their code of practice, but the detective informs him in unequivocal tones that he intends to remove the remains and get them to the morgue as quickly as possible for examination. It almost erupts into verbal warfare, when the detective says, 'This is a crime scene. Until I learn otherwise, anyone who interferes with my crime scene is going to end up in jail for corrupting the site. Got it?'

Ruari shares an amused glance with me, and I stifle a giggle under my breath. To laugh outright would be a good way of nipping my career in the bud – many academics, in my experience, having a tendency towards personal vendettas that are infantile in their pettiness and persistence.

We crowd as closely as we can to the site, but once the remains have been pointed out to the detective, we're all pushed to the fringes, leaving just the lead archaeologist monitoring the excavation. We watch him gasp with horror as the detectives go to work shovelling out the soil, sieving it for evidence before throwing it in a pile to one side. Gradually, the bones are recovered and laid on a stretcher, along with some other unidentifiable remains that might be hair or clothes. It appears to be the whole body. One of the detectives bends down and shines a torch into the exposed chamber of the souterrain. 'It's totally empty,' he yells, disappointed, and they finally depart, leaving the archaeologists to the field.

'Someone needs to go in and assess the souterrain,' the professor states, eyeing each of his colleagues in turn. I know him by sight as he's the Head of Archaeology at Cork University. He's totally blanked me out until the moment I suggest diffidently, 'As I'm the smallest, perhaps I should go?'

'No way,' Ruari says, glaring at me.

'I'm an archaeologist,' I say simply. 'Pass me a torch and a camera.'

'If you must, then I'm tying a rope around you,' Ruari says angrily, 'then if it falls in, at least I'll know where to dig!'

'Okay,' I agree, biting back the urge to laugh.

None of the professional archaeologists risk arguing, Ruari looks so furious. We wait in silence, aside from some quiet mutterings, while Ruari trots back to the farm for a piece of rope and a shovel, the detectives having taken theirs away with them.

I put my hands on his shoulders as he reaches around my middle with the rope and ties it with a swift, competent bowline. The very act of him putting a rope around me sends a shiver of delight through me, which is quite inappropriate, and his face, close to mine suddenly, betrays something far more than simple fear for my safety. He's as aroused as I am. A tight smile compresses his lips, warring with concern as he no doubt feels me quiver and rests his hands briefly on my waist before stepping back.

Then, suitably tethered, I slither feet first into the tiny aperture on my stomach and end up crouched inside in the chamber. I'm overwhelmed by a sense of awe. Am I the first person to enter this man-made cave in several centuries? It might even have been made a thousand years ago and lain undisturbed for all that time. It's a little over two metres in diameter. The ceiling is a neatly carved bowl over my head, made up of dry, compressed earth dotted with small stones. There are thousands of these souterrains across Ireland, and the wonder of it is that they don't collapse due to time and weather. The ancient people knew more than we do about the land they lived in.

Hunkered down in a space slightly too low to stand up in, I try to imagine what it must have been like, crawling urgently through a tunnel as armed marauders closed in on the settlement to raid the household above. The adults would be waiting, armed with stones, axes and anything that could be put to good use as a weapon. If I were a child, I would be waiting here, kneeling by the small bent tunnel with a rock in my hands, waiting to kill anyone trying to enter. A child could take out a grown man in that situation.

But after taking a series of pictures and examining the floor for irregularities, I'm forced to concede that the chamber is as empty as all the other ones that have been found, though one always hopes for that one magical moment when something unique is unearthed; some artefact that will provide a clue to past lives.

After positioning the yardstick that's handed down to me across the floor space, I take flash photographs. I call out that I'm handing the equipment back, then reach up to haul myself over the pile of rubble. Ruari takes both my wrists and pulls me out in a single, swift movement. He gives me a one-armed embrace of relief, but if we hadn't had an audience, I think he would have hugged me tightly, my personal-space issues notwithstanding.

I tug at the rope around my middle, and Ruari bends to unpick the knot.

The experts conclude that the souterrain was comprised of two chambers carved into the earth, joined by a small tunnel, and one of the chambers, weakened perhaps by the excavation of a shallow grave above, had fallen in, taking the body with it. As the skeleton obviously isn't ancient, the team of archaeologists wend their way back down to their cars, squelching through the boggy field in their unsuitable shoes, undoubtedly as disappointed as I am.

When they've gone, Ruari silently winds the rope into a hank around his arm and crooked thumb, and secures it. From his silence, I conclude he's not happy.

'It might not be Molly or Davan,' I comment. 'And even if it is, your great-grandfather is gone, so no one's going to blame your family for what happened fifty years ago.'

'It's not that,' he mutters. 'Damn it, Ginny. You could have died down there.'

'I had you to dig me out,' I say, grinning.

'It's not funny.' He grabs me by the shoulders, glaring, and for a moment I think he's going to shake me. 'I've just found you, Ginny. I don't want to lose you already!'

I must have my mouth open in surprise as he mutters, 'Sorry.' It's only after he removes his hands that I realise that I hadn't at all been spooked by him touching me. I've passed another milestone: Ben is long gone, and despite the similarities, Ruari isn't angry so much as justifiably concerned for my safety.

I hazard a guess. 'I think the bones are too long for a girl, unless she was very tall and quite well built. I imagine Molly to be fine boned, maybe even small. I might be wrong, of course – who knows? But I really don't want the bones to turn out to be Davan.'

His brow lifts. 'Why not?'

'I like to imagine that he and Molly rode off into the sunset and lived a full life together.'

'It's a nice thought.'

His tone suggests he doubts it, but in truth, the bones we just found could have been the result of something entirely different: a loved one lost in the famine, or a plain old-fashioned murder, the reasons for which might never be known. It might even be one of the English soldiers who were ambushed by the rebels in West Cork during the fight for independence, but we'll have to wait for the autopsy and see if the coroner can discover what the person died from, or whether that, too, will remain a mystery.

26

DAVAN, 1922

Davan woke slowly to the realisation that he was lying in a real bed. For a moment, he thought he was dreaming and any moment would awaken on the hard cot in prison, but his fingers shifted and encountered a smooth length of sheet, not the familiar thin, rough blanket.

He cracked open his eyes with an effort. Everything was hazy, out of focus, but there was daylight flooding into the room through tall windows, bright, angular shafts that drifted with dust particles. Painfully, he turned his head, and his eyes focused on a woman in a nurse's uniform, who was making a bed. She shook the sheet with a hard crack, like that of a sail jibbing with the wind at its back. He watched it settle in a cloud of bleached cotton. She tucked the ends in and folded the corner like an envelope, then seemed to feel his gaze on her and turned.

She came over and put her hand on his forehead. 'Welcome back,' she said. A tiny smile turned up the corners of her mouth and deepened into laughter lines. It had been a long while since he had seen a woman, and he studied her face with a sense of wonder. She wasn't young, but there was a pretty kind of vitality in her gaze, making her the fairest thing he'd seen in a long time.

'Where am I?' he slurred.

'St Finbarr's Hospital,' she said. 'Lie still. Those ruffians gave you quite a bad beating. You must have a thick skull to have survived that crack on the nob!'

His hand reached up to his head, which felt strangely large, and encountered a massive dressing on one side, then slipped down to verify what he suspected. He was naked beneath the sheet. A flush crept up his cheeks.

She smiled. 'Your clothes were filthy, and we had to wash you to assess the damage. When you're able to stand, we'll find you some clothes to get you home in. Whatever you were carrying is gone. You're lucky to be alive, you know. Can you tell me your name?'

'Davan,' he said.

'And your family name?'

He thought for a moment. 'I don't know.'

'Oh. Do you know where you were going?'

'No.'

He was frustrated by a sense of urgency. He had been going somewhere important, he was sure, and tried to rise.

She put a hand on his shoulder, pressing him back. 'Don't try to stand yet. I'll bring you some warm broth, now you've decided to come back to the land of the living.'

'What's wrong with me?'

'Bruising, mostly. Pretty bad bruising, but it was that crack on the nob that put out your lights. Nothing seems to be broken, though. You're very thin. Have you eaten recently?'

'I don't know.'

She didn't tell him the doctor's true words, that the blow to the head might have cracked his skull, but it would be a waste of his medical expertise to operate on a man, probably a vagrant or prison bait, who might be dead by the morning. They were to just wait to see if he would die or pull out of it.

'How long have I been here?'

'Five days. I was thinking you might not—' She flushed slightly and stopped herself mid-sentence. 'I told the doctor I saw your eyes moving, though, behind your eyelids, so I knew you were still in there somewhere.'

Had he been dreaming? If so, the dreams, or nightmares, had melted away into the darkness. The last thing he recalled was being in prison. How had he come to this place in this condition?

The nurse seemed to guess his unspoken question. 'The miller was bringing sacks of flour into the city and nearly ran over you. He found you on the road.' Her eyes twinkled. 'Luckily, he's a big strong man, and you're very slight. He loaded you onto his cart and brought you here.'

'I should thank him.'

'He said he was just doing what any good Christian would have done. He doesn't want you to know his name because' – she hesitated slightly – 'he said he thought you had prison pallor.'

He sensed a question behind her words, but although he recalled being in prison, he didn't know why. Had he escaped? If he admitted to it, would they just kick him out? Would they call the wardens to take him back?

He closed his eyes, and his mind drifted.

He'd been living on a farm. He vaguely recalled people he supposed were his mother and father, and some pretty girls he suspected were his sisters, but there seemed to be a huge black hole where his recent memory should be. He was sure he was not a bad man. He didn't think it was in his nature to harm or steal from anyone.

The thought gave him comfort.

Sleep washed over him. When he awoke the next time,

more memories surfaced, filtering back one at a time, as if his damaged head couldn't manage to find them all at once. He was Davan O'Brien. And he had been in prison because of a girl. Molly. That was her name. Molly Savage, from the farm next door. The girl he loved. A picture came into his mind, but he couldn't recall what had happened to her.

Several times, he tried to bunch his muscles to find the energy to stand, but the effort sent a bolt of lightning through his head; nearly made him scream out. Nurses brought in pillows, propped him up a little and fed him with a spoon like a baby. He had concussion, he was made to understand. He had to lie still and let his body heal itself. He wasn't getting up in any hurry.

A few days later, two nurses dressed him in a gown and assisted him to the latrine, but it was a further two weeks before he could stand unassisted and take hesitant steps, bent over like an old man. Over the following weeks, his headaches gradually receded, his bruises faded from black to blue to yellow, and eventually the doctor prodded his head, his middle and back with strong fingers, and pronounced him free to leave. They could do nothing to fix the double vision that the doctor said might stay with him for the rest of his life, 'From the blow on the head, you understand?

'You're a lucky man,' he added, though Davan winced and grunted in pain as his head was turned this way and that. 'Maybe your kidneys were bruised. There's no internal bleeding that I can see.' He shone a light in Davan's eyes. 'Good. So, just food and rest and exercise. Do you recall why you were in prison?'

So, they all knew but had still been kind. He was grateful.

'Molly,' Davan said softly, because although he sensed black spaces where memories should be, he did recall the love of his life and the events that had led him to prison. 'I fell in love with a girl who was too young. I would have married her, but her father had me brought down.' He blinked hard. 'I've been away for a year. I'm afraid he might have married her to another.'

The doctor's lips compressed slightly with compassion. 'If he did, well, it's done, and there's nothing on this earth will undo it. But he couldn't have married her against her wishes, not these days. Just bear in mind that whatever happened, it's obvious the father had Molly's best interests in mind, even if you can't believe that at the moment. Do you remember where you live?'

'My farm is south and west, near Roone Bay, by the coast.'

The doctor nodded. 'Right. Good. At least your memory is recovered. I'll see if I can find anyone going that way who can give you a lift.'

'Thank you.' Tears gathered in his eyes. It had been a long time since he had encountered kindness.

A week later, he was on the road, wearing second-hand clothes that were of better quality than the ones he had left prison in. He didn't like the thought that someone had died in them, but he had no choice. His own clothes, he was informed, had ended up in the furnace.

'Delaney Scott has kindly offered to bring you right to your farm, to save you walking the last three miles,' the nurse told him, adding in a low voice, 'The doctor didn't tell him about prison. He just said you were set upon by a gang of thieves in the city.'

Davan had nodded his thanks. It didn't matter whether he was innocent of any real crime, the very fact that he'd been in prison would frighten God-fearing country folk. He recalled his own mother often quoting: *Sure, when did a body ever see smoke unless there was a fire beneath?* His year in prison branded him an ex-convict, a stigma that would mark him for the rest of his life.

The driver wedged him between boxes of provisions, in the back of a wagon tethered to a sturdy dun-coloured Irish dray. 'Yous'll be able to rest a while, there,' he was told by the kindly old fellow. 'Don't you fret, now. We'll have ye at home soon enough. I'm sorry for your troubles.'

'Thank you,' Davan said. 'I'll make it up to you one day.'

'Aw, pshaw!' Delaney disclaimed. 'Sure, it's the Christian thing to do, to help a man in trouble, and it's not a bother, not at all. So just you sit back and take it easy.'

But travel wasn't something to take lightly in the rural areas, and Davan's endurance was sorely tried. He was thankful that Delaney didn't expect chatter as he negotiated the potholes, sliding and bumping along the narrow, pitted road that led west towards Bantry. He was more inclined to talk to the horse. 'Mind, now, Clara girrul,' he'd say, tweaking the reins or indicating the direction by tapping her rump lightly with a switch. 'Easy along, now.

'We'll stop overnight in Drimoleague,' the driver called over his shoulder as evening began to fall. 'Clara needs a rest, as do I. There was a time we might just keep plodding on, but as we get older, the road gets ever longer.'

Davan smiled dutifully at Delaney's humour. He was desperate to get home but liked that the man had a care for his ageing horse. A twenty-hour journey on these roads would be hard on the creature, big as she was. He nodded tiredly. In all honesty, a rest would be good. His head was banging like a stick on a tin can, and his vision seemed a little blurrier around the edges than before. It must be the travelling. He had done nothing but rest in the hospital, and the travelling was letting him know that he had a way to go yet.

'Have you got money for a lodging?'

'No. I have nothing,' he said. 'I can sleep in the wagon. It's not a bother.'

The wooden boards of the wagon were scarcely worse than

the hard bench he had slept on in prison, but the small, friendly hostelry provided him with fresh straw in an empty stall beside the horse. He wrapped an old horse blanket around himself and slept like the dead.

It seemed like only minutes later that he was being shaken awake to finish his journey. For this leg, Davan sat up on the wooden seat with Delaney, who broke bread and shared a jar of porter with him. The taste of fresh bread brought tears to his eyes, reminding him so much of his own kitchen, where his mother would bake fresh bread daily in the oven built in the side of the chimney breast. They travelled for several hours at a slow and steady walk, turning southward before Bantry, heading towards the coast.

It had been spring when Davan had been sent down, and it was spring again now, moving softly towards summer. He revelled in the open blue sky, the patchwork green of the meadows and, in the valleys, drills of corn freshly pushing out of the fields of rich loam that lined the streams. Light green leaves, speckled with sunlight, shimmered with promise. They made him think of Molly, with her fresh, youthful exuberance as they had lain in the rath, looking up at the birds wheeling above. He smiled softly, worrying about the future but hoping all the same. He had gone to hell and back, and surely God would extend some compassion now.

Delaney glanced sideways at his smile and echoed it faintly. 'Life always seems better when you can scent salt on the breeze,' he said.

Davan nodded. Delaney had no idea.

Despite his weakness, every step that brought him nearer to home injected him with determination. His life had somehow fallen apart, but he would rebuild it with Molly by his side, God willing. For a long while, that had seemed like a distant dream, but now he allowed himself to ponder on his future. That she had once loved him he didn't doubt. It might be that her love had faded with his absence, but he didn't want to believe that. It was more likely that her father had induced her to marry some other man for her honour – or for her father's honour, more like.

He tried not to worry, because if such a thing had happened, it would be too late to undo it, as the doctor had suggested. But it was a hard thought to contemplate as the one thing that had sustained him throughout the inhuman conditions of his incarceration had been the thought of finally being with her again.

He was eventually dropped off at the foot of the small track to his farm. He had rejected the offer to drive him to the door. 'You still have an hour's drive,' he said. 'I'd like to walk a little. It will be good to get a feel of home. I've been in the dark for too long.'

Delaney thought he meant the hospital, of course.

'God be with ye, Davan,' he said.

'And surely with you, too, for your kindness,' Davan returned.

Delaney clicked his tongue, and the dray mare heaved the wagon into motion. They drove on without looking back.

Davan walked slowly up the track, which had been carved deep by centuries of farm traffic. He saw no sign of activity at the house above, but smoke coming from the chimney spoke of the ever-burning fire, on which his mother cooked their dinners and heated the water, come rain or shine.

He stood at the open door, exhausted, tears in his eyes. He had once taken home for granted but now realised just how important it was. Inside the long, dark kitchen, his mother was tending to the pot, her back to him. He didn't want to startle her so said very softly, 'Mam?'

She froze, then turned as she arose, her face drained white with shock. Her hand went to her mouth, and she uttered a tiny noise between a wimp and a scream.

'Mam? It's just me,' he said again, frowning, stepping forward warily, as one would to not startle a skittish foal.

She reached out and tentatively touched his arm with the tips of her fingers, as if expecting him to be insubstantial, not there at all. 'Davan?' she whispered. 'It is yourself?'

'Mam, I'm come home.'

'Oh, God,' she said, her sobs rising in uncontrollable hiccups. 'Oh, God, we were told you were dead.'

27

GINNY

I make use of the improved weather to catch up on a few visits to farms, taking Ivy with me as we continue to deepen our new relationship as mother and daughter. We spend many hours talking as we plod up and down the boggy hillsides, and go over and over the reasons behind why I gave her up to my sister the day she was born.

Giving her up had made me really depressed and confused, but for Ivy to find out that her mother had given her away must be truly difficult to comprehend. The one truth is that we have always loved each other as family, so that already-established bond is helping her to climb over her own emotional obstacle course.

Today, we're sitting on a hill looking out over the Drombeg stone circle, staring out over a patchwork of tiny fields that slip towards a sea that twinkles with deceptive passivity on this cloudless day. We have a togetherness that is fragile, that I feel could erupt into condemnation at any time.

'Promise me,' I ask, 'that whatever ups and downs you have, you won't hate me. And if sometimes you do, I'll always wait until you don't.'

'Did you really want to be my mam?'

'More than anything.'

'And did my dad want me?'

I pause for a moment, trying to form a reply. 'He didn't get a chance to find out, love, but I'm sure he did..'

'But if you weren't married, why did you let him make you pregnant?'

She knows how babies are formed, in principle, anyway. Honesty is so hard when you know it's going to hurt. 'I didn't mean to, love. It just kind of happened.'

'So I was, like, an accident?'

'You mustn't see it like that. Me getting pregnant wasn't planned, but keeping the baby, keeping you, was. I could have gone over to England and got an abortion – you know what an abortion is?'

'When a doctor makes the baby go away before it grows into a real baby. The priest says it's murder.'

'Right. Well, I didn't do that. I didn't want to. But I was far too young to be a good mother, no matter how much I wanted to be. Don't forget, at the time, I wasn't so much older than you are now.'

Though, I guess when you're eleven, seventeen sounds really old, like being grown-up. I understand that as we get older the years compress and we measure time by the years we have left, not the years we've already lived. But that only happens when you look behind and realise half your life has probably passed on by.

'Will you have another baby?'

'I don't know.' This is already hovering on the edge of my consciousness. I'm approaching thirty, and though that's barely a stepping stone in a career path, my biological clock is ticking.

'But if you do, you'll love it more than me.'

I hug her close. 'I won't. But I can't ask Sarah to look after another baby, can I? It wouldn't be fair. And I'm older now. If I do have another baby, I'll have to bring it up myself. But the new baby will only have one mother, not two, like you.'

She sighs, then falls silent, knowing that I'm trying to find a way of making myself feel less guilty, but guilt settles on my shoulders in a way it never has before, because I did give her away. I can't deny that. What if she doesn't accept that I could love her and give her away in the same breath?

'But if you have another baby, will Ruari be the father?'

I flush despite trying not to and say carefully, 'I don't know. I like Ruari, though. I think you do, too.'

She nods. 'And Noah and Ted and their mam and dad. If you married Ruari, then they'd be my family, too, wouldn't they?'

'They would.' I wonder where this is going. I shiver, knowing that one day I'll have to tell her they already are. A cloud crosses the sun, and I clamber up slowly, feeling a little older than I was when I climbed out of bed this morning. 'I think maybe we should be heading back to Grandma's.'

'I think so, too. I'm getting hungry. But if Ruari's family is my family, would I be able to go there and ride the horses?'

I laugh. 'Even if I don't marry Ruari, I think his mam would be absolutely delighted if you did!'

Ruari is waiting for me when we get back. He'd called Mam, and she'd invited him to have dinner with us. His smile of welcome as I walk into the house speaks volumes. Mam's glance tracks between us, and I know the same thing is going through her mind that went through mine earlier: if I am to have any kind of relationship with Ruari, the truth has to come out.

But at dinner the talk revolves around political shenanigans: Ireland joining Europe bringing hope but also debt, rising costs and increased hardship for many. They touch on the escalating troubles in Northern Ireland that sometimes spike into the south, because the south is fighting for unification for the whole of Ireland, and some people in the north don't want it at all because it is largely financed by English commerce.

The men also touch on the social discussions that are in the news, regarding the contraceptive pill, homosexuality and divorce. Ivy, of course, listens to everything, her intense concentration hidden behind a bland expression and a deceitful concentration on her plate. She tries to answer Mam's questions about her day while listening to the men's conversation. I suspect such dialogue only happens in my sister's house after the children are safely in bed. I'll probably have to explain, later, what is meant by homosexuality and contraceptives. But Ireland is definitely England's poor relation when it comes to progress. The newspapers have started calling Ireland *the laughing stock of the progressive world*, which is incendiary to activists, Ruari says, likely to fuel further unrest.

'God help us if we don't have problems enough of our own,' Mam says indignantly, totally missing the point.

I'm a little distanced from politics, being rooted in the past, but Dad keeps an eye on the news, because it affects us all whether we want it to or not, just like the weather, he would say. Well, it does, but I'm with my late grandpa, who would stop discussions flat when they got heated: *Stop yer blathering, for pity's sake, why don't ye? Unless you're prepared to ride the donkey, stop talking about how best to do it!*

I suppose Dad is enjoying having another body at the table, one who is obviously well-informed on current issues. In this, Ruari is totally unlike Ben, who had been vested in his own love of the countryside to the exclusion of external influences. But then, all Ben knew was the land, whereas Ruari chose to leave the land behind to be a mechanic. It doesn't mean he's not interested; he just isn't consumed by it. I suspect the mechanics' bay has the radio blaring all day with pop music and news, whereas Ben would have been watching the wind ride the long grass, listening to the call of birds, the bark of the fox, and lifting his face to the air to see what the day was going to bring. In many ways, I find the brothers similar, but in some things, they're poles apart; *were, in Ben's case*, I think sadly. I thought I had reason to hate him, but should we hate a fox for killing hens when it's simply their nature?

'Well, that was wonderful, thank you,' Ruari says, parking his knife and fork neatly, and leaning back with a comfortable sigh that makes the old chair groan.

Mam preens. I doubt she's often praised for putting a dinner on the table. It's her job as much as being out in all weathers is Dad's and Micheal's, and it wouldn't occur to her to thank them for doing the milking.

'So, what's strange or new?' Dad asks Ruari, bringing things back to a more personal level.

'Well, there it is! I almost forgot. I did come up with news, after all. The skeleton they found? It's definitely male, a man of maybe five foot ten, now they've measured the bones. Judging by some bone buttons and the remains of a shoe, they think he was probably a poor person from somewhere near the beginning of this century.'

I'm prompted to voice the unspoken hypothesis. 'Then it could be Davan?'

Ruari is hanging on to the moment; his eyes are sparkling with information yet untold. 'They found he had a cracked skull. It was likely the cause of his death, because it showed no signs of healing.'

Mam gasps. 'So that spalpeen William did murder him!'

'It's not proved at all,' Dad grumps with a harrumph that could be interpreted as, *Women!*

'If it was him, that would be sad,' I comment. 'I've always liked that they ran away together and lived happily ever after. But if it is him, whatever happened to Molly?'

'I expect the mad eejit murdered her, too,' Mam says darkly.

Ruari laughs. 'Maybe he just sent her away somewhere?'

'Maybe, maybe.' Dad rolls his eyes in exasperation. 'We don't know that the skeleton is Davan, do we? Didn't they find anything else?'

'Just remnants of clothes and brown hair, but they were too far gone to provide any clues. He hadn't been buried deep, so the creatures had him ate,' Ruari says, in the local vernacular.

'Brings to mind one of Grandpa's songs,' Dad says with a grin, and breaks into a few stanzas from 'The Unquiet Grave':

> *Oh, where is your bed, my dearest dear, he said.*
> *And where are your white holland sheets,*
> *And where are the maids, my darling, he said,*
> *That do wait upon you while you are asleep.*

> *Oh, the grave is my bed, my dearest dear, she*
>   *said,*
> *And the shroud is my white holland sheet,*
> *And the worms and the creeping things they are*
>   *my waiting maids,*
> *They do wait upon me while I am asleep.*

'Eurgh,' Ivy says.

We all laugh. Dad has a fine singing voice, and it's a joy to hear him bring out one of the old songs, not that he has a bias. I heard him the other day, on his tractor in the sun, belting out 'Born to Sing', Ireland's contribution to the Eurovision song contest this year. It didn't win, but in Dad's opinion, it should have, by a military mile. But then, we Irish are a little precious about our birthright, with its music and legend. Not to mention the holy soil itself, blessed by St Patrick, our very own saint, who was, in fact, not Irish at all.

When the meal is over, Ruari makes his apologies.

Dad waves him out. 'Ye don't have William in yer head, lad.

Yous are welcome any time,' he says, adding with a sly smile, 'Right, Ginny girrul, show the boy out, why don't ye?'

Ruari doesn't take offence, and I walk him to the pick-up.

'Give me a minute of your time, Ginny,' he says. He holds out his hand, and with only the barest hesitation, I take it. His hand engulfs mine and squeezes with a hint of his natural strength. We walk on down the drive a short way, until we round the corner, out of sight of the house.

'Your parents seem to be okay with me,' he says, on the slight upward tilt of a question.

'Surprisingly so,' I respond. 'In the light of our history, I mean.'

'And are you okay with me?'

'Surprisingly so.'

He laughs and stops to pull me close, pressing me into the hard length of his body so that I have to lean back slightly to look up at him. 'So, will I kiss you, then?'

'If you will,' I say primly.

We've slipped into the old ways, and he laughs again before lowering his face to mine. I should be telling him about Ivy, but I don't want to ruin the moment. He makes me feel unexpectedly feminine and attractive and, let's be honest, physically interested, which, after me spending most of my adult life keeping men at arm's length, is quite a novelty.

I put my arms up around his neck and lift my heels from the ground. He bears the weight of me without faltering. We devour the flavour of each other, lost for a few moments in the age-old cry of lust. I feel his body starting to respond to mine, the blood rising, the tension springing, as they do in my own body.

Eventually, he lifts his head and pulls me around to hug me back into the curve of his body. 'Look.' The evening sun is sinking behind the hills in brushstrokes of orange and purple and red, before slowly fading to grey. 'That's for us, Ginny. A portent for our future happiness. You're going to marry me, be my wife.'

'I am?' I ask artlessly.

'Well, as you can see, I'm half-starved. If you can cook anything like your mam, you're a catch I'm not going to throw back into the water.'

I laugh, but actually, I don't cook half as well as Mam. He might discover that in time.

He nuzzles my neck as I lean back into the warmth of his body, whispering, 'I'd like to do wicked things to you.'

'Maybe one day.'

'So, you're not entirely averse to the idea?'

'Not entirely, no, but—'

'No buts. Keep that thought in mind. I don't want for you to one day say I rushed you and you were too young, or some other daft thing.'

I give a gurgle of laughter. 'I'm not so young already.'

There's a faint pause before he disengages and turns me back to face him. 'So, can we put Ben to bed?'

'What do you mean?'

'I think you have something brewing. You need to tell me about it before you can move forward.'

He senses that? I nod. 'I have. I will, but when I'm ready. I don't want to spoil today. I want to take this time and hold it, just in case... everything changes.'

He's intelligent enough to look concerned and props his hands on my shoulders to stare into my face with worried hunger. 'Ginny, I don't want to rush you – I mean that. But if you need to tell me something, I'm listening, okay? We started off on a wrong note, and that was entirely my fault, but you can speak to me openly. And if you can't do that, go up to the house and speak to Mam. There's nothing you can tell us about your past, about Ben, that will change the way I feel about you now.'

People make such bold statements before learning something that blows them out of the water. I shake my head. Now is not the time. I'm truly afraid of seeing his earnest expression morph into one of disbelief, cynicism, anger.

Because I'm not sure he will even believe me.

We walk back to the pick-up, hand in hand, and he pecks my lips before pulling himself fluidly up into the tall cab, his shoulders bunching beneath the ubiquitous check work shirt. I shiver with an intense need. I want him to reach down and grab me with ferociously cavemanlike ownership, and take me despite my protests. I wonder at myself and shake my head as I walk back into the house.

28

GINNY

I meet Ruari several times over the following weeks, and it's not by accident. We have coffee and buns in the little café in Roone Bay, we take walks up on his family farm or on ours, and we never run out of conversation. Mam smiles uncertainly, her eyes questioning, while I give a brief shake of the head. The time isn't right.

But when will it be right? I wonder.

Ivy is missing her school chums, and has a birthday party and a sleepover lined up, so although I've loved her company, when Sarah comes to pick her up, I feel a wash of relief. Ivy's interest in old stones has come to a grinding halt, and she'd been spending more time with Mam, sitting at the kitchen table, drawing. She was trying to copy Davan's drawings, and her efforts, though unskilled, show remarkable promise. Perhaps Davan's skill has just skipped a couple of generations and emerged in my daughter.

When Sarah arrives, I show her Davan's sketches and Ivy's attempts, and ask her whether she might find someone to nurture Ivy's skill, or at least give her the opportunity to discover if it's a real interest and not just one of those explorations all children go through while discovering themselves. I say I'll pay for it – it's the least I can do. And if it's music or something else, next month, well, so be it.

'Are you okay going back with your mam?' I ask Ivy. 'Despite what we've talked about, nothing has really changed, has it? She's still your mam.'

I'm lying, of course. The shift is subtle, but like all things in life, knowledge settles in its own time. It's all part of a girl's slow maturation, the ruptured-chrysalis moment of growing breasts and starting her menstruation. It's just another emotional bump in a journey that – although she doesn't realise it yet – will be filled with many, one after the other, for the rest of her life. I read recently that women spend one third of their lives in an emotionally distressed state, from periods to pregnancy, child-birth, pre-menopause, then the full-blown change. And that's without the added trauma of falling in love, and all its complications or disappointments. I feel sad that I can't shield Ivy in some way from all this trauma.

Once she's gone, I have no excuses left. I buy a bottle of wine and invite Ruari out for an evening drive. He picks me up, and I direct him to a lonely shore where we huddle side by side on a large rock that shelves down towards the water lapping impatiently below. I drink straight from the bottle and pass it to him. He knows it's time, and waits. An orange flare of sunset highlights a small tender rocking on the almost still evening tide. As I imbibe the fool's courage, night clouds gather over the Atlantic, roiling on the horizon, painting themselves blackly over the water. A faint breeze rises.

I shiver and take a deep breath. 'I never thought I'd be having this conversation,' I begin, then realise it's not going to be a conversation so much as a monologue. 'Mam and Dad had always told me to be wary of the Savage boys.' I smile because that includes Ruari. 'She said you were all up to no good. From what I recall about you in school, she was probably right.'

He turns hooded eyes towards me. 'You remember me from school?'

'Sure I do. You were good-looking, even then.'

'Did you fancy me, then?'

'Not at all. I just said you were good-looking. You were tall and skinny, and not at all interested in learning, so I thought you might be a bit slow.'

'I got a few CSEs.'

'That's what I mean. I recall you telling the teacher you were going to be a mechanic so what was the point in all that learning? Perhaps we both had our lives mapped out, just a little, without realising it.'

His lips quirk in an almost-smile.

'Ben didn't have any qualifications,' I add, leading the subject. 'Your mam told me that. He found school tedious and flat. He wanted to know what made the grass grow and why bluebells are blue, and the teachers couldn't answer his questions. He used to come out with these things – beautiful concepts – and he made me see the countryside in a different way.'

I reach out, and he hands me back the bottle. I take a swig and a shuddering breath. 'Ben was a fount of information about the land. Some of it was plain wrong, I learned later. But back then I thought he knew everything. He thought about things a lot and came out with his own personal philosophy.'

'About the land having a skin on it?'

'That was his favourite. He thought of the land as a living, breathing organism which needed to be nurtured. The land would provide for us, but in return it should be loved and cared for. I don't mean worshipped, like Gaia or that new-age hippy stuff. But he thought it should be respected, and maybe he credited the earth with some kind of sentience, because when there were natural disasters – like rockfalls, mines collapsing, you know – he talked about the earth getting its own back. He hated the quarries, you know, where we get gravel for the roads and whatever. To him it was like seeing an open wound, one that humans had made. That could make him angry.'

Ruari nods.

'I knew he had a temper. I'd heard of a few, ah, incidents. But he was always careful around me. I had the feeling he was holding back sometimes. When he felt something bubbling up inside, when he couldn't understand something, it made him frustrated, and then he could be a bit scary. There were a couple of times he made a fist and hit the ground. He frightened me a bit, then. And a couple of times he just got up and walked away, in the middle of a conversation, as though he knew he was about to get mad but didn't want to hurt me.'

Ruari's brows rise. Maybe he'd never seen that side of Ben.

I smile. 'He said he loved me, but I was very naïve and didn't quite realise what that meant. I loved our talks, and I thought he'd never harm me.'

There's a pause while I remember, and I feel Ruari grow tense, wondering what's coming.

'He told me I was going to marry him, and it sounded like an order.'

'Oh dear,' Ruari says. 'That's exactly what I told you the other day.'

I shush him. 'That's not the point. I was too naïve to realise that he meant it. He was a grown man, and I thought of him like my brother or a teacher. I trusted him that way. When he said I was to marry him, I said no way, I was still at school. He said I would leave, soon, and then we could be married. I told him that I didn't want to marry him, that I was going on to university.'

Ruari says, 'But you let him make love to you. He made you pregnant.'

'No,' I say softly; after all, this is the crux of the matter. 'I didn't let him. I went to meet him up on your farm, in the rath. When I got there, I realised he'd been drinking. There were bottles lying around the base of the big rock. The sun was shining. It was a beautiful day.'

I pause, close my eyes briefly, then carry on. 'He jumped down and began to kiss me, then...' I shudder with the memory. 'I told him no, but he didn't stop. I don't think he could. I was saying no, please don't, please don't, but he was out of control. When he'd finished, he leaped up and ran away, leaving me there, in the clearing, my clothes ripped and blood between my legs. I was hurting so badly I slipped trying to cross the stream and fell in, but I managed to get home. Mam cleaned me up, and she and Dad decided it was best not to say anything to anyone. They drove me over to Sarah's and decided I should finish school there, in Clon. Then a month or so later, I realised I was pregnant.'

Ruari is staring at me in horror. 'He *raped* you?'

'I honestly don't think he was rational. Not at the time. But when he ran, he knew then. Mam said he came around to their house several times after I'd gone away, begging to know where I was, begging to marry me, as if that would put things right.'

Ruari reaches out as if to hug me. His hand stops in mid-air, then goes back to rake through his hair. 'That's why you don't like being touched. Ben did that to you.'

I turn my head and smile softly. 'Ben did that. And you undid it, Ruari.'

He's lost for words.

The dark clouds have crept closer and turned the sea black. A spot of rain hits me. I feel as though a weight has gone from my mind. I breathe easily for the first time in years and heave myself to my feet. 'We've seen the best of the day. Time to go home, I think.'

'Yes,' he says blankly, rising to follow me up the track to the pick-up. He doesn't try to hold my hand. Is that significant?

On the way home, Ruari doesn't look at me, either. What I told him must be rattling around in his mind, taking shape and settling. His face is set hard, as it was the day I first saw him. His lips are compressed, setting his mouth into a kind of sneer.

Maybe I've lost him.

I want to cry. My throat has gone tight with fear.

At home, he squeals the vehicle in a circle and stops, facing back down the lane. His hands are clenched tightly on the steering wheel as if he wants to squeeze juice out of it.

'I'm sorry,' he says, still looking straight ahead. 'I'm so sorry. Now I understand why you left. Ben got moody after you disappeared. More so than before. We never quite understood what was going on. He told us he loved you and you were lost forever. We thought he would get over you, but he didn't. We – my family – wanted to know what had happened because we were worried about Ben, but we never thought... not in a million years... And we couldn't ask you, because you were gone and your family wouldn't speak to us.'

'Mam was afraid of the scandal. They never told anyone. And if I'd stayed, I wouldn't have been treated very nicely by the teachers or the clergy. They would have said it was my fault for even being alone with him. I'd been told not to.'

'But that's mad!'

'It's how it is. You know that.'

He scowls, swears horribly, then apologises for swearing.

'It's okay. You needed to know. I'll go in now.' I hesitate and add, 'I'd be pleased if you didn't tell your family. They don't need to know that about Ben.'

'They won't want to believe it, but they will, because the moment you told me, I knew it was true.'

'But please, promise you won't tell them? They were so kind when I came round with Ivy. I don't want to lose that just yet.'

'Mam was quite taken with Ivy. Your sister's done a great job, there.'

'She has. And she was there for me when I needed her, too. That's why I don't want your mam to only see me as the girl her son raped.'

Now his eyes widen as he turns to stare at me. 'For goodness' sake, Ginny. Were you keeping all this from us so my parents wouldn't be hurt?'

I give a snort of laughter. 'Not at all. My parents were more worried about my reputation and theirs.'

'They have to know, of course.'

'Okay,' she agrees reluctantly.

'Thank you.'

'Well, now it's all out can I hug you?'

I have tears in my eyes as I nod. We embrace silently, then he pushes me aside. 'I need to go home. I have some very heavy thinking to do.'

'Will I see you again?'

I had to ask.

He stares at me as if I'm nuts. 'I asked you to marry me, you daft girl. I think that means you'll see me again. If you still want to, that is.'

I give a wet chuckle and climb down from the cab. 'Okay, so. See you later, then.'

29

GINNY

The days go by and a storm squall passes through, making the land soggy once more, putting a halt to my outdoor work. I'm beginning to get nervous about how Ruari has really taken the news. I wonder whether, on reflection, he doesn't believe me, whether he's told his family, and they don't believe me, either. Maybe they think I'm just trying to blacken Ben's memory. My mind is running in circles, inventing scenarios, churning over all the possibilities and spitting them out in horrible dreams. Ruari hates me. Ivy hates me. Ben died because of me. I laugh internally, thinking of the childhood rhyme: *Everybody hates me, nobody loves me, think I'll go and eat worms...*

But depression isn't something I indulge in for long. I learned to compartmentalise early. If Ruari doesn't call, I'll leave the area as I did once before, but this time I'll never come back. I'd be too afraid of bumping into him and thinking about what might have been.

Secretly, I think it's not fair, but I'm sure Grandpa would have approved of my family's actions, if he'd been alive. It's how it is. If a girl gets pregnant out of wedlock, she's let down everyone: herself, the family, the community, the church. Never mind that it took a little input from a man. In this, society is clear: pregnancy is always the woman's fault, as if getting pregnant is a spiteful choice designed to make trouble for the man who had sex with her. But I've always wondered how intelligent people can truly think like that. The laws made by men try to be above the laws of nature. As if nature, in all its colossal, unpredictable, uncaring beauty, won't win a conflict, hands down. Those who propagate the myth of human superiority have allowed themselves to be brainwashed because it makes them feel good.

Of course, being a 'fallen girl', I have a different take on the subject than those who wallow in smug self-righteousness. Because I didn't choose: I was raped. There, I said it. I learned to pity Ben and fear all men at the same time, because they're physically so much stronger than me. I understood now that Ben was never quite in the real world, that the land itself was Ben's god. But he was also selfish. I have never admitted this to anyone, and probably never will, but I think he knew what he was doing when he raped me. He probably thought if I was pregnant, I'd have to marry him and stay in Roone Bay. I have no doubt that he later drove his tractor onto the steep slope on purpose to see if the land would punish him. It did, in the most final way possible.

Sarah calls one evening when Ivy is at a friend's house. Since Ivy discovered that I'm her birth mother, there has been much discussion, she tells me, which sometimes turns into outright accusation and argument. But Sarah says they always end up hugging and making up, and the family boat is gradually shifting back onto an even keel. After all, nothing can be done to undo the past; we just have to rationalise and live with it, and Ivy knows that.

Sarah says, 'Actually, I feel relieved now that Ivy knows the truth. I was always wondering how and when we could tell her, and the longer it went on, the harder it got.' This is followed by a long pause before she asks, 'Mam said you're seeing Ben's brother. Is that true?'

'It is.'

'Is that wise?'

'Wise has nothing to do with the way I feel about him,' I admit. 'It just happened. He's gentle and nice and kind, and I kind of, you know, *zing*, when I'm with him. He's not at all nuts, like Ben. He asked me to marry him.'

'Already? How long has it been. A month?'

'Two.'

'Isn't it a bit soon?'

'I didn't actually say yes.'

'Have you had sex with him?'

'Sarah!' But I know why she's asking, so add, 'No, not yet.'

'Does he know the truth about Ben?'

'I told him, the other day. But I didn't tell him about Ivy. He knows I was sent away because I was pregnant, and I didn't exactly lie but led him to believe I aborted the baby.'

'You should tell him everything. Ivy needs you to. She keeps asking who her real father is. I told her I can't answer that question. She took that to mean I don't know, but really she has to know. I think that's your job.'

'Oh. Right. But it's difficult. We visited his family, and his mam took quite a shine to Ivy and said she'd always wanted a granddaughter. How on earth could I tell her? Maybe I should have, but I didn't – so how can I tell her now?'

Sarah doesn't stand for nonsense. 'Just spit it out. Half the cat is out of the bag, and the other half is going to follow whether you like it or not, so just do it. Tell them everything. Then there will be no more secrets. If you're really going to be involved with this Ruari Savage, which sounds like a recipe for disaster, in my opinion, you've got no choice.'

'You're right, but it's difficult.'

'No, it's not. It's just words. Once you tell them, it's up to them how to react. Be brave. The secret will eat away at you, otherwise.'

She's so solid in her belief, but I've lived with this dirty little secret locked away inside all this time, and now I'm to get it out, dust it off and proudly show it to everyone? It's not as easy as she makes it sound. No, that's being unkind. She has pretended to everyone for years that Ivy is her daughter, and now they're all going to learn she lied, too. Somehow telling people I'd been raped made me feel unclean, though, as though I had deserved it – asked for it, they would say. And to tell people I have an illegitimate child is just as bad. I looked up illegitimate in the dictionary once. *Not authorised by law. Not sanctioned by society.*

But Ivy had had no choice about whether to be born and will have to live with the stigma. Society is more forgiving than it used to be. Attitudes are changing, about the role of women, about divorce, about contraception, about unmarried mothers. Unfortunately, they're changing far too slowly in Ireland.

Ruari phones and apologises for not being in touch. He's been busy with work, and he's going to come round and pick me up, later, if I'm free. He's taken some days off. He'll explain when he gets here.

All my miserable thoughts instantly disperse.

As he arrives, I run to the door trying not to seem too eager. He jumps out of the pick-up, all six muscular feet of him landing like a coiled spring. I envy him his strength. He smiles at me as if we had never had that conversation about Ben, and greets me with a kiss and a hug; asks if I'm okay.

'I've been better,' I admit. 'I've been worrying about what your family think.'

He looks surprised. 'They feel very bad about it, of course; not that it was anyone's fault, really, except Ben's, and we all know his brain was wired up wrong. Mam and Dad want to make it up to you, only they don't quite know how.'

Just by being nice, I think.

I'm inordinately relieved. I spent so long agonising about how his family would react and couldn't have got it more wrong. Suddenly, everything isn't as bad as I thought. Perhaps I'll find a way to unload the rest of the secret, after all.

'I'm actually off to Bantry,' he says. 'Remember my great-aunt, Winnie? She got brought into hospital the other day. Mam says it looks like she's on the way out. I've been instructed to go and make my final peace with her. They've called the priest just in case. You can wait in the truck, if you like, then we'll go on in to Bantry and, oh, I don't know. Go for a walk or something. Is that okay?'

I nod. I don't mind what we do. Just being with him is enough. 'I thought you didn't like your great-aunt.'

'Duty is duty. Mam told me to go, and I'll be on the other end of her tongue-lashing if I don't.'

I grin. 'You're not a child. And you're bigger than your mam by a long way.'

'You haven't seen her when she gets going. We're all terrified of her.'

I laugh, but I like that he takes his family duties seriously.

When we get to the hospital, I decide to go in, more to be with Ruari than to have anything to do with the old woman who had frightened Ivy. I was shocked at the time, but I realise, now, that she had mistaken Ivy for Molly's ghost. There's a familial similarity, which isn't surprising, under the circumstances. What

surprised me was that Ruari's brother saw it, and none of the
rest of us did until he pointed it out. But was it fear of the
apparent ghostly apparition that made Ruari's great-aunt react
so violently or something else? Guilt, maybe. I grimace at the
memory. Sarah's right. Secrets have a habit of unwinding at
inappropriate moments, so it's best to get it out and done with.

I don't like hospitals. The stench of cleanliness, the overt
friendliness of the staff, the wallpaper art, designed to make the
environment feel a bit more homely and personal but which
does nothing of the kind. Hospitals are for broken people who
need fixing, for the sick and the dying. Sure, women go there to
have babies, but really that's just to have the facilities at hand
for when things go wrong.

And for me, the memory of giving birth is something I try to
blank out. I had a social worker glaring at me the whole time I
was giving birth, because I wouldn't tell her who the father was.
Mam and Dad had a difficult time persuading her to allow my
sister to take the baby on. I'm sure she thought either my dad or
brother was the baby's father, that we wanted to keep an even
bigger scandal quiet. But in the face of my silence, rather than
put the baby in care, she caved in, because our solution meant
one less problem for her.

So, hospitals bring back bad memories.

We're directed to a small room where there are four old
people in various stages of exiting the world. They're hooked up
to beeping monitors, lying still and silent, just waiting. Surely
the waiting would be better done at home, in peace and familiar
surroundings? Why do people dying of old age end often up in
hospital? Those extra days, maintained by medical intervention,
offer little by way of quality, that extra time being consumed by
uncertainty and fear.

'I want to die at home, not like this,' I say softly.

Ruari glances at me and offers a twisted smile. 'Not for a
while, I hope.'

I don't think he's comfortable in this environment, either. But what happens at the end of our lives is out of our hands as surely as it is when we come into the world.

His great-aunt Winnie is a shadow in the bed, her diminished form lost beneath tightly managed covers. All we can see is the tiny face, shrunken and pitted as dried fruit, fine white hair settled around it in a halo. I can't hear her breathing, and if it wasn't for the faint rise and fall of her chest, I might assume her to be gone already.

'Auntie,' Ruari says softly. Too softly, maybe, because there's no movement.

A nurse brings a couple of chairs to the bedside and motions for us to sit. 'Talk to her,' she advises kindly. 'Hearing is the last thing to go, so even if she doesn't respond, she might well be listening.'

Ruari talks to her about the past, about his childhood visits to the farm she inherited and about her husband, his great-uncle, one of William Savage's brothers, who had been brought up on the Savages' family farm. Her eyes are moving beneath the lids, which have a faintly blue sheen like thin ice. After a while, it seems that Ruari's words have penetrated through her dozing, as her eyelids flicker and eventually rise. She turns her faded eyes towards him.

'William,' she whispers. 'You came for me after all.'

'I'm Ruari,' he says gently, 'William's grandson. William is gone these many years, Auntie.'

But she's lost in time, talking to herself or no one, I don't know. I strain to hear her words.

'Everyone said she was such a beauty. Even Cillian said she was beautiful. He never told me I was beautiful. Never. Not in all those years when I was loyal and true. I knew he only married me for my farm, but what could I do when you didn't ask, after two years of courting, and me getting older? Cillian didn't love me, but he always loved his pretty little sister. Like she was a saint, or something, but we know better, don't we? You chose Mairead instead of me because she was pretty. I always knew that. You should have been mine. I would have given you decent children. Not like *her*.'

She spat out that last word, spittle forming in the corners of her mouth. I'm shocked at the vindictive tone. Dad always said nasty young people don't become nice when they get old. They just become nasty old people.

She starts muttering again. 'They idolised her, all the daft men. Thought she was an angel because of her face, but she was soiled goods, wasn't she? Not like me. I did my duty by Cillian, went pure to the church. What was his name, the O'Brien boy? Ah, yes. Davan. He ruined her, of course. William sorted him out all right, and made out that she was still pure. In prison Davan was. And that's where Molly should have been, too, the dirty whore. The nuns got rid of her bastard.' Despite her situation, slyness creeps onto her face. 'Told William it died, but I know they sold it.'

Ruari glances at me, perhaps embarrassed or shocked by this relative of his. But I'm fascinated. William had been courting Winnie but had married Mairead, who was prettier, leaving one of his brothers to marry the jilted Winnie, not for herself but for what she'd inherited. She had hated Mairead for her beauty, and Mairead's daughter Molly for the same reason, and she's taking that hatred to the grave with her. There's no kindness in her, no forgiveness. Her bitterness is paramount, because it's so deeply embedded. There's silence for a moment, and I wonder whether she's quietly departed. But the eyes, staring at nothing, veer back towards Ruari.

'They both left you in the end, though, William. Got your just deserts, didn't you? Your precious daughter chose to follow Davan to the grave. You never told the priest Molly killed herself, but I did,' she says with satisfaction. 'I confessed so the whole time Mairead was breaking her knees praying for her whore daughter's soul, the priest knew the truth. Heh!'

As her vindictive laugh turns to a rattling cough, Ruari turns to me, shocked, and whispers, 'Did she just say Molly committed suicide?'

'That's what it sounded like to me.'

Ruari tries to get Winnie talking again, but her words become incoherent mutterings. Then Ruari's parents arrive with Noah and Ted, followed closely by the priest, who takes one look at Winnie and begins to perform his duty, making a sign of the cross over the bed, ponderously annunciating the traditional words designed to absolve the dying woman of all her sins and see her on her way to Heaven.

Ruari gestures a welcome and goodbye to his family, takes my hand and walks me out into the sunshine.

'What an evil old woman,' I state with a curl of my lip.

'She was bitter, which is kind of understandable. I never knew she was in love with William. Marrying Cillian on the rebound must have been an act of desperation. Perhaps she did that to still be part of William's family. And then she never had children. What a sadly disappointing life. She must have felt betrayed by everyone, including God.' He picks up where we left off when we were inside the hospital. 'Do you think Molly took her own life?'

'It sounded as if Molly did that because Davan had already died. She said she *chose to follow him to the grave*, didn't she?'

'But the story is, Davan was out of prison and they eloped together. Granddad said Davan came home. That's how we know what happened in the prison. He told his father.'

'Weird,' Ruari says. 'But if Molly did commit suicide, she couldn't have been buried in consecrated ground,' he muses, 'so what did William do with her body? He must have buried her on the farm somewhere. And if the other skeleton is Davan's,

William must have killed him. If that skeleton *is* Davan's, it would explain the cracked skull.'

'That's an assumption, but I agree. Grandpa said William told everyone in the townland that Davan had died in prison. It sounds like he planned it somehow, but maybe it backfired, then Davan turned up at the farm, alive. If William had already told Molly that Davan was dead, maybe she did kill herself. She'd had her baby taken away from her, and if then she thought Davan was dead – maybe it seemed like she had nothing left to live for. If Davan went to the Savage farm – your farm,' I amend, 'looking for her, maybe William killed him and buried him up in the rath.'

'All supposition, of course. But that still doesn't answer the question of what happened to Molly's body,' Ruari says. 'If she died, that is. William never told anyone that Molly was dead.'

'No, in fact, he came ranting to my great-grandpa Patrick, saying that Davan had stolen her away.'

'Maybe that was to cover his own back. You know what we have to do, don't you?'

'Find Molly's grave.'

'And what's the most sacred place on our land? A place no one would think of digging?'

'The rath. Where we found one body there, might there be another?'

He laughs. 'Or several, given William's temper.'

Ruari later rang and told me that Winnie died not long after we left the hospital. As she was the last member of the family who'd actually known William, I suspect she's taken the secret of Molly and Davan to the grave with her.

Our proposed visit to the rath to search for Molly's possible grave is put on hold as the wider Savage clan make plans for the funeral and organise a wake. From what I gather, none of the family had liked Winnie very much, but they still plan to send her off to God in the traditional manner. And, as Ruari reminds me, there's no proof that the skeleton we found in the rath is even Davan's, so maybe he did elope with Molly, in which case, there is no other grave to be found.

30

GINNY

The wake is held in the Savage farmhouse, because Winnie's house is too tiny and run-down to accommodate it. The day is overcast but not bad enough that the smokers in the party can't migrate outside.

Jenny has a hatred of smoking.

I have a hatred of wakes.

The whole tradition is kind of weird – make as much noise as possible in front of the dead person so if they're not actually dead, they'll wake up and not be buried alive. But having the dead person embalmed and on display through the event, like a precious museum piece, is a practice I find particularly gross. And all these relatives kissing Winnie's rigid, cold cheek and wishing her well in the afterlife, when most of them hadn't liked her while she was alive is dishonest at best.

Connie has bought crates of beer and wine, and Jenny has made enough scones and biscuits and sandwiches to feed the townland, but by the early evening most of the victuals had been demolished. When people are feeling a financial pinch – which equates in no way with the hardships of Ireland's past –

any excuse for a party is a good one, especially if the food and drink is free.

At the wake, I see a few surprised and questioning glances cast at me, but no one says anything. I can almost hear the telephone lines getting ready to sing as the news is later whispered and discussed: *Is the family feud over?* But let them make of it what they will. The past is the past. Like all scandals, another one will soon arise to take precedence in the community.

The noise winds down, and the cars drift away – most of the drivers not at all legal, but this seems to be normal practice. I realise I've drunk far too much to drive home and tell Ruari I'll just walk back across the fields, but he shakes his head. 'There's a usable bedroom in the old farmhouse that I'm doing up. Stay here for the night.'

I must look a little shocked, because he provides a rueful smile. 'I'd obviously like to, ah, make love to you, but it's your choice. If you want to wait until we're married, I understand. Staying over is a genuine offer. I'll call your parents, if you like. Then you can have breakfast with us before driving home. I'd like that. And besides, if you want to walk across the fields, I'd have to walk with you and then back again.' He puts on a fake sad face. 'It's dark and cold and lonely out there in the wild.'

'I can look after myself.'

'No, you can't – you're wobbling.'

He's right. 'Okay. But I'll call my parents.'

'Phone's in the hall.'

He leaves me to make the call, and I reassure Mam and Dad that I haven't been kidnapped or put under any kind of obligation.

Ruari leads me across the yard to the old house, which is definitely an ongoing project. The outside is sound, with new windows, doors and roof, but the inside boasts very little in the way of home comforts. The floor is exposed concrete, and the stairs and upper floor are just bare boards. Bits of wood and a pile of plumbing materials are stacked in a corner. There are boxes of tools exploded all around the living room, and a few sample floor tiles speak of a decision not yet made. The downstairs internal doors are leaning against walls instead of hanging in their allocated spaces. But there's an overall feeling of a work that hasn't been abandoned.

'You're doing this yourself?'

'I had some lads over to help with the roof and windows, but now it's all up to me. What do you think? Could you be happy here? If not, we can look at something else.'

'I think it's fantastic, but – look, we're not even engaged!'

'Well, I consider us engaged. We can nip into Cork and buy a ring in the week if you like.'

I blink, startled at the progress. He swiftly changes the subject.

'It's got good views at the back – look. And three bedrooms, so if you want children...'

'Do you want children?'

'I do, but...' He hesitates. 'If it's a problem, I understand.'

'Not a problem. It's just that... I'm feeling overwhelmed.'

'Good. Best to get that out while you're drunk. Maybe you won't remember in the morning.'

I laugh. 'I'm not drunk. Just a bit off balance.'

'Sure.'

Ruari shows me up to a bedroom containing a double bed. 'At least this one has a door on it. And a lock. I put clean sheets on, just in case.'

'Just in case you got lucky?' I ask snippily.

He cracks a sleepy smile at my drunken humour and gives me a full body hug that leaves me in no doubt that he'd like to 'get lucky'. 'No,' he says. 'You can beg all you like, but I'm not going to have you throw accusations at me in the morning. I'll be over in the new house. You'll be alone here.'

'Sorry,' I grump.

'Go to bed. The bathroom is over the landing, and there's aspirin in the cabinet.'

He laughs and leaves me to it.

I don't lock the door. It's a deliberate act of trust, though Ruari will never know that. I fall into the bed naked and drift almost immediately into a deep sleep.

In the morning, I find I need the aspirin and take three. My head is pounding. Wine has that effect, though I'm sure I didn't drink that much. I was walking around holding the glass, with a smile plastered on my face, answering questions about my work, sensing the underlying, unspoken curiosity about me and Ben and Ruari.

In the basic kitchen, I discover coffee and milk, and I'm sitting on a wide windowsill looking out at the view of the mountains behind the farm when Ruari knocks and enters.

'How are you?'

'Hungover. But I wasn't aware of drinking too much. I don't, as a rule.'

'Are you up for breakfast?'

'I'll give it a miss, if you don't mind.'

'Okay, I'll tell Mam. So, take it easy. Stay until the head's better before driving. I have to go to work. There's a job some-one's shouting for, and I'm short-staffed. I'll be back this after-noon. Will you be here?'

'I don't know. But I'm not up for strenuous exercise, so I won't be stonking up any mountains.'

He grins. 'I'll give you a call, later, to see how you're getting on. If you're not here, I'll come to your parents'.'

'Okay.' He's about to leave, when I say, 'Thank you.'

'What for?'

'For, ah, understanding.'

'Not a bother.'

He looks so sexy leaning in the doorway I could grab him right now and haul him upstairs myself. I wonder how strong his resolve would be, then. I'm genuinely amused by that thought and grin to myself.

He cocks an eyebrow.

I flush faintly. 'Oh, just a thought. It's nothing. I'll see you later.'

After Ruari's gone, I explore the house properly. Aside from the bedroom I was sleeping in, there are two smaller bedrooms and a bathroom upstairs. Downstairs there are the original rooms, comprising a big kitchen and two smaller rooms which would probably end up as dining or living areas. A new annex has been built on the side, containing rooms that I suspect are intended for utilities and maybe another bathroom. I stand there for a moment visualising the bare plastered walls painted with colour, and children playing somewhere nearby. I've only known this guy for a couple of months, and I'm planning a whole future with him.

Am I crazy?

But in a strange way, my past with Ben seems to have crossed over somehow into the present with Ruari. I feel that I've known him a lot longer than the three actual months.

I finish my coffee and go back upstairs, intending to lie down for half an hour while the pills do their thing but realise I must have slept again, because when I get up, the sun is high and my headache has receded.

I discover my bag inside the front door. I don't know whether I brought it over last night or whether someone put it there for me this morning. I pick it up and put it over my shoulder. I should call at the house and say hello to Jenny and Connie before leaving, but I find the thought strangely daunting. They won't have minded me staying here. Ruari is old enough to make his own mind up about the girl he invites into his bed, even if he isn't in it at the time.

I'm heading for my car, when Jenny comes to the door of the new house and waves me over. 'Please. I've been looking out for you. I saw Ruari go off to work, so I thought we could take this opportunity to have a chat.' She glances at her watch. 'Actually, he'll be back at any time. Will you stay for lunch?'

I must have slept longer than I thought, if it's nearly lunch time. The last thing I want to do is chat to Ben's mam, what with the history which isn't quite behind us, but I nod and smile as if it's no big thing.

The house has been tidied since yesterday, and the dead woman is no longer holding court in the living area, thank goodness. Jenny sees me glancing at the empty space where the coffin had been and says, 'She was picked up last night. The undertakers will look after her until the funeral, which is booked in for Thursday. Winnie was never the easiest person to like, but she was family. The last of the great-grandparents' generation. Would you like coffee or tea?'

I'm not sure I want either but to be polite say, 'Coffee, please.'

Connie walks in from the farm, bringing the familiar scent of hay. He scratches his head, grinning. 'Big night, last night, eh? We saw the old girl off in style.'

'Quite a crowd,' I agree, adding with a touch of sarcasm, 'She had a lot of friends.'

He laughs outright and sits himself at the breakfast bar, while Jenny spoons instant coffee into mugs, pours on the boiling water, then slides them over for us to add our own milk and sugar. She pulls out a tin of biscuits from under the counter, then slips onto a stool opposite me, hugging her mug with both hands. 'Look, I know this is going to be difficult, so

I'm just going to come out with it. Ruari told us what happened with Ben. I am – we are – absolutely mortified that it was our son who did that to you. What were you at the time, fifteen?'

'Sixteen.'

She swears softly. 'I can't tell you how sorry I am. We knew Ben had problems, but...'

'Noel told me what happened to Ben. It wasn't your fault. That must have been hard at the time, especially when you realised he wasn't the same, after.'

'True. Well, blame is something one apportions to oneself, rightly or wrongly. In my case, I think I was pushing Ben too hard with the riding, pushing my own frustrated ambitions onto my child. I suppose Noel told you what happened to me?'

'He did. He said no one expected you to walk again.'

'It was a bad time, all right. Two years in rehab, pretty much.' She dwells on that briefly, then casts a quick smile at Connie. 'But look at the positive side. If I hadn't had the fall, I wouldn't have gone to Kerry, I wouldn't have met Connie. I wouldn't have had Ben, of course, and my other wonderful sons. It's a strange old life,' she says. 'Happenstance,' she adds. 'I don't believe in fate.'

'And if I hadn't met Ben, I wouldn't be here now,' I muse. That's a strange thought. I wonder, in a different world, whether I still would have met Ruari, or whether I would have ended up somewhere totally different. Happenstance. I like that word.

'After Noel told me, I did wonder what Ben would have been like if he hadn't had the accident,' I admit. 'Because I don't think his underlying character was determined by that.'

'True. He was a thoughtful child. Always loved nature and the like.'

'It was his fault that I became an archaeologist, you know. He taught me to appreciate the landscape, the mountains, nature and the past. No one else saw things the way he did. I'm sorry he died.'

'That's very generous, in the circumstances,' Connie says.

Jenny nods. 'We were a bit worried when we learned he'd been seen with you. And then you disappeared, so we guessed something had happened. But we didn't have any idea that he'd...'

'Call it what it is, love,' Connie says.

Tears spring. 'I can't,' she says, a sob in her voice. 'How could he do that? Our son?'

'He was a troubled mind,' Connie says. 'He didn't fit well into this world of ours. I've wondered, since, if it wasn't an accident, whether he knew what he was doing.'

Jenny wipes her eyes. 'We'll never know. Sometimes I think his accident was for the best, but I'd never say that to anyone.'

Connie grins. 'You just did, sweetheart.'

'Well, you know what I mean. Oh, listen, is that Ruari, now? He's early.'

'Well, I guess he has reason,' Connie says with a wink that makes me blush.

'So, the thing is,' Jenny says, taking a deep breath and speaking far too quickly. 'Connie and I have talked about you and Ruari. Do you love him?'

'It's too soon,' I say honestly. 'But I do like him. A lot.'

A vehicle door slams outside.

'Well, we just want to assure you he's not at all like Ben. He's stable enough and has been running that business for three years, now, since he bought out Eoghan McCarthy, and he was apprenticed there for several years before that. There's not much he doesn't know about motors.'

'Are you providing me with a reference?' I ask, amused.

'Well,' Connie says, his natural smile lurking, 'sort of. We just want you to know we're okay with it. Whatever happened in the past died with Ben, and if you and Ruari can make a go of it, we'd be pleased. No pressure, of course. But it's about time Ruari thought about settling down, making a home.'

The door opens, and Ruari freezes in the opening. 'I'm not interrupting anything, am I?'

'Not at all, no, of course not,' we say in unison.

He laughs. 'Okay. I'll go out and come back in, shall I?'

'Don't be daft, lad,' Connie says. 'We were telling young Ginny here about all your faults. Someone had to before it was too late.'

Ruari walks over to the counter and makes himself a coffee while we each concentrate on our own circling thoughts. It's strange sitting here with Ben's parents, discussing what happened all those years ago. I never thought this day would ever arrive, to be honest.

I take a deep breath. 'So, Ruari told you that I was pregnant?'

'He did,' Connie says. 'He said you, ah, got rid of it.'

'She,' I say. 'The baby was a girl.'

They both look confused for a moment, then Jenny's mouth drops. 'A girl? You had the child?'

'I misled Ruari, I'm afraid.' I glance at him briefly. He's leaning against the counter, watching me intently. 'I said I'd got rid of it. I didn't say when or how. My parents would have sent me to England to get an abortion, but I couldn't do that. Never mind the manner of its conception, to me it was a baby, and I knew that if I'd done that, I would have regretted it for the rest of my life.'

Jenny's eyes are wide. 'So, we have a grandchild somewhere?'

I nod. 'She was adopted.'

'Is she— Will we be able to—' Jenny puts her hand to her mouth, unable to ask the question.

'My sister adopted her. You've already met her,' I admit. 'I'm sorry I didn't let you know that at the time. Ivy had only just learned, by accident, that she was my daughter, so it was all a bit traumatic.'

'Ivy is Ben's child?' Jenny asks, stunned.

'Right. So that's why she looks so much like Molly,' Connie says, amused rather than shocked. 'I thought that was a bit strange. It's all clear now. Oh, my goodness!'

'Are you going to tell her?' Jenny asks. 'Will she be all right, knowing we're her grandparents?'

'Sure, she will. In fact, she said to me the other day that it would be useful if I married Ruari, so she'd be family, and could come and stay here.'

'She said that?'

I laugh. 'She's a typical kid. Totally selfish. She wants to come and ride the horses and thought persuading me to marry Ruari might do the trick.'

Ruari's lips twitch with amusement, but he doesn't interrupt.

'She doesn't know Ben was the father, though I expect she'll work it out; she's not stupid. I told her that her father was a friend, but I didn't love him enough to marry him, and then he died. She knows Ruari's brother died in a farm accident. It's not a leap of imagination to join the two concepts.'

I stand up. 'Now, thank you for the coffee and the chat. I'll take a rain check on lunch. I need to go home. You have a lot to think about, and my parents will be worried.'

'Worried because you're here?' Connie asks, frowning.

'Not exactly. Worried about whether I actually managed to get the truth out and how you'll all react. Well, we do have history. Mam said it was time I told you, especially if...'

'You're going to marry me,' Ruari interrupts. 'No "if" about it. I have a feeling they're not too averse to the idea?'

I smile and look towards Ruari's parents. 'Mam wants to invite you all over for a meal with us. Would that be all right?'

'Absolutely,' Jenny says, and from her beaming face, I realise that the family enmity of the last century really is over.

Ruari turns up at my parents' home, later, just as we've finished dinner. Right on the doorstep, in front of them, he picks me up in a bear hug and swings me off my feet.

'Oof! What's that for?' I say, pushing ineffectually at his chest. He's like an immoveable rock, my fists making no impression at all.

'Because. I. Love. You,' he says, smacking a kiss on my lips between each word, 'and because you didn't kill Ben's child.'

'Oh,' Mam says, while Dad is looking slightly bemused, and Micheal is grinning.

Ruari puts me down and tries to brush an oily smear from my top, making it worse. 'Sorry,' he says, not at all contritely, then turns to Mam and Dad. 'I do hope you're okay with this?'

'Would it matter if we weren't?' Dad says, but there's a smile lurking.

'Well, it would certainly make things easier if you are, because I'm going to marry your daughter.'

'I haven't agreed,' I protest.

'It's about time all that bloody nonsense between our two families was done and dusted,' Dad states.

'Language,' Mam reprimands mildly.

'Well, it was you who wouldn't talk to Mrs Savage.'

'That was years ago. And I was understandably upset.'

'I said you were going to invite them to dinner,' I comment. 'They'd like that.'

'And there are no more surprises to crawl out of the woodwork?' Ruari asks, glancing at us all, one by one.

'No,' I say.

'Good,' Ruari says. 'So, is it a yes?'

My grin makes my cheeks hurt. 'Of course it's a yes.'

'Well, break out the beer,' Dad says. 'This has to be cause for celebration.'

31

GINNY

Ruari and I decide to get formally engaged later in the year. The beginning of autumn turns the sky steel grey, and for three days the rain is torrential. The farmers are grimly waiting to see if this year is going to be a disaster for the livestock, but on the day Ruari and I drive into Cork to buy a ring – which Ruari insists upon – the sky turns the taps off, and the surface water, which had been running in rivers down the boreens, begins to subside. After much deliberation, I choose a gold band made of Celtic knotwork, topped with a small sapphire stone. 'Diamonds are cold and hard and glitzy,' I tell him, when he queries my choice. 'The sapphire is my birth stone, and blue is my favourite colour. Do you like it?'

'I love it. It's like your eyes,' he says.

Well, not quite, but I'll take the compliment.

I go to take the wrapped package from the jeweller, but Ruari whips it away and puts it in his pocket. 'Nope. This is the only engagement I'm going to have, so we do it properly. With champagne and strawberries.'

'What, a party? I don't think I want—'

'No, silly. Just you and me. A picnic on a damp, cold Irish

rock up on a bleak hillside in the rain. I'll try not to kneel in a bog.'

'Oh,' I say. 'Suits me!'

In the end, we decide it's too risky to go up anywhere exposed, because if the torrential rains begin anew, we might have difficulty getting back down, or even put rescue services at risk.

'We could just light a fire and stay at home,' I suggest, half-joking.

At the moment, we don't share a home. We're busy decorating and finishing his house before we move in, so any firesides would be in the company of one or the other of our parents. Not exactly the romantic option.

'That's not going to happen,' Ruari says. 'I want this to be a memorable day. Wet and cold we can cope with. I want something we can look back on and have a laugh about. What about the big rock in the rath, then? We can splash up the hill and climb on it to at least get our feet out of the damp.'

I hesitate. 'Ben used to wait for me there, sometimes. He would sit on the rock with his legs dangling over the edge and lean back to stare at the sky. He loved clouds. And,' I hesitate, then add with a rush, 'the rath is where it happened.'

'Oh. Of course. That was insensitive of me. I'll think of something else.'

I shake my head. 'No. Let's do it. Let's overlay the bad memories with good ones. I want to remember the Ben who used to tell me the names of the butterflies and who could pick up bumblebees without getting stung, rather than the Ben who was brain-damaged and unhappy.'

So, on Sunday, when his workshop is closed for the day, we take strawberries, a bottle of champagne and two fragile glasses, and set off up the hill.

'Have you brought the ring?' I ask, halfway up the first field.

He stops short, looks horrified and bangs his head with his

hand before the lurking smile pops out. Of course he has. We plough on through two boggy fields, across a stream of water trickling down from the hills above, and make our way to the ancient stone wall that rings the lower part of the rath. I'm breathless from the uphill struggle, but Ruari leaps up and reaches for my hands. As he had, once before, he lifts me easily up onto the platform, and we fight our way through the ever-present gorse to the sanctuary within.

'I wonder why nothing grows in the middle?' Ruari says.

'If Ben were here, I bet he'd be able to explain it.'

Strangely, now that everything is out in the open, I'm able to talk about Ben with a sense of nostalgia, even here in this place, where we're going to overwrite bad memories with good ones.

We're in front of the stone, now, and to one side there's a pile of earth where the detective dug out the skeleton. The ancient chamber beside it has collapsed in on itself, undermined by the recent deluge. Ruari climbs up onto the top of the rock, by a raised rubble path that rises to one side. I don't know if Ben made that, or whether it was there long ago. I follow more carefully, feeling my way on the slippery wet rock. I wonder whether this is a good idea.

Ruari looks around the muddy platform. 'Can you imagine living here? All year, I mean.'

'That's what I'm working on at the moment. An education presentation for the schools, to help children understand what it might have been like. It's assumed that the early tribes were savages in animal skins.'

'It's how they portrayed it in the history books when I was at school.'

'Me, too. Which is the whole point of the exercise. They would have had good homes, for the day. Circular wooden huts made of thin woven branches. Maybe double-skinned, lined with wool to keep out the draughts. And a wooden fence around the perimeter to keep out wolves and two-legged predators. And fires to warm themselves and cook on. They were primitive through lack of technology, not intelligence.'

'We're lucky, I guess. Living today.'

'True, but you only have to see the beautiful artefacts they made to realise that they were a civilised people. They were tribal, probably warlike, with different values, but I bet they loved their children, enjoyed a good meal and gained pleasure out of seeing the sun come out, the same as we do. Actually, they were cleverer than most people today. Put anyone from today back then and they'd be dead within a few months.'

I heave myself to my feet on the rock. Ruari puts his arm around me. 'King of all I survey,' he jokes.

I laugh, because the Savages' land is obliterated by the ring of trees.

Then he looks at me. 'Am I your king?'

I look up into his eyes. I think of all sorts of reasons why I wouldn't, being a modern woman, honour him and obey his every command, but as I look up into his eyes, which are shadowed by his own face, all I can see is the depth of his love for me. 'You are,' I say softly.

'Will you marry me?'

'I will.'

'When?'

'Right now. If there were a druid handy.'

He makes a big show of looking around. 'Never a druid when you need one.'

He crouches down to his backpack; pulls out the champagne glasses. We sit on the edge of the rock and dangle our feet over the edge. I hold the glasses while he pops the cork and quickly tips the foaming clear liquid into the glasses. We wait until it subsides and clink glasses.

'To us,' Ruari says.

'To us and the future and our children,' I add.

'Are you sure?'

'Absolutely.'

He takes a sip and screws up his face. 'Do you actually like this stuff?'

'Not much,' I admit.

He roars with laughter and downs the rest of the glass, like medicine. 'Give me a jar of porter, any day!'

'Well, it cost an arm and a leg, so we can't waste it.'

Overhead, dark clouds churn and tumble, but they no longer have the power to destroy me. Perhaps I have finally put Ben into context in my mind. He was a damaged soul, but I never loved him the way I now love his younger brother.

'I can imagine living up here,' I muse. 'Just think, if the trees weren't here – which they wouldn't have been – we would be able to see right across the valley. We would know where the other people lived, because we would see the smoke of their fires. We'd keep sheep or cattle below. We women would be spinning, weaving, cooking and looking after the children while you men would be guarding the perimeter, keeping a weather eye out for marauders. Mostly standing around doing nothing but looking manly, in fact, while we women did all the work.'

He puts his arm around me again. 'Your primitive women-folk don't have a very high opinion of the men in their lives.'

'They come in handy when there's a skirmish.'

'Is that all?' His arm tightens around me, and then I'm tipped back on the rock, my outstretched arms firmly pinioned, while he's inched his knees between my legs.

'Well, that, too,' I say, laughing. 'Ow, let me up.'

He grins as he releases me. 'See, that's why men invented beds.'

I pull the strawberries out of the rucksack, and we sit and munch. Then, with fingers sluiced in red juice, he pulls the ring out of its little box and slides it onto my proffered left hand. 'There, so,' he says with satisfaction. 'Now we're properly engaged.'

I feel the chill of rain on my face. 'I think we're about to get wet.'

'Yep, let's head down.'

He leaps to his feet, gives a yelp and slips instantly down the other side of the rock as if it's made of ice. Then there's silence.

'Ruari!' I scream and scramble for the path we came up. I slip down hastily on my backside, barely stopping to find footholds, then scramble around the rock to find Ruari leaning against it, on his feet, but encased in a tangle of gorse. He looks a bit dazed.

'Are you all right?' I ask breathlessly.

He gives a shaky laugh. 'Whoa, that was a little unexpected.'

'Can you get out?'

'If you pass me the rucksack, I can wrap it around my arm. This stuff is lethal. But look.'

He's pointing in front of him. The ground has turned into a mud slide and exposed what looks like another chamber.

'Oh,' I exclaim. 'It was a three-chambered souterrain all along. It was the middle chamber that initially collapsed.'

'Rucksack?' Ruari reminds me.

I look up.

'You left it up there?' He rolls his eyes. 'Well, don't slip or you'll be joining me in the thicket of thorns, which, you might notice, I'm still stuck in.'

I scramble back up the rock and collect the bag, descending more carefully. I empty the contents onto the grass and hand him the bag, which he uses to push the thorny branches aside, then squeezes out amidst a muttering of under-the-breath language.

He emerges, scratched and bleeding, and I laugh outright. 'People are going to think I did that.'

'Suits me.'

I kneel beside the exposed chamber, lean right over the edge and squint.

'Careful,' he warns. 'Don't go falling in.'

'Oh my God, there's a skeleton,' I say.

Ruari laughs. 'Good one!'

'No,' I insist. 'Really, there is.'

The guard thinks it's a joke, too, when we call it in, but eventually the whole circus is re-enacted as a stretcher is brought up the hillside and the remains are carefully lifted out. This time it's obviously a woman as the clothes are recognisable as being from the beginning of the century. Once the coroner has examined the body, along with our snippets of folk memory, a story begins to emerge.

DAVAN, 1922

Davan's sisters trickled in from their chores one by one, their shock and confusion at finding their brother not dead, after all, followed by the delirious joy only such a momentous event could give rise to. They cried and fussed like a clutch of hens, bothering him with a chatter of exclamations and questions. They thrust him into his father's chair by the fire. He closed his eyes and smiled. He was, they all agreed, as pale as the ghost his mother had assumed him to be and far too thin. He was bent and diminished from the cruel treatment he had suffered, and lines etched his face. But they would soon have him right, with food and exercise, and the sun on his face. Life opened up before him. He was home. The hardships of the past year flooded from his soul.

Everything would be all right now.

Davan's father came last from the fields, fetched by one of the sisters, and stared at his son for a long moment, then surreptitiously wiped his face with his sleeve. Davan had instinctively known that his father loved him, but in his adult life, he had never experienced physical affection. Their love was stored deep in the soul. His father nodded, and sat at the rough wooden table and asked for a drop of the pure. For once, his wife fetched it without nagging, and he lifted the jar to toast, 'You're welcome home, son. Most welcome.' He wiped his face again, then his features settled, as they always did.

When the family had eaten their supper, Davan's father explained, 'Two weeks ago, I drove up to the prison with the cart to bring you home but learned you were already gone. I was told that some of the prisoners had given you a bad beating before you left, but they didn't know anything after that.'

'It wasn't the prisoners,' Davan said. 'It was the guards.'

'Why would they do that?' his mother queried, shocked.

He shook his head. She had no idea of conditions in the prison, and Davan wasn't about to enlighten her. 'Why did you think I'd died?' he asked.

'William Savage said he heard it,' Davan's father spat. 'He has a cousin who works in the prison. He couldn't keep the glee off his face.'

Davan hid his shock. He had already worked out that Molly's father had instigated the beating; the guards had as good as told him so. Money had obviously changed hands. William must have assumed the guards had done what they had been paid to do: make sure Davan never came home at all. He wondered why the guards hadn't killed him, if that was the case. Maybe their consciences got the better of them, but it was more likely they were afraid of being had up for murder if he didn't leave on his own two feet.

He said nothing of this to his family. 'So, what news of Molly?' he asked.

There was a brittle silence. 'Best forget young Molly,' his father advised. 'It was herself that caused the trouble in the first place.'

Prison had taught Davan to temper his anger. 'It wasn't Molly, Dada. William was right in saying it was me. I was wrong to take advantage. I was the older one. She didn't know what would happen, and I surely should have.'

He'd had a lot of time to ponder on his actions, as the judge had advised. At first, he had assumed William had instantly betrayed him to the police in hasty, righteous anger, but later, especially after this recent beating, he recognised the calculated coldness of such an action. He felt a flutter of alarm. If he could be like that to Davan, how had Molly fared?

As the end of his prison term had come near, he had decided he would go and speak to William, man to man, see if he could pave the way towards a future. But in the light of this new revelation, that didn't seem such a good idea. It was more likely that William and his batch of braw and hardy sons would finish the job the prison guards had started. No, he needed to find out about Molly, first. Find out if she was wed and learn her mind regarding himself. He hoped she wasn't wed, because Molly had a deep faith, and if she had made vows, even to another man not of her choosing, she would keep faith to the end of her days.

He reached to cover his mother's wrist, where it lay on the table. 'Mam, tell me. Is Molly well?'

'Leave it, boy,' his father growled. 'Haven't ye learned the lesson yet?'

'I love her,' Davan said simply. 'Tell me she isn't married.'

His mother took pity on him. 'She's not married, son. She was sent away, and everyone knows why, though none would dare say so. I've seen her across the fields, from a distance only. The boys and the father don't let her stray.' She added, in a troubled voice, 'I haven't seen the poor girl in church, either. Surely her family would want her to receive the Holy Communion?'

Davan's guilt rose afresh. They had made a prison of her home. Not hard to do when she lived in a house with eight strapping menfolk and her mother, once beautiful, now meek and straggled as a pecked hen. Poor Molly, who loved to run wild and watch the hares play, who had enchanted him with her childish trust, which he had surely betrayed. 'And the child?'

His mother shrugged. 'There is no child, son. Molly was but a child herself. Maybe she was too small, maybe it died at birthing. It's not as if we can ask, now, is it?'

But he was determined to speak to Molly, find out her own mind. If she no longer wanted him, he would respect that. But if she asked, he would steal her away from her own family. If they eloped, he knew they could never come home again. She would know that, too. He was sorry that his actions might impact on his own family but trusted that William was not so lost to reason that he would commit murder in his own townland. This would be the first place William would come, like an angry bull, to claim back what was his own.

Careful interrogation of his mother the next day brought the news that the Savage family would likely attend mass on Sunday, except for Molly, who they said was unwell and would stay indoors, but which his mam said was a downright untruth.

When Sunday arrived, he professed himself too weak to attend mass. He wasn't entirely lying as the headaches could come without warning, sending rainbow flashes that obscured his vision and caused bile to rise in his throat. They would no doubt pass, in time. But on Sunday, despite his plea for secrecy until he was well, he knew his father would not be able to stop himself from gleefully spreading the news of his son's unexpected appearance, as if risen from the dead like Christ.

The family left, walking down the lane as he had once done, too. His father was in the lead, his mother and the girls trailing behind in a descending line. In past years, he would have been behind his father. It had seemed perfectly normal to him at the time, but seeing it from a distance, he smiled, as they looked for all the world like a line of ducks.

Then his smile died. The moment they turned the corner,

he took to the fields. He walked down the valley, through three fields to the boggy patch of ground that was the unlikely source of his father's and William's disagreement. He waded through the flat rush of water, with its trailing fronds of duckweed, onto William's land.

There was smoke rising from the farmhouse chimney, and William carefully peered in through the kitchen window. There was no sign of activity, and as the house, like his own, was a single-storey cottage with just three rooms, he was able to establish quite easily that the family were not present.

He went to the half-door, which was always propped open, and called softly, thinking that there was an uncanny stillness to the house.

He felt awkward, trespassing inside, where he had never set foot before, but he had to be sure. The big family kitchen, similar to his own, was scrubbed clean. The two bedrooms, one for the parents and Molly, the other for the boys, were cluttered with beds and little else. Where would Molly be, if not here? Maybe she had gone to mass, after all. But he needed to make sure she wasn't around, doing her chores, chattering to her hens as if they were the sisters she had longed for.

He left the house and walked to the small barn, where the cows would be milked and the calves brought in during the winter, and there he found her.

They had lain her on a door propped on two trestles, as was the custom. She lay on her back, her eyes closed as if in sleep, her sweet rosebud mouth stilled forever. Her hands had been crossed over the breast of her one good dress, which he had never before seen without its wrapping of a bleached linen apron. Her skin was not just milky pale as he recalled but almost transparent. He recognised her mother's raw grief in the way her hair had been freshly washed and brushed until it shone.

Her only daughter.

His only love.

He dropped to his knees and wailed as he had not done since birth, a raw, agonised cry of denial. A while later, he found himself curled on the floor, as he had on that last day in the prison, but this time it was not for the physical torment of his body but a mental torment that he knew would never heal.

How had it come to this?

He finally stood and examined her with clinical analysis. Though she was cold, her body was soft and pliant and unmarked. She had lain here for a day, at least. Why had they not called the priest? Why had she been left here, lying on her own, with none in attendance?

The answer flooded in.

She had poisoned herself; an unforgivable sin, according to the fifth commandment, in which God proclaimed that his people had a duty to preserve and love their own lives. The family could not ask the priest to give her absolution, and she could not be buried in the churchyard. She would remain forever beyond Christ's love, in purgatory. He realised, with cold clarity, that the family intended to bury her secretly on the farm and would probably invent some story about her going off to get married. They did not want the stigma of a suicide in the family.

That she had died for love of him, Davan did not doubt, and his reasoning soon worked out why. As William had gloated to Davan's own father about his son's presumed death, he had probably told Molly the same thing. Davan could only suppose that it had taken her these last few weeks, while he was – unbeknownst to her – recovering in hospital, to decide she couldn't live without him. As far as she knew, they had stolen her baby and her true love, leaving her with nothing to live for.

Maybe her father had even boasted that Davan's presumed death had been caused by his own hand. That would surely have sent her towards the kind of madness that would make her commit such a dreadful act.

The thought of his love spending eternity in the loneliness of an unknown grave was too much for Davan. He would join her, at the risk of his own soul. He lifted her in his arms and staggered up the hill to the rath where they had spent so many dreamy hours. He kicked away the gorse from the half-collapsed souterrain they had once explored and backed in, dragging her inside, carefully shielding her head from damage. He rearranged her body on the carved earth floor, composing it in the traditional manner.

But she must have flowers to take with her into eternity. And it was too dark. He wanted to see her, to watch her as he waited for his own demise. He would gather wild roses and fetch candles to light her way, and sit with her until they lay together as close in death as they had been in life.

But as he climbed back out of the hidden cave, the headache he had been holding at bay lashed out ferociously. He cried out and fell back down. His mind seemed filled with rainbow colours in the darkness, and as the earth cascaded back on top of him, he thought, maybe, after all, God had come to take them both into His arms.

GINNY

'How are you doing?' Ruari asks. He's just back from work, traipsing oil into the house on his black work boots.

'Feet!' I yell, just as my mam used to do – and probably still does, when Dad and Micheal come in tired from the fields.

Ruari obediently steps back to the little porch he's built on the front of the house and removes his boots. Why does he never remember? In just his socks, he pads in and kneels before me, putting his ear against my belly. 'He's sleeping,' he says.

'She's been kicking up a storm,' I say.

He stands and kisses me softly, gently, as if I might break. 'Are you well?'

'Of course not,' I grumble. 'I'm pregnant. I waddle like a duck. I can't breathe. I can't sleep, and I want to pee all the time.'

'Well, wife, that's soon going to be over.'

'It will, and I'll be thankful for it.'

'So, anything new or strange?'

'Well, actually, yes. I had a visit from the museum director at Cork, who seems keen to take on Davan's sketchbook. He wants to make a case especially for it, and says would we mind if he wrote an article and published the pictures, which he says are unique and amazing.'

'He's right – they are. What did you tell him?'

'I said I'd talk to you, because of the sketch of Molly, and her story, but I can't see a reason why not. It would be kind of nice if Davan's work was out there for people to see, wouldn't it?'

'It would,' he agrees. 'She's too beautiful to lie hidden away in a hot press.'

'That was just to keep it from getting damp. And it's the nature pictures that fascinated him, more than the image of Molly. I think we were all taken by her, because it's personal. We knew the story – or some of it – and it's kind of emotional actually seeing her image. Maybe I'll keep that page, frame it.'

'No. It's the best image in the book. Let the museum have it. Let the world see that illiterate Irish farm workers from back along were real people, sensitive, clever.'

'And the story?'

He shrugs. 'Tell is as it is. Tell it how we think it was. There's no one left alive who is going to be hurt by it now.'

'Oh,' I say, with shock.

'What?'

'My waters just broke.'

The look of absolute terror on Ruari's face makes me laugh. 'Go and tell Jenny. She'll know what to do. Then let my parents know. And my sister. Well, actually, no, don't tell Sarah. She might think another baby is coming her way.'

'You can joke, at a time like this?'

A contraction hits me, and I fold over, groaning. 'What better time to joke. Off you go, now.'

I'm a bit frightened, but it won't be like last time, with the social worker scowling at me, my father pacing in the next room, my mam and sister waiting to take the baby from me the moment it arrives. I was made to feel like a criminal, then. I'd been terrified of the whole process, just living through the experience with the bare minimum of knowledge of what was about to happen. Despite my family, I had felt so alone.

The midwife who attended the birth had been decidedly unpleasant. After the final, ripping pain of birth, there had been a moment when all the pain was over and I lay there stunned when she told me with casual disregard that I'd given birth to a girl. She wrapped the newborn baby in a towel and dumped her in my arms. After a few distressed yells, the baby had quietened down against the warmth of my body, her eyes closing from the exhaustion of the birth. I had never seen anything so tiny, so perfect. I wanted to hold her, keep her, but all too soon she was taken from me.

I watched Sarah feed my baby, and nurse her, while I went back to school. I wonder I didn't go mad, the ache in my empty arms a burden I didn't know I could carry. I cried for that baby and think from that moment onward I was never fully in the present. Not until Ruari came along and brought me back into the land of the living.

Sarah had been annoyed that I insisted on calling the child Ivy, which was considered to be a weirdly hippy choice, not at all traditional. *Why?* she asked. I couldn't tell her that it was Ben's favourite plant, its sticky flowers like green snowflakes that magically keep the bees alive in winter in our barren winter landscape. She would never have understood. Even then, after all I'd gone through, I knew Ben hadn't meant me harm. I hadn't known, then, that I would never see him again.

Ivy, now twelve and growing up fast, is fascinated by her new sister. We'll be a strangely united family, I think, with our secrets kept, for the time being, anyway, until Ivy is old enough to decide for herself who she tells about her real parentage. She knows, now, that her father was Ben, Ruari's older brother. She accepts that I loved Ben a little but not as much as I love Ruari now. It's best she doesn't know the truth and can think of her unknown father as the man I portray; the one who was so in tune with nature he was like part of the landscape itself.

I never thought I would end up living on the Savages' farm, in the old farmhouse Ruari renovated. But with three houses tumbled onto an acre of land, Jenny is close by, presently behaving like a mother hen, popping in at all hours to make sure I'm okay.

The second skeleton is assumed to be that of Molly Savage, but there are no marks on her body to tell how she died. The coroner assumed poison, of which there is plenty around if one knows the countryside.

That she had been placed reverently in the old souterrain by Davan, before he died of his head wound, seems to be the logical explanation. It's sad to think they hadn't eloped and lived happily ever after, as rumour had suggested. But I'm sure their sad story will be told over the firestones and turned into a folk memory handed down for generations, before that, too, dissipates on the winds of time.

EPILOGUE

GINNY

I thought that was the end of Davan and Molly's story, until one day an unknown woman drives up to the house and knocks on the door. I open it with our baby Molly in my arms and a query on my face. The woman is maybe the same age as my mother. She's tall and neat, with what looks to me like an expensive cut to her clothes and silvering hair. She holds in her hands a rolled-up magazine.

'Are you Ginny Savage?'

'I am,' I answer suspiciously.

Ruari comes to the door behind me. Since the discovery and speculation about the skeletons discovered in the rath, we've had a few unscrupulous reporters trying to barge their way in, seeking seedy background stories about our lives.

'I'm Angela Benedict. You don't know me. I'm sorry to come unannounced, but I wanted to talk to you about this.'

She unrolls the magazine to show me the front of a well-thumbed copy of the magazine containing the article, 'The unsolved mystery of Davan, his life and art'.

I feel Ruari tensing, seeing her as a different kind of reporter, maybe, when she explains, 'I'm an artist. I subscribe to this magazine, but this article floored me. It was so beautiful, so moving. And the mystery behind it is somewhat intriguing.'

'It is,' I agree, not mentioning that the reporter knew all too well what we believe happened. 'Have you come far?'

'Not so far. I live in Middleton, east of Cork city, but apparently my grandparents came from this part of the world. I was never too curious about their past until I saw this article.'

I'm curious now, and Molly is becoming a dead weight in my arms. I step back, and Ruari opens the door in invitation.

'Come on in. You'll take a cup of tea?'

'I will, thank you.'

She seats herself at the pine table in the kitchen and lays the magazine open at the page illustrated with a small selection of Davan's beautiful drawings, which includes the exquisite image of the long-disappeared Molly Savage. Ruari makes the tea while I peruse the images again, never losing my fascination for both the story and the skill that lay behind them.

'So?' Ruari asks somewhat belligerently, placing the mugs on the table and pushing one towards her.

Angela is unfazed by the understated antagonism. 'Thank you. I always wondered where my love of art came from. Neither my parents nor my grandparents had the slightest hint of talent. 'I always knew I was good, though, and have managed to carve a career for myself in illustrating. But when I saw this article, I had the strangest feeling that I was connected to it.'

I'm fascinated by the quiet strength behind her words. She's neither boasting nor self-aggrandising, just saying it as it is. She has the air of someone who is self-confident, used to being listened to, someone of importance in her own sphere, maybe.

She reaches into her bag, pulls out a small cloth bag and tips a necklace on the table. It's a fine chain with a tiny silver-plated cross, nothing special, discoloured with age. I glance at her. She smiles gently at my confusion. 'I inherited this from my grandmother.' She pushes the chain closer to the image of Molly, and suddenly I see it.

'Oh Lord! It's Molly's,' I whisper.

'Or similar,' Ruari says warily.

'When I saw the article,' Angela carries on, 'I started to do some research into my family lineage. I was never inclined, before, but that intrigued me. It turned out that before she married, my grandmother Evie's surname was O'Brien. I began to wonder if she was one of Davan's sisters. I don't know their names, of course, but I understood he had several.'

'He did, but we were never close with them. They married away before I was around,' I tell her.

She pauses, passing her finger gently over Molly's exquisitely drawn features. 'I can't prove it, of course, but I suspect someone secreted Molly's necklace with the baby, like a token to say she hadn't been willingly abandoned. I read that they used to do that back in the 1700s in Venice, but the abandoned babies there weren't so badly treated.' She sighs. 'I'm sure not all nuns here were horrible in the way it's sometimes portrayed. I have an idea that Davan's sister went in search of Molly's baby, intending to bring it back and bring it up as her own. If that's true, Davan and Molly's child would be my mother, Mairead.'

'But that was Molly's mother's name!'

Her face lights up. 'Another little clue, maybe?'

'Perhaps the O'Briens knew that Mairead Savage wouldn't have abandoned her daughter in the way it was told,' I suggest, trying to paint Ruari's great-grandmother in a better light than the article suggests. 'She would have had no say in the matter, not back then, especially if her husband was as violent as he's portrayed. The poor woman apparently spent her last few years on her knees in church, praying for her daughter.'

'Yes, her daughter's suicide was suggested in the article. And certainly, she would have been terrified for her daughter's soul in that era.'

I'm trying to take this all in, when Ruari says, in amusement, 'But if it's true, that would make you not-so-distantly related to myself and Ginny!'

'It would.' She smiles and pushes a business card to me. 'I'm not trying to gain anything from you, you realise. I don't need to. I'm quite successful in my own right.'

She reaches into her bag again and pulls out a book on Irish plants, opening it, with peculiar coincidence, on a beautiful line drawing of an ivy flower. 'I illustrated this book. Most of my work is nature related, though I have been known to do a few portraits. I like to believe that my gift came down from Davan.'

She taps her chest, right above her heart. 'If that's the case, Molly and Davan are still alive, in here.'

A LETTER FROM DAISY

Dear reader,

Thank you so much for reading *The Irish Family Secret*. I would love it if you kept up to date with all my novels and any other significant news from Bookouture, so do make sure to sign up at the following link. Your email address will never be shared, and you can unsubscribe at any time.

www.bookouture.com/daisyoshea

A rath, as mentioned in the story, is a man-made pancake of earth on which a homestead is thought to have been built. There are some 40,000 in Ireland, and another 10,000 might once have existed. A souterrain, also mentioned, is a monument from pre-history, often comprised of an entrance tunnel and three caverns joined by two small tunnels that one has to crawl through, as Ginny does. These souterrains have been discovered in their thousands, dotted all over Ireland, and the pattern seems to be fairly standard.

A few years ago, knowing that my husband studied archaeology, a local farmer called us up and said his tractor had nearly gone into a souterrain and were we interested? Tractors plough more deeply than they did in the past, and are heavier, so this souterrain, which had lain undiscovered for hundreds, if not thousands, of years, had been exposed right in the middle of his large field. Its existence had been previously unsuspected, though it was not far from an impressive rath.

We immediately took a torch and measuring equipment and drove over, in some excitement. The end chamber had collapsed, leaving a rubble slide into the middle chamber. I slithered down this to take photographs and dimensions for the national Irish Monument Database. I hauled myself through a six-foot-long passage on the far side, on elbows and stomach, and peered through into the last chamber. I didn't go in fully, worried that it would collapse and bury me. If it did, my husband said, he'd best go home and make a cup of tea, because no way would he manage to dig me out!

Being the first person to enter this souterrain since it got lost to history was amazingly moving and also provided a huge sense of the necessity of such a place. As the tunnel was tiny and there was a bend halfway through, it clearly indicated how a marauder would have had difficulty in negotiating it, and would have been unable to wield a sword or any kind of weapon. Anyone hiding in the far chamber – even a child – would be able to do serious damage the moment the infiltrator popped a head through, so the souterrain was an incredibly safe environment. It is generally accepted that souterrains would also have been used for food storage, too, being safe from animals and, being underground, maintain a fairly stable temperature.

That experience provided the idea for why Davan and Molly's disappearance was such a mystery, their final resting place lost until excessive rains caved it in, exposing them and their story.

One of my most gratifying experiences as an author is to know that readers enjoyed the novel and closed the last pages with a sigh of satisfaction, even maybe a little tear. If you did, then I'd be delighted if you would leave a review to let other readers know how much you enjoyed the story. Be sure, though, to dwell on the characterisation, the writing style and your own emotional responses, and don't give away any critical plot points.

I've lived in West Cork since early retirement, and it's been the most fulfilling time of my life. The wild countryside, the rocky seashores, the call of the sea, the scarred history, the underlying myths and legends, and most of all, the inclusive warmth of the dauntless Irish people. There's a wisp of fey here, in rural Ireland, that subtly underpins all our lives and which quietly infuses my stories. I do hope you're looking forward to my next book as much as I'm enjoying writing it.

All the best, Daisy

www.daisyoshea.com

 facebook.com/DaisyOSheaAuthor
x.com/westcorkwriter

AUTHOR'S NOTES

DISCLAIMER

Roone Bay isn't a real town, and any individual homes and businesses mentioned are fabrications. There are many families in the area with the surnames I've chosen to use, but any similarity to real persons, alive or dead, is entirely coincidental. All views in the work are those of the characters, not the author.

OVERVIEW OF IRELAND

Ireland is divided into the four provinces: Connacht, Leinster, Munster and Ulster. Cork is located in Munster, the bottom-left section of Ireland, where its rocky fingers reach out towards America. Within the four provinces, there are thirty-two counties containing around 64,000 townlands: historic areas that once might have been clan boundaries and which can be anything between a hundred and five hundred acres. Roone Bay is set on the southern coast of Ireland, in the mythical townland of Tírbeg, somewhere between Bantry and Skibbereen.

PRONUNCIATION, TRANSLATIONS AND EXPLANATIONS

- O'Shea: Oh Shay
- Molly, mo chroí: Molly, mo kree (Molly, my love)
- Cú Chulainn: *ku hu* (as l*oo*k) *lenn* (mythological Irish hero)
- mo chroí: *mo kree* (my friend/my dear)
- A 'hot press' is an airing cupboard. Press is old English for a cupboard where fabrics were stored. In Ireland a fridge is a 'cold press'.

ACKNOWLEDGEMENTS

My thanks go first to my husband, Robin, who's believed in me in every way from the moment we met. A staunch supporter of my passion for writing, he's the first critic of my work, my best friend and also my 'til-death-us-do-part' love. Thanks to my lovely mother, Alma Yea, one-time librarian and teacher, for encouraging me to read fiction when I was a child. Thanks to the whole team at Bookouture, who manage the process so efficiently. Last, but certainly not least, thanks to all the readers who enjoy my fiction. Without you, my work would be pointless, so don't be afraid to reach out and provide me with much-needed reassurance.

PUBLISHING TEAM

Turning a manuscript into a book requires the efforts of many people. The publishing team at Bookouture would like to acknowledge everyone who contributed to this publication.

Commercial
Lauren Morrissette
Hannah Richmond
Imogen Allport

Cover design
Dissect Designs

Data and analysis
Mark Alder
Mohamed Bussuri

Editorial
Kelsie Marsden
Nadia Michael

Copyeditor
Jon Appleton

Proofreader
Laura Kincaid

Marketing
Alex Crow
Melanie Price
Occy Carr
Cíara Rosney
Martyna Młynarska

Operations and distribution
Marina Valles
Stephanie Straub
Joe Morris

Production
Hannah Snetsinger
Mandy Kullar
Jen Shannon
Ria Clare

Publicity
Kim Nash
Noelle Holten
Jess Readett
Sarah Hardy

Rights and contracts
Peta Nightingale
Richard King
Saidah Graham

Milton Keynes UK
Ingram Content Group UK Ltd.
UKHW040939141024
449705UK00005B/183